SNOWED
UNDER MURDER

SNOWED
UNDER MURDER

A Sierra Pines B&B Mystery

KATHRYN LONG

CAVEL
PRESS

Kenmore, WA

A Camel Press book published by Epicenter Press

Epicenter Press
6524 NE 181st St.
Suite 2
Kenmore, WA 98028

For more information go to:
www.Camelpress.com
www.Coffeetownpress.com
www.Epicenterpress.com
www.kathrynlongauthor.com

This is a work of fiction. Names, characters, places, brands, media, and incidents are either the product of the author's imagination or are used fictitiously.

Cover design by Scott Book
Design by Melissa Vail Coffman

Snowed Under Murder
Copyright © 2022 by Kathryn Long

ISBN: 978-1-94207-860-9 (Trade Paper)
ISBN: 978-1-94207-861-6 (eBook)

Printed in the United States of America

*In memory of my high school writing teacher,
Miss Finley, who inspired me.*

ACKNOWLEDGMENTS

None of this journey would have been possible without my fantastic agent, Dawn Dowdle. You are my rock through all this. Thank you for believing in my work. And to my editor at Camel Press, Jennifer McCord, you put me on the right path and gave me very helpful advice to make this a great series. Thank you for your guidance and patience.

Without the support of my family and friends I could never write a single page. A special shout out to our Brain Trust group of authors—though our get-togethers were virtual for a time, you continued to inspire me with your words of encouragement and advice. Sisters and Misters in my local chapter of SinC have helped keep me connected to and engaged in the writing world.

Again, my gratitude goes to Theresa Atashkar who resides in Folsom, California and a short distance from my fictional town of Sierra Pines. You've been a treasure of information when I needed to learn about the Lake Tahoe region.

I thoroughly enjoyed my research for this story, especially about the California Gold Rush days. This helped me to set the scene for Ali and guests when they visited the local gold mining sight and to add realistic details to Clive Schumacher's story about his ancestor discovering gold. Also, I experienced a personal joy in finding the perfect lines for Gladys Bellwether to say whenever she commented about the golden days of Hollywood. Here's to all the wonderful classic movies and stars of years gone by.

Finally, to all the wonderful cozy mystery readers! Your love of this genre helps keep writers inspired. Thank you.

CHAPTER ONE

*E*VERYTHING IN LIFE BECOMES A BEFORE-AND-AFTER *moment, sweetie. You've got to expect the unexpected and roll with it.*

Aunt Julia comforted me with those words whenever I struggled with the bumps and bruises of awkward teenage embarrassment, career choices, job losses, and boyfriend drama. She was a smart lady and my calming force every single time I needed her. I'd give anything to pick up the phone, call, and hear her voice again.

Less than a year ago, I was a happily employed screenwriter in New York, until the infamous pink slip changed things. Julia convinced me to come visit her. We could chat, drink hot toddies, and eat special desserts baked by her dear friend and employee, Gladys Bellwether, she said. I was enthused by her energy, but those before-and-after moments, the ones to throw you off your game, came hurdling back.

When Aunt Julia died suddenly, I became the owner of the Sierra Pines B&B, and life settled into a somewhat pleasant state, at least for a few minutes. Then, the murder happened, rattling the folks of Sierra Pines like a California earthquake. And those aftershocks people talked about; I got mine in other ways.

"Hand me the roll, please. I see a spot we missed." I glanced down and wiggled my toes to relieve the cramps due to standing on the chair for too long.

Gladys placed the roll of weather-proofing tape in my hand. "I can't believe this storm. Winter brought us a doozy . . . again. If only we had the money to finish replacing these front windows." A frown curled her lips, and, with the corner of her apron, she wiped a smudge clouding the glass.

Yesterday's snowfall had left more than a foot on the ground with a prediction of more to come. An angry wind howled and seeped through drafty window seams that no amount of tape could completely fix. I gave my arms a vigorous rub. "No point in discussing what we don't have." I lifted my chin for a second to boost a look of confidence, but Gladys's frown told me I wasn't fooling her. "We have plenty of firewood to keep the place warm and the guests comfortable." I pointed to the parlor. "And a beautifully decorated tree to cheer up everyone."

The ten-foot pine nearly reached the ceiling. Many older homes like this Victorian were built with rooms of impressive heights. Of course, the design wasn't so practical when it came to heating the place. Christmas ornaments ranged from colorful bulbs to tiny figures with old-world charm, and twinkle lights and popcorn strands curled around the branches. An angel with iridescent wings perched on the very top while a red skirt circled the base, covered with a meager display of gifts. My shoulders sank. I'd yet to do my shopping, and Christmas was less than two weeks away.

Gladys cut the strip of tape I held out. "Firewood to keep the place warm. Yes, your aunt said the very same thing, every year for the past twenty years." She shrugged. "We'll make do, I guess."

I smoothed the taped surface then stepped down from the chair to stand next to her. "There. Now, we have the bedroom windows left to do, whenever the guests are out of the house."

"I believe the Smiths are staying here this afternoon. But Abby Lewis and Faith Ritter went shopping. I heard from Clive Schumacher early this morning. He claims in the past couple days business has been booming at the hardware shop as well as at the other stores. He's already sold out of snow shovels and scrapers. And Bobby told him there are no more tire chains left in stock at Retread Tire and Repair. He's called in a special order from Placerville." Gladys clucked her tongue. "Nothing like a holiday storm to push shoppers to fill their lists."

I shook my head. "Too bad some wait until a storm is here to buy those winter necessities." At least the white stuff put everyone in a festive mood. As expected, skiers by the dozens poured into Tahoe Pine Ski Resort, eager to take on the slopes. As for business in Sierra Pines, a trip into town yesterday took me forever to get my errands finished. Dozens of shoppers filled the streets and sidewalks, carrying bags stuffed with gift items. On the upside, I imagined the constant jingle of cash registers certainly pleased the merchants.

If only the B&B fared as well. We had two vacancies when normally the house was full during the holidays. I puzzled over the situation and, after a little snooping, figured out what could be the cause. The Tahoe Pine Ski Resort was under new ownership this season. Morton Enterprise, whose businesses spanned the globe, hired Tabitha Wells, a well-known, successful resort manager. With a quick Google search, I learned Wells was super smart and armed with some serious business savvy. I drooled imagining the fat expense account that came with her job. In the meantime, I checked my email a dozen times a day and waited anxiously for the mail to arrive each afternoon. After two months, I'd received no word from the publisher that had Julia's journal. The book advance we discussed would solve a lot of financial problems for the B&B. At least the modest life insurance and what Julia had in her bank account would keep the business afloat for a while.

A good friend of Gladys who worked at the ski lodge claimed Wells lured guests with plenty of incentives—lodging packages that included free ski lessons and discounts on all the amenities like the spa and gift shop.

I twisted my mouth into a scowl. All we offered were breakfast and a weekly game night with complimentary snacks. However, Sierra Pines B&B provided guests the personal, downhome touch. Tabitha Wells couldn't possibly match that perk. We needed more in order to compete, though. I had some great ideas to spark business, but that would take money we didn't have.

I clasped my hands together. "You know, I'm starving. Why don't we take a break and have lunch before our new guests arrive?" A heavy dose of fortitude would keep me positive, especially when facing the couple who'd show up on my doorstep today. Gladys's leftover chicken salad was in order. That and a generous slice of homemade pumpkin pie. I squeezed my love handles and moaned. I'd gained ten pounds since arriving here in October. A combination of mourning the loss of Aunt Julia and running the B&B was to blame. Or maybe Gladys's delicious recipes were anybody's downfall.

"Chicken salad sandwiches, rice pilaf, and my special brown sugar and sour cream pumpkin pie should do the trick." Gladys wiped a stray curl off her forehead and smiled.

"Bless you." I wrapped an arm around her shoulders and rested my chin on her head. Gladys Bellwether was tiny but full of energy. In her eighties, she could take on the biggest of tasks and never complain. With a twinkle in her eye, she remained positive even during the sad times or hard ones. Coming from a generation that taught you to pick yourself up when you fell then dust off and keep going, Gladys was tough, inside and out. So was her brother, Ollie. The Bellwethers and my aunt Julia were cut from the same cloth. Maybe some of that resilience had to do with those experiences during their Hollywood years. Of course, after decades of working on movies, attending Oscar galas, avoiding the relentless paparazzi, and recovering from a rather tragic romance, Julia escaped to Sierra Pines. The Bellwether siblings quickly followed. All three of them had devoted heart and soul to the profession, leaving little to no time for personal commitments like marriage. The B&B became their do-over.

I rubbed Gladys's back, then released my hold to walk with her to the kitchen. I tapped my fitness watch to light up the screen. "I'm guessing we have maybe an hour before you know who shows up. In the meantime, we can eat, chat, and relax." I released a trembling breath from my lips.

"I don't understand how you could agree to such a decision. Your cousin, who you've said more than once is an unbearable man, and his bride coming to our B&B?" She wagged a finger. "You are a true saint with a generous heart, Alexis."

I chewed on my lower lip. I'd held back what really worried me about the situation. Cousin Nathan's bride, Isadora Lane, never held a spot on my list of favorite or even friendly people. "Don't give me too much credit. I couldn't say no to my mom. Nathan is her sister's son. She asked, or more like pleaded with me to agree. She's doing Aunt Betts a favor, and so am I. Sure, he's boastful and rude and selfish, but he's family." I sighed. "Besides, what else was I supposed to do? Refusing would make me no better than him, which I'm not." I clenched my fists and paused to glance sideways for a brief moment but got no response. "Come on, Gladys. I can't help that the ski lodge messed up their reservation and—"

"And the newlyweds just had to honeymoon in Sierra Pines, right?" Gladys snorted. "Sounds suspicious to me. Maybe his bride had everything to do with the decision." She wagged a finger. "I don't forget much, and I remember you mentioning the infamous Isadora Lane once or twice. According to you, she's the kind who loves to toot her horn."

I frowned. "I won't go that far. I doubt Isadora ever gives me a second's thought." My words rang hollow. The Isadora I remembered schemed and manipulated every situation to gain her advantage. The infamous stage and screen actress had a reputation. I knew firsthand what she was capable of doing. The real question was why she decided—because my gut told me Gladys was more than likely right—to come to Sierra Pines.

Gladys poked my arm. "Maybe they'll find our quiet B&B boring and leave by tomorrow."

"Gladys Bellwether. Are you saying we're boring?" I grinned.

"No, of course not. What I'm saying is Sierra Pines and New York are miles apart in what they offer. Nothing wrong with stating the obvious." She bristled but with a kind voice.

"Whatever their reason for coming here, we'll be the perfect hosts and—"

The doorbell chimed a few notes of the festive tune, "White Christmas", and in an instant, the picture frame fell to the floor, shattering the glass. Gladys gasped. "Oh dear. I'll get the broom and dustpan to clean up while you handle the door." She pattered to the kitchen.

I spun around to face the entrance. I couldn't know for sure, but I sensed who rang the bell because the tingle of nerves crawling up my spine grew intense. Nathan had always terrified me when we were kids. As we grew up, that emotion changed to annoyance. Our relationship was like siblings who fought and rivaled each other. I held my breath and took impatient strides to the front entrance. Heaving my chest, I pinned a smile on my face. In one quick motion, I gripped the handle and pulled the door wide open. "Nathan. Long time no see." I almost eye-rolled at my corny greeting. With a quick recovery, I stepped sideways. "Please, come in."

"Hey little cousin. You sure look great." Once inside, he shoved me against his chest in a bear hug then pulled away and smiled.

I tried catching my breath, then a quivering laugh escaped, thinking how I was the older one by two years. He hadn't changed much. The spikey hair with tinted blond tips was new. He dressed with the usual don't-I-look-fine expensive threads that didn't suit him and an overdose of cologne. He wore the same smile that was more sarcastic than sincere. Even though she was hardly a prize catch, I couldn't imagine why Isadora would marry him. "Well, how about you? Married and all."

"Oh!" His eyes widened as he moved backward and pulled Isadora to his side. "You remember my cousin Ali, don't you, Izzie?"

Isadora scrunched her face. "Please, Nathan. We've talked about nicknames." She extended her hand. "Nice to see you, again, Alexis. Apologies for the last-minute reservation. I hope it's not an inconvenience. Anyway, thank you for putting us up in your, ah, little B&B. Rebecca insisted you wouldn't mind." She shifted her gaze from side to side. "Such cute décor. Victorian, isn't it?"

I winced. Aunt Betts hated when people called her Rebecca. I stepped farther back into the foyer. "Um, yes. We like the place. It belonged to my great aunt and her mother before that." I pressed my lips together before I began rambling. My anxiety spiked because Isadora was intimidating. Her gorgeous willow-like figure, graceful posture, and flawless complexion, not to mention the deep, sexy voice, were lethal weapons. And that was only on the outside. What went on inside was something I feared to encounter. I remembered how she attacked my parents. Her words were cruel and meant to be destructive. She called them theater has-beens who lost their talent and shouldn't be allowed near a stage. Of course, Willa and Robert Winston were Broadway stars with plenty of Tony Awards to prove the fact. Isadora acted out because she was jealous. The comments didn't hurt any less, though. Maybe the battle of insults would stop since she'd become family.

Gladys moved next to me. Every inch of her five-foot frame stood erect. "So glad you made the trip safely. I'm Gladys Bellwether and a very good friend of Alexis."

She'd added emphasis to the words *very good friend*, like it was a warning. I covered my mouth to hide the grin.

Gladys narrowed her eyes and stared at Isadora with a stern set to her jaw, then shifted her gaze to Nathan. "You're lucky Alexis is such a sweetheart." She shook her head. "Anyway, your room is first door on the right, which comes with a private bath and fireplace, you know."

She swung back to face Isadora. "The house may be small and old, but it has plenty of comfort and amenities. Breakfast is served every morning until ten. Any special requests need to be made at least a day ahead. Now, if you'll excuse me, I have work to do." With that, she turned on her heel and hurried down the hall.

I cleared my throat and ignored Isadora's look of surprise. "Let me show you to your room. If you like, there's a parlor with plenty of reading material and a piano. Do you still play, Nathan?"

"He does." Isadora placed a hand on his arm. "And I sing, but I'm sure we'll find more entertaining things to do in the evening, won't we?" She winked at Nathan.

I rubbed my neck and turned away. "Also, we have a library with a large screen television and plenty of videos to choose from, if you want to watch a movie." I pointed down the hall. "The kitchen is open in the evening with snacks and hot cocoa." I smacked my thighs. "That's about it. Oh, if you like, I'd be glad to take you on a tour of the town. Most every business has extended hours for the holidays. Lots of places to shop, and restaurants where you can dine. We don't serve lunch or dinner, obviously." I tapped my lip. "Then you'll want to visit the museum and our town theater. Sierra Pines has lots to offer." I sounded like a walking advertisement from the Chamber of Commerce. Shrugging my shoulders, I let out a nervous titter. "Sorry. I can't hide my enthusiasm about this place."

"Sounds like you've found a nice little town and a profession that suits you," Nathan said.

Discomfort heated and rushed through me. Acting was always a competition for him. Never once, did he compliment me on landing my screen writing job or Mom and Dad's theater career accomplishments. He loved talking about acting, but only when the conversation was about him and his latest commercial set to air during prime-time television. The most frustrating thing, though, was he was brilliant in them, and one actually received an award. Not anywhere near a fame-worthy Oscar, but he bragged anyway. What really depressed me was how his paycheck put mine as a screen writer to shame, which he also loved to point out, every chance he got. I shifted my weight from one foot to the other. "I'm happy, so I guess you're right."

"Well, I'd find living here a total bore." Isadora pulled off her coat and tossed it on the rack. "Really, Ali. Don't you miss New York and working in television? I mean how much shopping and eating can one person do?"

"How about skiing?" I spilled out a response, quickly sidestepping the remark about my former job. Most everyone in my family worked in the arts—theater and television, from acting to prop design to screen writing. To take an abrupt turn by running a B&B surprised no one more than me. I cleared my throat and smiled. "I mean, I figured since you planned to stay at the resort . . . do you ski?" I knew Nathan did. In fact, he'd entered competitions and placed in a couple of them. I sighed. Yet another thing he lorded over me.

With lips narrowed, she cocked her head. "I'm from the north."

As if that answered my question, I nodded. "Then it's settled. We'll add Tahoe Pine Ski Resort to your agenda. I good friend of mine can set you up with ski wear and equipment. He owns a sports apparel shop in town, and his partner works the rental booth at the resort."

Isadora leaned her head against Nathan's shoulder. "I'm exhausted from our trip and the ridiculously heavy lunch we had at that diner on the corner. What's it called? Never mind. What I need to do now is rest." She yawned and glanced up at him. "Maybe we should stick around the B&B this afternoon before we get a bite for dinner. Then I think I'd prefer turning in early."

I widened my eyes. "Oh, of course. We'll take that tour tomorrow morning after breakfast. No hurry." I pointed at the stairs. "If you'll just follow me, I can take you to your room." I turned.

"Really. There's no need. I'm sure in a place this small we can find it on our own." Isadora said.

I scratched the back of my head and convinced myself those tiny jabs weren't meant to insult. Besides, why cause waves with a guest, even when the person was Isadora? "Okay then. You'll find bottled water in the mini fridge. If you'd like another beverage, just holler."

Nathan patted my back. "Thanks, again, little cousin. You're the best."

I waited in the foyer until he and his new bride reached the top of the stairs, and then I made my way to the kitchen. "Yeah, you're the best, Alexis Winston. And a colossal idiot." I wagged my head and mumbled. "What was I thinking? No amount of money is worth—"

"Worth that pain in the patootie?" Gladys met me at the kitchen doorway and shoved a plate of cookies in my hands. "I thought maybe a little sugar might sweeten the bride's sour disposition."

I rolled my eyes. "I doubt cookies would do the trick." I skirted around her and approached the table. Setting down the plate, I plopped in a chair. "Isadora hasn't changed a bit."

"Her kind never does, I'm afraid. And I think I've figured out why the two of them are the perfect match." Gladys made her way to the sink and unloaded dishes from the drying rack.

"Why? I'm dying to hear."

She chuckled. "Can't you see it? The both of them are boastful, self-centered, and love to throw out those hurtful jabs. In fact, she reminds me of Anne Baxter in *All About Eve*. Released in nineteen-fifty, I believe. Conniving and cold-blooded enough to fool the wisest of her victims." Gladys turned and slapped the dishtowel against her side. "We should lock up the valuables and keep a close eye on her."

I raised my arms. "Oh, for goodness sakes, Gladys. Your paranoia and flair for the dramatic is showing. Isadora might be stuffy and selfish and sometimes inconsiderate, but she's not a thief, and calling her cold-blooded is going too far." I purposefully left out the other adjective. The incident with my parents came pretty darn close to describe conniving behavior. In any case, I'd keep watch and derail any of Isadora's talk or behavior that would upset the other guests. They came here for a relaxing and quiet stay. Plus, the last thing we needed were bad reviews about the B&B. I traced my finger along the table edge. This week was bound to be long and stressful.

"Say! How about we skip the chicken salad and go straight for the pumpkin pie?" Gladys set a plate in front of me with a generous helping of dessert.

I smiled. "Why not? There's therapy to your baking, after all." I forked a bite with lots of whipped cream and shoved it in my mouth. Pie and determination filled me with optimism. Gladys might have been right in warning me not to accept Mom's request. However, no way would I let the newlyweds ruin the Christmas spirit of Sierra Pines.

I devoured my dessert and washed down the last bite with a glass of milk. Eying the cookies, I considered what Julia would do. *Put aside your petty feelings and be the gracious host* would be her advice. "You're a hard act to follow, Julia Winston." I mumbled under my breath.

"What did you say, dear?" Gladys set the last of the dishes in the cupboard and pivoted on her heel to face me.

I nodded. "Just me having a conversation with Aunt Julia."

"Oh, yes. I have them quite often. I only wish they weren't all one-sided." Her brows puckered. "Does she answer you? I think a spiritual connection would be quite nice." She nodded with a wistful smile.

I swallowed. In the days following Julia's death, Gladys acted quirky and a bit off, and sometimes a lot off. My suspicions had turned into concern when she mentioned conversations with her dearest friend and implied Julia gave her advice.

I stood and picked up the plate of cookies. "Nothing spiritual in my experience. Keep the chicken salad in the fridge. I'm taking these to Nathan and Isadora. Kind gestures and hospitality. Isn't that what Julia would do?"

"Absolutely." Gladys approached and hugged me. "She'd be proud of her niece. And so am I."

"I try my best." I called over my shoulder as I walked down the hall to the stairs. My decision was mine to own, good or bad. Sure, I wasn't comfortable with Isadora, and not so much with Nathan either, but I could manage for the family's sake. Maybe I needed to search deeper to recognize a positive trait or two in both of them. I groaned as I hit the top step. "Here we go."

Approaching their door, I heard voices, and they didn't sound happy. I chewed on the inside of my cheek and sorted through options. If they were arguing, I shouldn't interrupt. I could set the cookies on the floor next to the door and walk away. On the other hand, interrupting might be wise, before things got out of control. I'd witnessed Isadora's angry tirades once or twice. I winced. None were a pleasant scene. I took a few more steps to the door.

"I don't care what you want. This was my decision to come here. My career is at stake, sweetheart. You may be my husband, but you will never be my boss. Got it?" Isadora's voice raised with a nasty edge to it. "Remember, I could ruin your career and those pathetic commercials you always brag about in a heartbeat."

"Izzie, sweetie." Nathan drew out his words.

My stomach rolled at the sound of his whiny voice.

"Don't call me that. How many times do I need to tell you? Now, let's get into bed and make up."

Her tone softened and deepened on the last sentence. That seemed to end the conversation. The sound of kisses and moans quickly followed. I gagged. Interrupting wasn't a great idea after all. I clutched the plate and tiptoed up the stairs to my room. Maybe I needed the cookies more than the newlyweds did.

I sat on my bed and munched on a bite of sugary confection while contemplating Isadora's words. What did she mean about her career being at stake? Last time I'd checked, Broadway theater news claimed she was at the top of her game, headlining in a successful play that had been running for a year. I set down the half-eaten cookie and slid the plate out of reach. Something was missing from this story, but what? I leaned back against the headboard and stared up at the ceiling. The way she talked to Nathan wasn't nice. She threatened to end his career. Did she have something on him, some damaging secret that he was hiding? Maybe I could sum this up as a petty quarrel, but one thing I was sure of, Isadora was most likely up to no good.

CHAPTER TWO

I ENTERED THE KITCHEN AND MOANED. Succulent aromas of bacon, warm bread, and fresh-brewed coffee permeated the air. The winter storm had exited Sierra Pines, moving east, and the sun peaked out from the clouds. Light streamed through the kitchen window and bathed the room in a warm glow.

"Help yourselves, folks. A hardy breakfast will get you through the morning." Gladys lifted her spatula then scrunched her nose and eyed Ollie. "Just look at my brother. He's a perfect example of hardy eating."

Ollie patted his ample stomach and shoveled another bite of cheesy omelet into his mouth.

I grinned. Ollie certainly lived up to his motto—*love life and every morsel in it.* To look at him, you'd never guess he was Gladys's sibling. In everything opposite of his sister, Ollie was tall, rather large-boned, and bald. One trait they shared, though, was having a kind and generous heart. I never witnessed them refusing to help a friend or stranger in need. Shivers ran through me thinking of this past October and how they came to my rescue. I was forever grateful.

"The food is delicious, Gladys." Abby Lewis refilled her coffee cup and added spoonsful of melon and apple slices to her plate.

Abbey had traveled from Oregon where she helped with the family-owned business, an inn on Coos Bay. This was her first vacation in over a year, she claimed. Tall and slender, she glided through a room, graceful as a cat. With those striking blue eyes and thick, blonde hair, she reminded me of a runway model. Neither the Bellwethers nor I got her to open up much, so Abby remained somewhat of a mystery.

I spooned a healthy portion of scrambled eggs on my plate and added strawberries and blueberries before taking a seat. My job was to help with the clean up since cooking wasn't exactly my strongpoint. I also took care of the financial end of running the B&B and other sundry duties while Ollie handled maintenance. The arrangement worked. As I sipped coffee, my gaze took a sideways glance when Nathan and Isadora entered the kitchen.

"Good morning, everyone." Nathan greeted us with a smile.

Isadora yawned and nodded without comment.

I stood then moved to the other side of the table and sat next to Gladys. "Take those two spots. There's plenty of coffee and hot water for tea. Plates are next to the warming pans." I tried keeping my eyes on Nathan while I talked, but couldn't avoid Isadora whose scowl deepened as she lifted each pan lid with a heavy sigh.

I cleared my throat. "Ollie, Abby, meet Nathan Goyer, my cousin, and his wife, Isadora Lane."

Isadora sighed. "I don't suppose you have poached eggs and fresh avocado, do you?"

I could hear Gladys grinding her teeth and mumbling under her breath. Before she said what I guessed would be a scathing reprimand, Nathan interrupted.

"Now, Izzie, Miss Bellwether told us to make any special requests a day ahead. Why don't you have some coffee and a plate of fresh fruit?" He stroked her shoulder.

That seemed to relax her, which relieved me. I patted Gladys's hand. "See?" I whispered. "Everything's fine. Nathan can handle her."

"If you say so." Gladys speared a strawberry and shoved it in her mouth.

Before conversation about the lack of poached eggs and fresh avocado continued, Margaret and Paul Smith, and Faith Ritter came into the kitchen.

"Good morning," I greeted then pointed at Faith. "Nathan, Isadora, this is Faith Ritter. She's a history professor who's come here to collect stories about the gold rush days for an article she's writing. How is that research coming along?"

"Very well, actually." Faith patted her chest then pulled a pair of glasses out of her shirt pocket and shoved them on. "That's better. Can't see as well as I used to, but I'm always forgetting where I put the blasted things.

Anyway, thank you for the advice. Some of the folks in Sierra Pines have wonderful stories about their ancestors. The information is priceless."

"I'm glad I could help." I turned to the Smiths and made introductions. "Did Gladys give you the tour of Julia's collection room yet?" The Smiths were classic movie fans and had written several books about the golden years of Hollywood. When they read about Julia's acting days and her move to Sierra Pines, they arranged to stay at the B&B.

"We're planning to this afternoon," Margaret said. She squeezed Paul's hand. "And we're pleased to announce that our proposal for the new book has been accepted by our publisher."

Gladys squealed and clapped her hands. "Why that's wonderful news! Isn't that wonderful news, Ollie?"

Ollie shoved another bite of eggs in his mouth and gave a thumbs-up sign.

"Julia would be pleased." I gestured for them to take a seat then rose to carry my plate to the sink. Tears dribbled down my cheeks. The Smiths intended to include a chapter about Julia in their book.

In a short while, everyone left to get on with their day. I breathed a grateful sigh of relief, thinking our trip into town might help distract Isadora from her moodiness. Even with his strong influence, Nathan couldn't possibly keep up those pep talks on his own. He needed lots of holiday cheer and festive surroundings to help.

THE SNOW-COVERED GROUND GLISTENED IN THE SUN. I led the way into the heart of town. My pride swelled as I took in the festive trimmings of Sierra Pines. Twinkle lights sparkled in the Western Redbud trees lining the sidewalk along Main Street. Snowflakes, Santas, and reindeer cutouts decorated frosted store windows. Every merchant advertised their holiday specials on an assortment of goods—bagels, sugar cookies, scented candles, tree ornaments, and more.

With the B&B only two blocks away from the heart of town, I suggested we make our journey on foot. Gladys declined to come along, leaving the three of us. I hoped to find safety in numbers by persuading one or two of the other B&B guests to join the tour of Sierra Pines, but the effort failed. I was on my own to keep up the conversation and entertain Isadora while Nathan played on his cell phone. *Lucky me.*

Stopping in front of Meeka's Mementos. I pointed. "If you're looking to buy souvenirs for people back home, this shop is full of touristy trinkets."

Isadora huffed. "I think we should wait. L.A. will be a better place to shop." She squeezed Nathan's arm. "Don't you agree, sweetheart?"

I turned away for an instant and rolled my eyes.

"Oh, I don't know. Those snow globes are nice. I'm sure my little sister would love one. What do you say, Ali? Don't you think Kinsey would enjoy the one with Santa and his sleigh?"

I screwed my mouth into a stiff smile and turned to face him. Kinsey was only three and Aunt Betts doated on her. Having a child late in life filled a void Nathan left when he moved out of the house. She was spoiled and temperamental, but Betts ignored the behavior. Much like she'd done while raising Nathan. Kinsey had enough toys to fill every room in the B&B. I shrugged. "I guess any young girl would like a snow globe."

"Of course, she'll love it." Isadora pulled Nathan to her side and walked to the door. She turned to look over her shoulder. "You don't need to join us. We'll be only a few minutes."

Rude gesture aside, I was relieved to be alone for a moment. "Five days, Ali. You can spend the next hour or two with the happy couple. Then, Ralph will do his part and take them to the lodge. With any luck, I can avoid contact for the rest of their stay." I yanked on the flaps of my hat to cover my ears.

"Ali Winston! Why in the world are you standing out in the cold all by yourself?"

The chirpy, high-pitched voice of Florence Greeley came from behind and made me jump. "Florence! You startled me." I puffed out air and then grinned. "I'm waiting for a couple of B&B guests to finish their shopping. What brings you two out this morning?"

I studied the woman standing next to her. Dottie Sample owned Boxes and Bows. The stationery and packaging business was one of the oldest in Sierra Pines. Her auburn-tinted hair styled in a curly perm took years off her age. She was short in stature but had the muscular build of someone half her age—probably from lifting heavy packages every day. "Hi, Dottie." I smiled.

"Good morning, Ali. Beautiful day for a stroll through town, isn't it?" She pulled her shoulders straight and cleared her throat. "As for Florence and myself, we're on a mission. Now that I'm SPACA's event coordinator, you know, I suggested we make the rounds to find out who's participating in our holiday gift giving."

I covered my lips to stifle a chuckle. For the past two months, Dottie prefaced every comment with words about her title. People began referring to her as that newly appointed SPACA coordinator. The job had belonged to another member who took over the treasurer position.

The Sierra Pines Alliance of Cultural Activities organized many programs, including the Christmas event where distributing gift baskets and toys to needy families was the central focus. Florence had been the president of the group for over ten years and prided herself on presenting the entertainment portion. Starting with the famous names, she'd reach out to celebrities and work her way down to semi-known locals, until one accepted the invitation to our tiny town that barely showed a blip on the radar.

"That's nice." I nodded then turned to face Florence. "Any nibbles on the entertainment guest this year?" Since Julia's passing, I replaced her as the SPACA secretary and kept records of all activities.

Florence pressed her hands to both cheeks and shook her head. "This will be a disaster. A last-minute cancellation puts me back to square one. I swear, no matter how small the name, the diva persona in a celebrity will rear its ugly head. Reese Blaine is nothing but a has-been from that eighties' sitcom." With a tip of her chin, she sniffed. "The misguided diva had the nerve to say her agent advised her not to appear in our holiday event because it would ruin her career." She raised her arm in a careless gesture. "As if. Her career died decades ago along with frizzy perms and stretch pants. I should've gone with the cross-country skier."

I blinked without comment while working my brain to recall who the heck Reese Blaine was.

"To top it off, she had agreed to also MC our event. You know, since Minnie no longer wants the job. She's off to take sky-diving classes and hip-hop dance lessons. I ask you, what woman in her nineties hip-hops? And now, I have two roles to fill." Florence slouched her five-feet-something frame while her penciled brows formed squiggly lines.

Still, I knew Aunt Julia's long-time friend fairly well. Despite the display of theatrical drama, Florence never quit a challenge, not with that inflated ego and fierce determination she wore like a medal of valor.

In a moment of silence, Dottie cleared her throat. "I know someone who'd love to take over the job as MC. In fact, I, erm, *she* has been eying that position for quite some time." With a tilt of her head, she pasted on a smile.

Florence adjusted her scarf. "Of course, I have others on my short list. I'm expecting a phone call from one of them any hour now. Not exactly what I hoped for, but he's been a game show host and has a gorgeous singing voice." She sighed.

I shifted my gaze to Dottie whose face flushed red as a ripe tomato. With palms facing up, I shrugged. The poor woman wanted the job and spoke up every chance she got during the SPACA meetings. From what I witnessed previously; the request always fell on Florence's deaf ears.

Before I could say words to soothe Dottie's anger, Nathan and Isadora burst through the doorway of Meeka's Mementos, carrying several bags overflowing with boxes. I chuckled. So much for waiting to hit the trendy L.A. stores.

"This shop is absolutely adorable." Isadora squealed as she shoved her bag into Nathan's arms. "I found an original Tiffany table lamp shaped like a globe. Meeka certainly has exquisite taste. Idina will love this."

Florence gasped. She nudged my arm then moved closer to whisper. "Idina? As in Idina Menzel?"

"Um hmm, that would be my guess," I said then cleared my throat to grab the happy couple's attention. "Nathan and Isadora, these are my friends, Florence Greeley and Dottie Sample. Ladies meet my cousin Nathan Goyer and his wife, Isadora Lane."

Florence's eyes popped as she squeaked a hello. She pumped Isadora's arm with a bit too much enthusiasm.

"Oh, my goodness. I do love your Broadway performances. The role you played as Barbara in *Beetlejuice* was to die for." Florence giggled. "Literally."

Dottie narrowed her eyes and pursed her lips. "I'm sure she's heard all this before, Florence. So, what brings you to Sierra Pines? This town isn't hopping with excitement like Hollywood or New York."

"Nathan and Isadora are spending part of their honeymoon here before heading to L.A."

"My little cousin is such a sweetheart. When Izzie and I lost our reservation at the ski resort, Ali was kind enough to offer us a room at the B&B." Nathan grinned and slapped me on the back.

I lurched forward at the forceful gesture, then landed firmly on my feet. "Only because my mom and yours asked nicely." The words came out before I could take them back, but Nathan didn't seem to catch on to their meaning.

"Are we going to tour this town, or what?" Isadora tapped her designer boot in rapid tempo. "The morning is cruising by, and I want to go skiing while there's still some daylight left." She tugged Nathan's arm.

"Oh, wait!" Florence dropped her mouth and gasped. "I have a brilliant idea. Isadora Lane, would you do us the honor of being the MC for our Christmas event the Friday after next? I mean, if you'll still be in town." She touched her arm. "Now, before you say no, this event will be covered by newspapers across the state. It's for charity, and I always request the most celebrated stars to help. You definitely are one of those. Stars, that is." Florence blushed.

Isadora removed her hand from Nathan's arm. Narrowing her eyes, she gave her head a slight shake. "I'm not sure. You said news coverage? How big? Would the *Hollywood Star Gossip* mag be one?" She reached to curl a lock of hair around her finger and stared at no one in particular.

Florence bobbed her head. "Oh, yes. I'm sure we can get Tiffany—she's the reporter for the magazine and personal friend of mine—to do a writeup."

I studied the both of them. Isadora wore the face of total disinterest while Florence showed desperation. Give her paws and a tail, and she'd sit up and beg, if it would help her case. I almost felt sympathy for the SPACA president because Nathan's bride was the queen of tortuous behavior, and she dished it out with gusto. Meanwhile, poor Dottie looked ready to blow like Mount St. Helen. She'd coveted the MC role and done everything but come right out to beg Florence for the job. I guess she lacked the confidence and worried about rejection.

I mouthed the words *ask Florence, now,* but Dottie shook her head.

"Maybe we should give Isadora time to think about her answer." I blurted out then snapped my mouth shut.

"Nonsense." Isadora scowled at me. "Publicity can always boost my career, and the *Hollywood Star Gossip's* coverage and your little program will fit perfectly in my work schedule. After my meeting in L.A., we can return here for the event. Thank you, Florence."

I winced as Florence squealed while Dottie's face color deepened to a shade of purple. This was an awkward moment because Isadora and Florence completely ignored her.

"I'll be in touch." Florence glowed with her smile stretching earring to earring. She grabbed Dottie's arm and steered toward Bagels and Buns. "We should let you go. Enjoy your skiing!"

"Well, it's always nice to do something for the little people." Isadora brushed a palm across her coat.

I scrunched my nose. "You mean the vertically challenged? I wasn't aware you were a supporter."

"Seriously, Alexis. That's not what I meant." She huffed then twisted on her heel. "Can we finish this little excursion and stop for lunch? After that tiny breakfast, I'm famished."

"Little. Tiny. Seems we have a theme going here." I mumbled under my breath and led the way down Main Street. Deciding to skip our stops to the theater and the museum, we moved on to Emery and Treadwater Winter Apparel for a talk with Ralph Emory about ski equipment and to arrange a trip to Tahoe Pine Ski Lodge and Resort.

I'd done my very best to bow out and let Ralph take over but couldn't resist the pleading look in his eyes.

"I owe you another lesson, and it's been two weeks since your last one. What if you forget all I taught you?" Ralph raised his chin and eyebrows.

Ralph was one of my best friends in Sierra Pines. We'd met at the B&B when he was a guest. He and his life partner, Owen, moved here a month ago to open a second store. They fell in love with the warm, cozy feel of the town as well as its people and decided to stay. Owen's cousins agreed to manage the other shop, making this move possible.

I sighed. "I guess." I turned to Nathan and Isadora. "We should go. I can show you a couple places to eat, then we'll stop for lunch before heading back to the B&B. I'm sure you'll want to rest and freshen up before the trip to the lodge."

"I'll meet you up there at three." Ralph waved at the newlywed couple and waited until they stepped outside. He gripped my hand. "Thank you. I truly don't think I could handle that woman without help."

"Isadora?" I snorted. "She's more bark than bite."

"I'm not so sure." His brow furrowed. "See you later on, Ali."

Lunch passed without one grumble of complaint. Maybe food was Isadora's recipe to soothe her agitated state. In any case, I was pleased. Noting his relaxed posture and animated conversation, I assumed Nathan felt the same, or maybe he'd been totally oblivious to his wife's behavior.

Close to one, we arrived at the B&B, only to be greeted at the door by Gladys. She twisted her apron while shaking her head.

My brow wrinkled and a hint of concern trickled through me. "What's wrong?" I skipped over hello.

She leaned in close to my ear and cupped a hand to the side of her mouth. "Erm, well it seems the furnace might need a bit of work."

Nathan and Isadora didn't wait to hear more of the conversation. They slipped by us and headed upstairs.

My shoulders sank along with my mood.

"Well, we better call for the repair service to check on it." I pressed my lips together. "Tom is out of town, isn't he?"

Gladys nodded. "Ollie is friends with Glenn Timmons. He owns a furnace repair shop in Placerville. I'll have Ollie give him a call. Sorry, Alexis."

I patted her shoulder. "You know better than to apologize. We have enough in our emergency fund to pay for whatever's needed." I groaned. Except a new furnace. I'd have to call about a loan for that.

"Oh, and another guest arrived while you were gone. Miss Beth Rawlings from Cleveland, Ohio. Since she requested privacy, I put her in the rear left room."

"We aim to please." I smiled. "The newlyweds and I are heading to the ski resort this afternoon."

Gladys raised her brow, and I added, "Not the way I planned to spend my day, but Ralph needs moral support."

"Huh. If you're referring to Frankenbride and Mister Toot-Your-Horn, I do believe that support would take an army."

I wagged my finger. "Now, Gladys. We don't talk about our guests that way." I leaned in. "But thank you. Guess I can use a little of that support too."

"Always, dear." She squeezed my hand, then put her steps in gear toward the stairs. "Now, if you'll excuse me, I promised to deliver lavender bath salts to Miss Rawlings. She wants to freshen up after her long trip."

"I'll go. Gives me a chance to meet her." I walked to the stairs. "Top shelf in the hall closet?"

"Yes. Let me know if we need to order more. Lavender does seem to be everyone's favorite. Thanks, Alexis."

I waved to dismiss her and jogged up the stairs. Pulling out several packets of bath salts, I overheard the mumbled voices coming from the newlyweds' room. No way would I experience a repeat performance. Whether arguments or sappy make-out sessions, all of eavesdropping made me uncomfortable, especially when one in the conversation was my cousin.

I sprinted to the rear end of the hall and skidded to a stop in front of Beth's door. I knocked. "Hello? I'm delivering your lavender bath salts, Miss Rawlings."

The door inched open. Wide, blue eyes peeked out at me. Beth stuck her arm through the opening and wiggled her fingers.

I placed the lavender packets in her hand.

"Thank you." She whispered but accompanied her words with a warm smile.

I nodded. "My name's Ali. I'm owner of the B&B. So, if you need anything or have questions about local spots, restaurants, things to do, just ask."

"Yes, um, I hear there's a ski resort nearby?"

She eased open the door, giving me a better view. I took in her appearance. Tall, muscular but with a curvy frame, shoulder-length black hair, and striking blue eyes. I blinked. "Skiing? Of course." My brain raced and thought of the opportunity in front of me. "Tahoe Pine Ski Resort is about forty minutes east of town. Say, would you like to go there later this afternoon? Another couple and I are leaving here around two." I said a silent prayer she'd agree. With someone else besides me to accompany Nathan and Isadora, the trip might be bearable.

Beth straightened and grinned ear to ear. "Yes! Absolutely I would. Thanks for the invite. I'll meet you in the foyer at two."

The door closed before I could respond. "Huh. That was easy." I whistled while sprinting up the stairs to the third floor and my room. Like Beth, I'd take time to freshen up. Two o'clock was only an hour away.

I wondered about our latest guest. With only a five-minute talk involved, I couldn't assume she was shy, but the topic of skiing sure made her come alive. I made a mental note to grab one of the brochures with descriptions of all the Lake Tahoe region ski resorts, along with a discount coupon, and give them to her.

Adding to my list would be another call to the editor. I understood the world of publishing moved slow as a turtle, but I was desperate for good news. In the meantime, I couldn't put off much longer the other solution to our financial worries. My parents and their handout was a tempting offer. No twenty-eight-year-old woman wanted to admit she couldn't manage on her own, but I'd swallow my pride and take the offer rather than lose the B&B.

I pulled my hair into a ponytail and shoved my legs into ski pants. My ideas to boost business were great ones, but I needed time and money.

"Might as well add a call to Mom and Dad to my list." I blew out a puff of air. Or maybe a miracle would fall in my lap. I grabbed my parka and gloves out of the closet. "Yeah, and money grows on trees."

CHAPTER THREE

No surprise, Nathan and Isadora came out of their room fifteen minutes late. Beth and I had time to chat, which kept me from growing too irritated. I promised Ralph to meet on the slopes at three. I hated breaking a promise.

My brows lifted as Isadora led the way down the stairs. A fur hat—fake or real I couldn't say—covered her head, and she wore fur-trimmed white leather boots to match. A florescent pink, puffy jacket made her look like a marshmallow and twenty pounds heavier.

"So very sorry we're a tad bit late. The water pressure in this place is atrocious. Took forever to draw my bath. Really, Alexis, you should have something done about that."

Beth, who stood close to me, gasped then mumbled words I couldn't catch.

Heat flushed my cheeks. "That happens in the winter. The pipes get a bit sluggish. Run hot water for a couple of minutes next time." I pulled on my parka when a quick glance at Beth reminded me. I gave her a nod. "Nathan and Isadora, this is Beth Rawlings who enjoys skiing and comes from Ohio." I gestured toward the couple. "Beth, these are the Goyers from New York, who also enjoy skiing." Call it petty, but I got some satisfaction out of referring to Isadora as a Goyer. The sour expression on her face told me I hit a bullseye.

"Glad to meet you, Beth." Nathan greeted with a wide grin and one hand extended.

I covered my laugh with a cough. Maybe he got some thrill out of my introduction too.

"Thanks. Same to you." Beth blushed and shook hands. She turned to Isadora who, without a word, walked across the hall to study the foyer table display of photos and mementos.

I caught Beth's casual shoulder-shrug, which seemed to me a polite dismissal. If only I could excuse Isadora's rudeness that easily. "We better get moving or Ralph will think we deserted him."

We piled into the all-terrain SUV, a Land Rover. Julia bought it last year, after deciding the B&B needed official transportation for guests. I'd stored her cute convertible for the winter out of necessity. I loved that sports car, but its light weight and compact size were useless on snow-covered and icy roads. Of course, Ollie offered the use of his ten-year-old pickup on occasion, but it only seated two. Most of the time, the gas-guzzler sat in the garage.

I drove east out of town on Lincoln Highway. The road surface was still slick from the past storm, but chains on the tires kept the vehicle from sliding. Afternoon sunlight peeked through the tall pines and created a blinding, white glare on the snow-covered ground.

I pulled the sun visor down and slipped on sunglasses. "I'm guessing we'll arrive at the lodge around three or maybe a little after."

"Have you skied much, Ali?" Beth asked.

I chuckled. "Only if a dozen or so lessons count."

The rearview mirror reflected the smirk on Isadora's face. I cleared my throat. "Seriously, I have an unhealthy fear of heights and moving at fast speeds. Skiing involves both. Ralph Emory—he's co-owner of a sports apparel shop in town—has been helping me get over that fear, thank goodness." I'd taken one brief lesson with the resident ski instructor, Kyle Steele. He wasn't as tolerant.

"Ralph sounds like a kind and patient person." Beth stuck out her lower lip. "Too many people aren't."

I flipped on my left turn signal. "Unfortunately, I'd have to agree."

"How about we listen to some music? All this chatter is making me anxious." Isadora's tone grew edgy.

"We're almost there. Twenty more minutes, I'd guess." I flipped on the radio and turned to a local station playing soft rock.

The sounds of Nathan humming and tapping his hands to the rhythm hinted he'd tuned out his wife. Was that the way he coped with her moods?

As I pulled into the drive of the ski resort, a light snow began to fall. The twinkling gold lights lining the lodge's walkway and massive porch showed in the distance. The two-story structure was built of redwood and stone with metal roofing that was added a couple decades ago after lightening and fallen pines damaged the original. The place was small compared to Sierra-at-Tahoe and Squaw Valley, but the slopes were excellent, and the resort had its own lodging with ski in ski out accommodations.

I'd learned plenty on the bunny slope and, after a dozen lessons, I'd graduated to the intermediate level. Ralph was serious about training. He'd sent me to the gym to work out to strengthen my muscles and improve cardio. His confidence gave me confidence.

I braked the car at the entrance. "I'll meet you inside. If you spot Ralph, tell him I'll be a few minutes. Looks like the only free parking spots are several rows back."

As I drove away, I glimpsed Isadora sprinting ahead while Nathan hung back to walk alongside Beth. Something was weird about the newlyweds, but what? Not coming up with an answer bugged me.

I steered the car into an open space then grabbed my bag off the seat before exiting. Shielding my eyes with one hand, I studied the nearest slope. Specks of colorful ski parkas stood out against the snow-white background. To the far right, near the back entrance of the lodge, Kyle Steele approached. I scowled, and my heart thumped as the uncomfortable and embarrassing day with him as my instructor came to mind. After less than an hour, he'd thrown up his arms while commenting I had two left feet and neither one could ski—not at all nice.

"Well, Kyle Steele, it turns out I can ski just fine." Gripping the strap of my bag, I held up my head and marched across the parking lot.

Once inside, I searched the lobby for familiar faces. Beth stood at the rental counter, alongside Ralph, while his partner Owen handed Beth a pair of skis. Situated several feet from them and near the manager's office were Isadora, Nathan, and Tabitha. I tilted my head to one side and puzzled over the scene. Isadora and Tabitha stood almost nose to nose. A lot of finger-pointing and scowls soon crescendoed into raised voices. A groan escaped my mouth. "Oh, boy."

I hurried toward them, weaving around obstacles in my path. I winced at the gawking faces and dropped jaws of the resort crowd and feared my own confrontation with the manager. All the B&B guests, along with me, would be banned from Tahoe Pine forever if the situation got any worse. Tabitha Wells would make sure of it. Truth was we weren't exactly best friends.

"You certainly don't deserve a five-star rating." Isadora snapped as her eyes flashed angry green and those crimson-painted lips grew pencil-thin.

Tabitha threw up her arms. "How many times do I need to say it? The reservation date you gave us was for *next* week. Hardly our fault." She lowered her voice, but clenched her teeth as she spoke. "Besides, we've reimbursed you the total amount and given you a voucher for a free stay the next time you visit."

"Are you kidding? I wouldn't come back to this dump if you begged me. In fact, I . . ." Isadora paused to take a breath then stabbed Tabitha's chest with one polished fingernail. "I plan to tell everyone I know, along with a call to the California business bureau, and warn them about you. Let's see how that precious five-star rating holds up then."

Tabitha's chest heaved as she gripped the counter to steady herself. "Making threats? I could have you arrested for that and for libel. I'd be careful if I were you, *Isadora*."

I wiped my brow while sorting through possible options. Intervening might make matters worse, but those clenched fists at Isadora's sides warned me she was about to lose control. I pictured a hard sock to the jaw, followed by a major lawsuit.

However, breaking up the argument fell into Nathan's hands as he gently pulled Isadora away and whispered in her ear. Then he turned to Tabitha. "I'm sorry. My wife has been under a lot of stress lately. Please forgive her." He led Isadora to the far end of the lobby while Tabitha marched to her office and slammed the door.

I blinked. What just happened? I knew Isadora had anger issues, but this display went beyond that. Like Nathan remarked, maybe stress triggered her behavior. I was doubtful.

"Quite a spectacle, though I think she over-played the dramatic performance."

I squealed then turned to face Ralph. "Oh! Hi. So, you think Isadora was putting on an act?"

He shrugged. "Hard to tell. Either that or she's having a mental breakdown. Of course, I don't know the woman well enough."

I shook my head and let out a nervous chuckle. "The display you witnessed? That's pure Isadora. She'd sooner cut you into tiny pieces with her social media trashing than to forgive and walk away. She's an insecure actress with plenty of anger. Nobody should cross her." I shuddered.

Ralph narrowed his eyes and tipped his chin. "Thanks for the warning, but I don't intend to spend time with the grand diva." He patted my shoulder. "Let's get your equipment. Oh, and Beth said to tell you she's heading to the expert slope and will meet us back at the lodge after."

I followed Ralph to the rental counter. After an exchange of hellos with Owen, I gathered my equipment, ready to head outside and gear up.

"I'll be just a few minutes behind you, Ali. Owen and I need to discuss a missing order from Sacramento," Ralph said.

I waved and continued to the exit, lugging my gear. I struggled to keep my thoughts on skiing. Visualization was one of the ways I prepared. Picturing myself going down the slope as graceful as a world ski champion kept the queasy terror inside from taking over. Right now, that wasn't working. My mind was consumed by images of Isadora. Not to mention, I puzzled over Nathan's kind and gentle handling of his wife. This was not exactly the Nathan I remembered. He leaned more toward the date 'em and dump 'em relationships. My suspicions leveled up a bit. He couldn't have changed that much. What was the saying? A zebra can't lose its stripes, and my guess was this zebra must be hiding something.

I hit the automatic door button with my hip and quickly stepped outside. Leaning the skis against the building, I then zipped up my parka and shoved the flaps of my hat over my ears. As I lifted the goggles off my chest, I caught sight of Isadora. She sat on a bench near the ski lift with her head lowered. I could see her upper body shaking as if she might be crying. Nathan was nowhere in sight.

Before I could reach her, Kyle came into view. He laid one hand on her shoulder, but she shrugged it away and stood up to face him. Within seconds, she shouted something I couldn't quite hear. As she stepped back, Kyle grabbed both her arms.

Off to the far left, I spotted Nathan marching toward them. It was hard to tell from several yards away, but his face looked tense. "This can't be good." I hurried to reach them as fast as my boots could move through snow, which was little to nowhere.

"Let go of me." Isadora snapped her words while attempting to wiggle her arms free. Her head suddenly turned, and our eyes met. With a final tug she freed herself from Kyle's grasp. Raising her voice, she added, "I'm perfectly capable of skiing without anyone's help. So, get out of my way."

Kyle's face reddened. "I'm telling you. It's not that easy."

"Hey! What's going on?" As he reached Kyle, Nathan gripped his arm and spun him around.

"Get off me, man." Kyle jerked loose and shoved Nathan backward. His jaw tensed as both fists came up, ready to fight.

Isadora took advantage of the distraction and hurried toward the ski lift. "Isadora! Wait." I shouted, but she didn't turn.

I winced at the sounds of a thud and groan. Tumbling to the ground, Kyle lay still as Nathan ran toward the ski lift.

I trudged through snow, stopping for a second in front of Kyle. "Are you okay?" A grumble and nod were enough assurance for me. I moved on to catch up to Nathan and Isadora who, by now, stood next to the lift.

"Go away, Nathan." Isadora shrugged to dismiss him. "Seriously, you hurt me. As my husband, it would be nice if you supported me instead of talking like I'm some kind of mental patient." She stepped into the next available car then turned to face him. "Truth is, I don't really need you interfering. I can handle this myself." She stabbed her finger at him. "Say one more word about it, and I'll tell everyone everything."

I stood close enough to see the details of her face—a brow etched with anger and thin, rigid lips contrasted with tears on her cheeks. Cold shivered through my body and made me tremble. Despite the obvious pain in her expression, all I could think was she didn't love Nathan. Maybe she didn't love anyone. Or maybe, like Ralph said, this was all a dramatic act. Still, she mentioned the warning again. I heaved a breath. What was Nathan hiding, and why was Isadora so upset?

"There you are. I hope you aren't thinking of skiing on this slope." Ralph shook his head and tugged at my sleeve to lead us in the other direction.

I glanced over my shoulder. Nathan sat on the bench by the lift, as if undecided on what to do. I wanted to reach out, offer some consoling words or give him a hug. Instead, I followed Ralph.

Tugging on my ski boots, I tightened the straps, then stepped into the skis. With a couple of clicks, I fastened the heal and toe pieces. Breathing a sigh, I straightened and stuck the ski poles in the ground, ready to take on the slopes.

"Now, remember what I've taught you. Keep your skis parallel. And when you turn, make sure your skis are flat on the ground but stay balanced on your outside leg. Right?"

"Parallel, skis flat, and balance on outside leg." I tapped my head. "It's all in here. Promise."

"Great." Ralph opened the next available lift. "After you." He stepped to the side to clear my way.

Once the cable set in motion, the car swayed side to side then jerked forward. I peered below us as we were suspended hundreds of feet above the ground. Skiers became tiny images sliding gracefully down the slopes. "Peaceful, isn't it?" I smiled at Ralph.

"One of my favorite places to be, especially after the stress of a busy day at the shop or a spat with Owen." Ralph chuckled.

I shifted my waist sideways to face him. "How's that bundle of cuteness? I hear from Gladys she's the star of the stage in the youth acting classes the Bellwethers teach." I winked.

"Our sweet Sophie." Ralph moaned and placed a hand over his chest. "We couldn't be more blessed. Owen asks me every day when I think we'll hear news from the lawyer about the adoption. He's so anxious, I'm afraid his hair will turn white." Ralph shrugged. "Comes with parenthood, I guess."

"What does?"

"Worrying about your child."

"Hmm. Guess so." Maybe one day, I'd find out, but the idea of marriage and parenthood wasn't on my mind. At this moment, my concern focused on Isadora and the uncomfortable scene with Kyle. I knew he was crabby, impatient, and not at all a people person. However, what I witnessed didn't make sense. Grabbing hold of Isadora as if forcing her to . . . what? Take skiing lessons? I tapped my fingers on the lift door. That explanation didn't work in any way.

"Why so quiet? Did I miss something before I came outside?" Ralph raised his brow.

I let out a puff of air. "Where do I start?" I gave him the abridged version of what transpired, starting with Isadora's confrontation with Kyle and ending with her telling Nathan to get lost. "Weird, right?"

"After the scene in the lobby with Tabitha, I'm not surprised by Isadora's behavior. She's got to be off her nut."

I squinted as sunlight glared through the windows. "Maybe so."

The lift car swayed again as we came to a stop. Ralph jumped down and held my hand as I followed.

Wind whipped through my hair and a spray of snow stung my face. I placed the goggles over my eyes and took a deep breath. Cold air traveled into my lungs and invigorated me. From up here the world below and everyone in it seemed so small and insignificant. Somehow, I felt stronger.

"Are you ready to go, Miss Winston?" Ralph nudged me.

To answer, I pushed off with my poles and, leaning forward, schussed down the hill. The force of cold air tingled my skin as I picked up speed. A rush of adrenaline ran through me and, for a moment, surprised me. Up to now, all my concentration had been on keeping the proper stance so I wouldn't lose my balance and fall. This feeling was so much better. I laughed out loud as I shifted weight to my outside leg and slalomed across the slope. Amazed at how the movement came without effort, I tried again, turning to the opposite side which came closer to the expert slope.

Wind whistled in my ears, yet somehow, I heard a mournful, high-pitched cry echoing from the line of pines on my right. As if my gut instinct took over, I slalomed toward the trees and that sound, ignoring Ralph who shouted my name again and again. Maybe I acted paranoid. After witnessing the dramatic and confusing displays back at the lodge and the anxious mood they put me in, who could blame me?

With a sharp turn of my skis, I stuck my poles in the ground and came to a stop. I held my breath and, for a few seconds, heard only the soft rustle of branches swaying in the breeze. Could the sound have been the screech of a bird or wildcat? Plenty of wildlife lived in the Sierras. I shrugged and stepped to bring my skis around, pointing toward the slope, when a scream pierced the silence. I tensed. The frightening sound came from beyond the pines and in the same direction as before.

Without hesitating, I pushed off to steer around the grove of pines and find a path. In several hundred yards, I came to a clearing, which led to the more difficult slope, but I didn't stop to consider any other option. Those screams might be a cry for help. I couldn't ignore that.

The path descended. Soon, I spotted a sign that warned skiers of the drop-off ahead. Catching my breath, I kept going, only at a slower pace. The clearing grew narrower, and I could see another cluster of pines up ahead. I pulled to a stop. Shielding my eyes from the sunlight, I scanned the area from left to right. Movement far off to my right made me freeze. *Red parka and black cap.* My heartbeat skipped then raced faster. Nathan wore a red parka and black cap. I pushed off with the poles and skirted around the trees to reach him.

He stood with his hands clasping the back of his head. Shifting his upper body side to side, he let out a mournful cry.

"Nathan?" I stepped behind him and gently placed a hand on his shoulder. "Nathan?" I spoke softer. "What's wrong?"

In a slow and awkward gesture, he raised his arm, trembling as he pointed to the drop-off.

I swallowed and leaned over to peer into the ravine. A tiny whimper escaped my lips. A florescent pink jacket stood out against the background of white. Arms and legs spread in awkward directions. And a fluffy fur hat lay to the side. I squeezed my eyes shut then opened them wide. The image hadn't disappeared. Gripping Nathan's coat sleeve, I steadied my wobbly knees. "Isadora?" My voice whispered, carried away by the wind. In all the dramatic fashion she'd be proud of, Isadora had given her final performance.

CHAPTER FOUR

R ALPH WRAPPED HIS ARM AROUND ME in a tight hug, but I couldn't stop from shivering—or worrying. Medics had gathered at the cliff with their equipment in hand. Reaching the base of the ravine, they hoisted the gurney with ropes. I turned and buried my face in Ralph's shoulder. I couldn't gather the courage to view Isadora's body lying on that gurney, wrapped in a body bag.

"I should be with Nathan in case he needs me." I pulled away from Ralph and swiped my wet cheeks with the back of my sleeve.

Ralph patted my back. "I think maybe you should take a breather. Your cousin will be fine. He's in Sheriff Sterling's hands."

I cringed. "You don't know Nathan. He's the kind to shoot off his mouth before thinking." My gaze shifted to study the two men. Nathan shook his head and backed away at one point while Quint wrote in his little notebook which I knew meant he was collecting plenty of information for his case. Whether that was good or bad for Nathan I didn't know. However, I'd lean toward the not-so-good side. He got into more scrapes than the average teen and a man in his twenties, mostly due to impulsive, immature, and sometimes angry behavior. He was a child in a man's body and needed a body guard to keep him out of trouble. I shuddered to imagine what Aunt Betts would have to say—like Nathan was her baby boy, and I should be looking out for him.

"Why don't we head back to the lodge for a warm beverage? I'm sure the, um, questioning will take a while. No point in freezing while we wait, is there?" Ralph smiled and squeezed my hand.

I wound a curl of hair around my finger, uncertain what to do. With a final sideways glance at Quint and Nathan, I shrugged. "You're right. They'll be fine." My words didn't quite fit my confidence level, but I couldn't think of anything else to change it. "Let me give Quint a heads-up, then we can leave."

With skis still attached, I slid my way across the snow to where the men stood, several yards from the ravine. I couldn't hear the exact words of their conversation, so I inched closer. Quint hadn't noticed me approaching. He continued with his questions while Nathan ran fingers through his hair and paced back and forth.

"I tell you. I don't know what happened. I heard a scream coming from this direction, and I looked around but didn't see anyone," Nathan said.

"What made you look down the ravine?" Quint tapped his pen tip on the notebook. "If you didn't see anyone, and I'd guess after the fall the victim didn't make another sound, why look there?"

My stomach rolled hearing him say victim.

"I don't know." Nathan shook his head. "I guess because of the scream. People scream when they fall, right? All I remember is one minute, I was standing on the other side of those pines, then the next, I was looking down the ra-ravine." He sobbed and covered his face with his hands.

My heart tore. I wanted to stop Quint from asking all those questions. Nathan was miserable. He'd just lost his wife. What was Quint thinking? In the next second, I took a deep breath then cleared my throat to get his attention.

"Don't mean to interrupt, but Ralph and I are heading to the lodge to wait." I shot a look at Quint. "I mean, if that's okay with you?"

He fixed his gaze on me.

I stiffened. This situation was awkward. Sometimes, mixing roles of boyfriend and sheriff didn't fit the moment. Like now. "Okay then." I pointed behind me. "I'll just leave you two to finish."

"Nathan will need to ride back to the station with me so I can get some more information," Quint said.

I nodded. "Okay." My gaze darted from him to Nathan and back again. "I guess I'll see you later?"

"Yep. I'll follow up to get statements from you and Ralph." Quint shoved his notebook and pen back inside his jacket pocket.

At last his face relaxed as he approached me. He closed his hand around mine and his lips turned up at the corners just a bit. "I'm doing my job, Ali. You know that, right?" He kept his voice low.

"I do know. It's just . . ." My insides quivered as I glanced at Nathan, who stared at the ravine. Couples squabbled, even newlyweds. I pictured Isadora and heard her angry words, but remembered Nathan's calm response. "He's my cousin. He's *family*, and I can't believe he killed her. He loved Isadora." At least I hoped he did.

Quint gripped my shoulders. "I'll work the case like I always do. If he's innocent, that will come out in the end. You have to trust me."

"Sure." I stepped away and out of his hold. "Give me a call when you need my statement." Overwhelming sadness rushed through me. I was exhausted both emotionally and physically.

"Are you ready, Ali?" Ralph stepped close and touched my shoulder before facing Quint. "Sheriff Sterling." He tipped his head in greeting.

"Ralph. I was telling Ali that I'd be in touch to get your statements." After a silent pause, he cleared his throat. "We'll work through this. Don't worry."

I wrapped my arm around Ralph's as we moved away. "Let's get that hot beverage. I'm thinking of White Russians with extra whipped cream and sitting by the fireplace while we wait. What do you say?" At least I could try to put on a brave front.

"I'm absolutely on board." He cleared his throat. "Giving Quint our statement isn't the real reason you want to stick around, is it?"

"No, it's not." The desperate look on Nathan's face haunted me, not to mention picturing Aunt Bett's angry expression. Going back to the B&B now felt like I abandoned him. I couldn't, not just yet.

We finished our trip down the slope, entered the lodge, and approached the rental booth.

"Why don't you go ahead and order for us. I'll turn in the equipment and speak with Owen. I'm sure word about the accident has spread," Ralph said.

My heart sank at the thought of people gossiping about such a tragedy. "Look for me at a table near the fireplace." I steered a path to Tahoe Eats and Beverages to place my order and stood behind two other customers. While waiting, I scanned the lounge area. Soft murmurs of conversation and laughter filled the air where people congregated, drank beverages, and nibbled on snacks. The impressive stone fireplace in the center opened on two sides to project the heat. Several tables, seating, and benches surrounded the area.

To my far left, Kyle Steele set a steaming mug on an end table then sat next to a female guest. He wrapped his arm around her shoulder for a brief moment.

I pulled off my hat and ran fingers through my hair. I recognized the woman—Beth Rawlings. What was Kyle doing there? Consoling her, perhaps. At least that's what the scene looked like.

In the next minute, Kyle stood and walked away.

After setting the mug on the end table, Beth leaned her head against the sofa and closed her eyes. With finger and thumb, she massaged her temples.

I contemplated whether to join her. When I was feeling poorly—not that I was certain that was her case—I only wanted to be left alone. On the other hand, someone showing compassion was always welcome.

"What can I get for you, Miss?"

I shifted to face the server. "Hi. I'll take two Hot White Russians in mugs with extra amounts of whipped cream, please. Oh, and go easy on the vodka. We're driving home." Though I would've liked my drink extra strong to help sedate the worry and shock attacking my emotions, I erred on the side of caution. I strived for control in my life. This situation wouldn't allow it, and neither would Quint. What a mess.

"Here you go. Light on the vodka. Heavy on the whipped cream." The server, a perky blonde with a dimpled chin, smiled and slid two frothy mugs across the counter.

I exchanged mugs for cash then took my beverages in hand. Steering a path to where Beth was seated, I braced my shoulders. If she looked at all displeased at my intrusion, I'd find another spot for me and Ralph to sit.

"Hi, Beth. Looks like you're ready to call it a day." I twisted my mouth into what I hoped was an encouraging smile.

She gasped and her eyes popped open. "Oh! Wow, you startled me."

She straightened and placed both hands at her sides, but not before I noticed the trembling. I gestured to the sofa. "Mind if I sit? I mean, unless you'd rather be alone?"

She shook her head and relaxed her shoulders. "No. I could use the company."

I sat and leaned against the arm of the sofa, facing Beth. "Is everything okay? Did something happen while you were skiing?"

She closed her eyes and rubbed her temples again. "Migraines. When I get one, nothing much helps. This came on so suddenly. One minute, I was enjoying my trip down the slope. The next, I was seeing stars. Bright lights. They call those visions an aura. I call them disturbing. Happens to a lot of migraine sufferers. After a good night's sleep, I'll be fine." She gave her shoulders a slight shrug and attempted to chuckle. "Anyway, enough about me. How was your skiing?" She lifted her mug and took a swig.

I pressed my lips together and searched for the right words. Her blank expression told me the gossip vine hadn't reached her. "I guess you haven't heard. There was an accident on the slope." I gauged her reaction. She lowered the mug a few inches, along with her jaw.

"What? Oh my. I hope no one was hurt." She set down her beverage and placed both hands together on her lap. While lines creased her forehead, her chin quivered.

"There you are! I made a complete circle around the fireplace to find you. Hello, Beth." Ralph's smile dipped southward. "What's wrong? You look upset."

I patted the seat next to me then pointed to his mug. "One Hot White Russian as ordered. I was ready to tell Beth about Isadora when you arrived."

"Oh. She doesn't know?" As he furrowed his brow, Ralph took a healthy swig of his drink.

"Not yet." I patted Beth's hand. "Isadora fell off a cliff into a ravine. Unfortunately, she didn't survive."

Beth clutched her throat. "That's horrible! How did it happen? Who found her?" She shook her head. "Poor woman. And her husband. How awful. Didn't they just marry?"

Beth's words sent my emotions into a spiral. At this point, I'd need several White Russians to calm me. "They did. In fact, Nathan was the one who found her." My voice trembled on that last part.

"I think I'm going to be sick." Beth cradled her head with both hands.

I shifted my gaze to Ralph. "Migraines."

"Would you like me to call you an Uber? We might be here awhile. The sheriff wants statements from both Ralph and me," I said.

Beth lifted her head and blinked. "You were there too?"

"I heard a scream and found Nathan at the cliff. Seriously, you look ready to pass out. Let me call for a ride. We need to get you back to the B&B. I'll let Gladys know so she can make you some tea or whatever you like. Okay?" I squeezed her arm.

"Sure. That would be nice. Oh, and if you see that ski instructor? His name is Kyle. Would you tell him thank you? He was coming down from the slope to the lodge while I was struggling with my skis. He helped me inside. Poor man was limping too. I hope he's all right."

My gaze flickered. "Limping?" Suddenly, I pictured the scene when Kyle had walked away after consoling Beth. His gait hadn't appeared stiff or awkward. Maybe I missed that detail. I'd been busy focusing on Beth and wondering what was wrong.

"I asked him about it. He grumbled something about a client, but I didn't listen closely because of the pain in my head." Beth shrugged.

"Yes. Your migraine. I'll be sure to tell him when I see him." Even though he'd most likely tell me to butt out of his business, I was anxious to see Kyle's reaction after I mentioned Beth's comments.

We sat and finished our drinks while chatting small talk, anything but the topic most on our minds. Isadora's death was horrific and left so many unanswered questions. I worried about Nathan. In his grieving state, how could he handle being interrogated by authorities, or worse, being accused of murder, if that was where Quint would take this?

"You know, she had to have enemies. Somebody like Isadora angered and alienated a lot of people." I voiced my thought aloud to Ralph as we watched Beth get into the Uber.

"Hmm. I can't argue with that." He scrunched his nose. "Not to speak ill of the dead, but she was hard to like. I picked up on that in a matter of minutes. Oh, and from your accounts." His brow arched. "Better watch those stories, or your boyfriend might consider you a suspect."

A shaky laugh escaped my lips. "Too late. He's already heard plenty." I peeked at my watch. "Speaking of Quint, I wonder how much longer he'll be? You'd think he and Nathan would've returned to the lodge by now."

Ralph put his hand on my shoulder. "Ali, he will be fine."

"Yes, I realize." I turned. "I hate this uncertain place my mind is trapped in. I hate my cousin being in the thick of it. A possible murder case, no less. I mean, what will my mom and aunt say? That I screwed up, that's what. Growing up, I was always the responsible one while Nathan was the goof who got into trouble. My job was to keep an eye on him. What a horrible mess." My voice hitched and trailed off while I blinked away tears.

"Ali, it's not your job any longer. He's a grown man who should be watching out for himself, don't you think?" His hand rubbed my shoulder.

"Some habits are hard to let go of, I guess."

"Why don't you let me drive you home? You can send for your car tomorrow."

I shook my head. "I don't need—"

"I insist. Now, let's get you back to the B&B. I'm sure Gladys is frantic with worry." Ralph wrapped his arm around my waist.

"Fine. You're right. No good waiting here." I walked with Ralph to the exit door. Rather than worrying and moping about the circumstances, I should be working to figure out who most wanted to harm Isadora. If the accident wasn't an accident, that is. I kept my fingers crossed for good news from the coroner's office, but that glass of hope was more empty than full.

On the drive home, I stayed quiet. My thoughts rambled and poked holes in my numerous theories of who could be a killer. None of the people I knew seemed capable. Sure, everyone had their flaws, but to commit murder? I shuddered.

As we pulled in the drive, sure enough, Gladys was peering out of the front window. Ralph was right. She wouldn't rest until seeing me alive and well. I pulled on the door handle. "Thanks, Ralph. You're a true friend." In quick motion, I leaned to give him a peck on the cheek. "Talk to you tomorrow."

I ran up the sidewalk and toward the front porch. The door flew open as I reached the top step.

"Oh, thank goodness. When Beth told me the whole story, I nearly fainted. I'm so very happy you're safe." Gladys shut the door behind me then wrapped me in a tight hug and wouldn't let go. "I couldn't bare it if anything happened to you. Julia would never forgive me." Her words muffled into my chest.

I rubbed Gladys's back. "I'm fine, Gladys. You and Julia don't need to worry." With more than a little effort, I loosened her hold and stepped away. "Question is, are you okay?"

"Oh, of course, dear. Now that you're home." She clucked her tongue. "That poor man. What a horrible thing to happen, even if his wife was such a—"

I squeezed her hands. "Now, Gladys. Let's not finish that thought."

"Yes, of course. I'm not in my right mind. With everything that's gone on today, who would be? Perhaps a hot toddy or some chamomile tea will help. Would you care to join me?"

"Some tea would be perfect." I followed her into the kitchen. "Did Beth retire for the evening?"

"Yes. The poor dear is positively frazzled. I sent her off to her room with both warm and cold packs and advised her to get plenty of rest."

"Ali. There you are." Ollie entered the kitchen through the back door.

I blinked. He didn't greet me with his usual smile. Instead, his wrinkled brow and the rigid line of his lips hinted that something was wrong. "Ollie, what is it?"

"Come, sit." He motioned at the table.

I pulled up a chair across from him while Gladys stood off to the side, fiddling with the tea kettle. Resting my hands on the table, I stared at Ollie. "Okay, tell me the bad news. Does this have to do with the B&B?"

He nodded. "The furnace needs to be replaced. Glenn Timmons tried everything he could, but it's done for. Glenn will find us the best deal for a new one, but . . ." He covered my hands with one of his. "Ali, the cost will set us back a tidy sum."

I sank deeper into my chair. "A tidy sum which we don't have." I'd researched prices already. Thousands of dollars for a furnace was not in our emergency fund. "I guess my next step is to pay a visit to our bank." I slid the chair away from the table and stood. "Maybe we can brainstorm on other ideas tomorrow." I walked over to the counter. "Gladys, I'll take my tea to go. I'm heading upstairs to my room. If there's any energy left in me this evening, I plan to make a list of things to do." Things like how to solve the mysterious death of Isadora Lane without implicating Nathan and ways to somehow save my B&B from bankruptcy.

"All right, dear." She handed me a cup.

"Let me know when . . . or if Nathan returns tonight. Okay?" I smiled and patted her shoulder. "Thank you. I don't know what I'd do without you." I shifted a glance at Ollie. "Without both of you."

Ollie raised his cup. "You, too. We are all in this together, remember."

"Yes, we are." I held up my cup. "Night." My steps grew heavy as I trudged upstairs. A possible murder, a family member as the prime suspect, and the B&B heading toward financial ruin shredded my usually confident mood into tiny bits. Who knew if this was the last of what looked like bad karma? I shivered. In one day, our holiday spirit had gone from merry to scary.

CHAPTER FIVE

I TAPPED THE DOLLAR SIGN KEY OVER and over while staring at the screen of my laptop—a mindless and nervous act triggered by a morning spent shuffling ideas. I digested them and discarded most until my brain was fried. How to raise eight-thousand dollars in the next twenty-four hours was impossible to answer. Anyone could see that, but I refused to quit. "Stubborn willpower won't get you anywhere this time, Alexis Winston." I grumbled and stabbed at the dollar key several more times.

My gaze strayed to the front window. Sunlight filtered through the stained glass and spread a rainbow tint that brightened the floor, the walls, and the desktop where I sat. I stretched my upper body, releasing the rubber bands of tension, then, closing my eyes, I leaned back against the chair.

Raising the cost of rooms at the B&B was the only practical solution I'd come up with. Asking the bank manager for yet another loan was a longshot, but worth a try. I'd jazz up the website, maybe turn to someone with web design experience for help. Unfortunately, a shiny, new site would take time to attract customers and build the B&B bank account. I needed money now. "What am I going to do, Julia? I have to save the B&B." I twirled around in my chair to face the hall and gasped. "Oh! Gladys, you startled me."

"Sorry, but I was on my way to the parlor when I heard grumbling noises coming from this way. Are you all right? You sneaked out of the kitchen this morning before we had a chance to discuss our situation." She stilled for a few seconds then pulled something from behind her back.

I tilted my head. "What are you holding?"

She moved closer and sat on the sofa near me. "A photo album. I was tidying the cabinet hutch in the kitchen when I found it." Her eyes brightened and she giggled. "Such a treasure. Julia, Ollie, and I had so many adventures back then."

"Your days in Hollywood, you mean." I nodded. I'd heard so many stories of the movies, the stars, the parties, and how lucky they were to be a part of that scene. Of course, not all of those memories were happy ones. My mind flashed for a moment on the worst story of all. Aunt Julia had fallen head over heels in love with Cary Grant. They'd had a passionate but brief affair before he dumped her to marry another actress. After that breakup, Julia decided to dust off the glitter and glamor of Hollywood and return to Sierra Pines to take care of her ailing mother. Before long, Julia turned the nineteenth century Victorian home into a bed and breakfast, and her dear friends, the Bellwethers, arrived to help her run the business.

"Yes. As you know, Ollie was a talented stuntman. I took bit roles in a few movies, of course. And your aunt was the most beautiful actress. She could've won an Oscar one day." Gladys shook her head.

"Just like me, she didn't care for being in the limelight, so she turned to prop design." I smiled. Julia and I often talked about our common interest in the craft. I helped her with projects she made for the local theater productions, which soon made me consider that as my career path. However, fate steered me to screen writing then as an assistant researcher, and prop design became a hobby. That same turn of fate led me to run the B&B, at least for the time being.

Gladys patted the sofa. "Come. Sit with me and take a trip down our Hollywood memory lane. Besides, you need a break. If those frown lines on your forehead get any deeper, you'll look as old as me." She chuckled.

"Fine." I stood and circled the desk to join her. "I do need to take my mind off of this growing list of problems."

"Here, look at this one. Julia received her award plaque for her designs on the movie *Notorious*. My how happy and proud we all were." Gladys sniffed. "Too bad he had to go and ruin the moment."

"Hmm." I knew the "he" she referred to. Cary Grant announced his engagement, and Julia responded by throwing the plaque at him.

"Oh! Here's where we stayed while filming in San Francisco. The hotel manager explained his passion for movies. He boasted how many celebrities came to his establishment. Jimmy Stewart and Myrna Loy in *After the Thin Man* and of course Humphrey Bogart in *The Maltese Falcon* were just a few."

I studied the photos more closely and flipped through the pages. There were at least a dozen shots. Julia posed in front of what I guessed was her room and pointed to the name plate over the door which read, *The Lady from Shanghai.* I recognized the title as one of those classics Gladys and I had watched together. Inside Julia's quarters, views of various frames hanging on the wall with scenes from the movie, like Orson Wells and Rita Hayworth as they sailed to exotic ports, were on display. Mementos such as a safari hat and a miniature replica of the yacht *Circe* decorated the room.

I flipped through more pages and stopped when I found one with a brochure tucked inside the plastic sheaf. In bold print and centered at the top was the name "Old San Francisco Hotel." My breath hitched as I read the description. "A movie theme. How clever is that?"

"It is, or I should say *was* unique. The owner turned his passion into a hotel dream. Too bad the business folded in the nineties." Gladys shrugged. "I would've loved to return for a visit and reminisce about those days."

I straightened and smacked the album with one hand. "Maybe you still can. Reminisce, I mean." The idea seeded and blossomed in my mind. Images flashed, and, with each one, my grin expanded.

"Oh." Gladys widened her eyes to saucer-sized. "Oh! You want to turn our B&B into a movie-themed attraction." Her head bobbed. "Excellent thinking, Alexis. I love the idea."

I set the album on the coffee table and shifted in my seat to face her. "We pick a half-dozen films Julia worked on. Name each room with a title and take items from her collection and add framed photos of candid movie shots, hopefully some with Julia in them, to decorate the rooms. Make a few changes to our website, and bingo! We have a winner. Right?" I bounced off the sofa and paced the library. "Let's get started on planning today. After the holidays, we can move forward and make this idea a reality." I stopped in front of Gladys and pointed. "You and Ollie decide which films would mean the most to Julia. Then I'll go through her collection to take inventory of the items that will match."

She clasped her hands together. "I'm so very excited. The Sierra Pines B&B with a classic movie theme will be one of a kind."

"Or maybe not." I frowned. "I'll do an internet search. If there are any hotels, motels, or B&Bs with a similar attraction, I'll find them." I picked up my pace again. "Even if there are, let's say, a dozen or so in the country, we can claim we're one of the few who offer a movie experience."

Gladys smacked the sofa back. "How about film clips? We set up televisions in each room to play clips from the movies. When guests arrive, we have the videos playing for them."

"What about cost? Six television sets won't be cheap." I chewed on a thumbnail. "Unless Abe Victor at the electronics store can offer us a deal. You know him better than me, Gladys. Can you give him a call?"

She lifted her chin and winked. "Better yet, I'll pay him a visit with a plate of fresh-baked cookies."

"Great. Now, if only I can solve our immediate problem." I flopped down on the sofa.

"Thousands of dollars for a new furnace." Gladys shook her head. "Too bad it's winter. I don't think guests will appreciate living in a true Victorian age."

"With only a fireplace to keep you warm?"

"Or bed warming pans and stocking caps at night." Gladys nodded.

I chuckled. "No, we want to attract guests, not scare them off."

"So, are you going to call the bank manager today?"

"Maybe I'll drive into town and talk to Sheryl in person." Even if she refused to help, I had to try.

Gladys stroked my arm. "Let Ollie meet with Glenn. Maybe he can persuade him to accept monthly payments."

"Every idea is worth a try. Thanks, Gladys." My breath quivered. Financial woes were only one problem the B&B faced. When news got out about Isadora's death, potential guests might think twice about staying here or even recommending our establishment. After all, this was the second tragedy associated with the B&B in less than two months. "Has Nathan come out of his room?" Working on my problems with the B&B had kept my mind off of Nathan. Now that I had my game plan, Isadora's death and Nathan's predicament came to the forefront of my thoughts. I'd knocked on his door early this morning, but all I got was grumbling to leave him alone. At least Beth had taken a turn for the better. She'd been chatty and all smiles this morning at the breakfast table.

Gladys shook her head. "I haven't heard a peep from his room. Anyway, I left a tray by the door. Maybe he'll answer if he hears your voice?"

"I'll give it a try after I call my mom and give her the bad news." My stomach rolled.

"You mean about Nathan."

"I'm sure Nathan hasn't told his mom yet. I can't find the guts to call Aunt Betts, either, and that makes me feel guilty." I heaved a sigh.

"I think you're doing the right thing. Your mom is close to her sister, closer than you are. She'll know better what to say." Gladys managed a smile.

"I guess. Still doesn't give me comfort."

"Are you going to tell them about the B&B?" Her brows peaked.

"Probably not. We'll see." I gathered my list and empty coffee mug. "First, I need another hit of coffee. Then I'll head to my room to make the call."

Gladys took the mug from my hand. "Let me bring you the refill. Just promise me you'll come down to the parlor at noon. I've been baking all morning and have dozens of cookies, nut roll, and fudge to share. Most of the guests will join us. Coffee or tea and dessert. What do you say?" Her eyes sparkled along with an encouraging smile.

I stared at the ceiling for a second and tapped my lip. "Hmm, well, let me think. Stuck alone in a room, tortured by my problems or eating sweets and chatting with my best friends." I poked her in the shoulder. "Never could turn down dessert." I winked.

Gladys walked out of the library and toward the kitchen. "Please invite your cousin. I'm sure you can persuade him to come out of his room and join us."

I jogged up the stairs, but suddenly paused to listen for any noise inside Nathan's room. I raised a fist to knock then dropped my arm. "Nathan? Are you listening?"

The door opened. "Hey. I'm just . . ." Nathan swiped an arm to point behind him.

I peeked around his shoulder to look inside the room. My brows curled upward. "Planning to do a bit of housekeeping?" Clothes were draped over the chair and bed, and some bunched on the floor. A plate with a half-eaten omelet and a bowl of fruit sat on the end table next to a glass of juice. I sniffed and wrinkled my nose. Unpleasant odors I couldn't identify wafted from the room.

He raised an arm to rake fingers through his hair. "Sorry. I got back late last night."

"No apology needed." I hesitated, but decided to dive right in. "How did things go with Sheriff Sterling?"

"About as well as you'd imagine." A short burst of laughter escaped him. "Our honeymoon. This was supposed to be our honeymoon, Ali."

"Nathan. I'm so sorry." I reached to touch his arm, but he pulled away. Gone was the usual sarcastic smile and his voice of confidence.

"You know what's worse than your spouse dying while on your honeymoon? Being accused of murdering her. Can you believe that?"

My breath hitched. "I'm sure Quint wouldn't accuse you like that. He'll investigate every angle and find the real killer. Trust me."

"I've been warned not to leave town." His voice flattened. "I just want to get back to my job. Some sense of normal, you know? Keeping busy is what I need."

I lifted my voice in an encouraging tone. "Why don't you come downstairs later? Gladys baked several desserts and plans to serve guests in the parlor around noon. I'm sure getting out of your room will help take your mind off everything." I didn't know what else to say. I couldn't assure him things would turn out well.

"Sure. Dessert sounds nice. See you then."

Nathan closed the door before I could respond. A heavy mood threatened to swallow me up. I shook my head, determined to fight it. Things I could control should be first in line as far as my agenda went. A couple of phone calls were at the top of the list.

I marched down the hall and up to the third-floor attic, each step giving back my determination. Once inside my room, I shut the door and pulled out my phone. I stabbed number one in my favorites and waited to hear my mom's or dad's voice.

"Hello, sweetie. How are you doing?" Mom said.

I dropped into the chair situated next to the window, my tightened muscles released in a sob or two. I hiccupped and caught my breath. "I'm good."

"Hmm. You don't sound good. Tell me what's wrong."

Her voice switched into mother-mode, a warm and tender sound that soothed me. "Okay. I'm not good. Not at all." I drew my knees up underneath my chin and relayed what had happened in the past twenty-some hours—Isadora's accident, Nathan's questionable involvement, and, since my emotions reeled out of control, I blurted out the news about my troubles with running the B&B. That last admission made me ashamed, and the guilt in me resurfaced. The news about Nathan was enough to handle. "Sorry. I should be focusing on Nathan and . . . I'm sorry." My voice quivered.

"Oh sweetie. I'm so sorry we can't be there for you and Nathan. Don't worry. I'll talk to Betts. Nathan is probably too ashamed to tell her. Poor thing. What he must be going through. Maybe if I reserve a flight, your dad and I could come, though tomorrow would probably be the soonest available, and I doubt Betts would be able to since she has Kinsey to deal—"

"Mom, let me stop you right there. Please." I gripped the phone. "I'm sure Nathan will be cleared of any wrongdoing before the day's up. Trust me. Coming here won't help any."

"You're probably right." She sighed. At least let us help you with the B&B. What about a loan to help pay for the new furnace?"

I bit down on my tongue, but grateful to switch topics. "Actually, I was thinking of something a bit different. A way this doesn't come out of your pockets."

"Oh?"

"How about a GoFundMe sort of event?"

"I don't follow."

"Through your play's profits. If your producer would allow it, that is." I snuggled deeper into my chair. "Whatever the theater takes in through ticket sales, a portion, just a small portion, could be marked for the Sierra Pines Bed and Breakfast. I mean, what do you think?" I'd read about those funding campaigns, people raising money for everything— weddings, concert tickets, all sorts of items, big and small. Funding for a new furnace seemed reasonable.

"That's an excellent idea, Ali!" Her voice lifted. "Even if Mr. Swallow doesn't agree, your dad and I will donate our salary to your cause."

I groaned. "Then it comes out of your pockets, which I'm trying to avoid. Please, run the idea by Mr. Swallow. If he doesn't agree, I'll find another way. Promise?"

She clucked her tongue. "I don't know why you're so determined to refuse our personal help. We care about you and your venture, even if it turns out to be a foolish one."

"Mom." I gritted my teeth and refused to take the bait and argue a point that had been discussed numerous times. "Just ask Mr. Swallow. Okay? I have to go. Another phone call to make. Tell Aunt Betts I'm sorry and trying my best to help and support Nathan. Love you. Give my love to Dad too." I punched the end call button. My idea about a fund-me campaign was a longshot. I worried if she kept trying, I'd finally cave and take the loan offer.

I tapped on my phone and stood facing the window. Frost etched in the corners, forming an oval frame. I could see through the center and view the Sierra Mountains. The New York skyline couldn't compete with this snowcapped majestic scene. I was both humbled and grateful to be close to such an example of nature's beauty.

I scrolled through my contacts and selected the number of Sierra Pines Community Savings and Loan. Sheryl Gibbons, the bank manager, answered on the first ring.

"Hi Sheryl. It's Ali Winston. How are you today?" Always start with pleasantries, as Julia would say.

"I'm doing well, Ali. How about you?"

We went back and forth, talking a bit about the holiday, the weather, and our families before I got down to business. "I need to make an appointment to see you, today or tomorrow morning, if you're available?" I held my breath.

"Sure. I have an opening at eleven tomorrow. How's that sound?"

"Perfect." I smiled.

"May I ask what this meeting concerns?"

"Um. Well." I scratched behind one ear. "Can we wait to discuss the particulars tomorrow? I hear Gladys calling for me."

"Sure. See you then."

I exhaled and relaxed. If Sheryl was going to deny me a loan, she'd have to do it to my face. I checked my phone. I had one hour until meeting for dessert in the parlor and plenty of time to take a shower and fix my hair.

"Thank you, Gladys." I took the mug of coffee she offered and sat on the sofa next to Nathan. He kept quiet while he munched on a frosted snowman cookie. I turned sideways and tucked one foot under my thigh. "I'm glad you decided to come and join us." My eyes narrowed as I studied his expression. Rather than fix his gaze on me, he lowered his chin to stare at his plate.

"Sorry if I snapped at you earlier. I'm frustrated, is all. Frustrated and angry." He finally raised his head and shrugged.

For an instant, my gaze met his, and my heartbeat hiccupped. His eyes glistened with tears. I grasped his free hand and squeezed. "Of course, you are. Remember, I'm here for you. No matter what happens."

He nodded. "Thank you, cousin."

An awkward silence followed while the hum of chatter and laughter from the other guests echoed in the background.

"I didn't do it."

He mumbled his words in a whisper so I barely heard. "I know you didn't. And Quint will come to that conclusion too. Give him time."

"Did I mention the sale going on at the hardware store? Best Schumacher has offered since ninety-three. Or maybe it was ninety-four." Ollie slapped his knee. "Whichever it was, I'm cashing in. Bought a whole new set of garden tools."

I grinned. "Did you buy anything for me or your sister while you were shopping?"

Ollie scowled. "Now what out of everything in the hardware store could you possibly need? You ladies should stick to those frou-frou shops, like Meeka's or Bagels and Buns."

"I've noticed you shopping in those frou-frou places, as you call them, many times." Gladys gave me a wink and chuckled.

Ollie blushed redder than Santa's suit. "Saint Genesius! You two and your caterwauling about nothing. I'm talking about the hardware sale. Can't you leave it at that?"

Gladys burst out laughing. "You and your patron saint of actors. Can't you take a bit of razzing, brother?"

"I'm taking my dessert somewhere quiet, without all your noisy talk." Ollie piled cookies, a couple of muffins, and several pieces of chocolate fudge on his plate then exited the room.

I shook my head and patted Nathan's hand. "See the fun you'd miss if you had stayed upstairs?"

"Yeah, I guess so."

His smile barely surfaced but at least he tried. I turned to the Smiths who sat on the loveseat in the far corner next to the fireplace, almost cheek to cheek. "Any updates on your research, Margaret and Paul?"

"So much to learn!" Margaret brightened while clutching her husband's arm. "We took the tour of your aunt's collection room and have started writing her chapter. I didn't realize how far back her career in the industry went. Were you aware she knew the Barrymores and once had lunch with W.C. Fields?"

I smiled. "Yes, she told me Fields joked how he didn't like children, but Julia was polite so she was the exception."

Margaret reached inside the pocket of her jacket and pulled out a pad and pen. "Oh, I will add that gem to our story. Thank you, Ali."

"Speaking of research, I've found some fascinating places to explore." Faith nodded. With one finger, she slid her glasses up her nose.

"Wow. Looks like Sierra Pines is delivering everything you all hoped to find," I said.

"There's an old mining sight just outside of town. I was told some of the original settlers discovered gold there in the early days of the gold rush."

"A few years before our town was officially established," Gladys added. "According to Clive Schumacher, his grandfather was there that day in the year eighteen hundred and fifty, I believe. Afterward, everyone in town celebrated with punch and carrot cake." Gladys snickered. "I'd venture to guess many of the men drank something a bit stronger."

"I'll be sure to speak with Mr. Schumacher. Oh, and I plan to visit the mining sight later this week and take some photos." Faith punched buttons on her phone. "Just adding a reminder to my calendar."

"Maybe we can join you?" Abby straightened in her seat. "Is there a tour and maybe a hiking trail? I sure could use the exercise." She stared at her half-eaten muffin then set both coffee mug and plate aside.

"I'm not sure about a tour or hiking trail, but there is some walking involved." I checked Google Maps. "The mine is far off the road, near the lake. I'd say a quarter mile?"

"Perfect." Abby rested splayed fingers on her thighs and rose from her chair. "In the meantime, I think I'll take a walk into town and burn some of these calories. Delicious treats, Gladys. Thank you."

"You're perfectly welcome, dear."

Everyone seemed to take Abby's cue as they gathered their dishes and started for the kitchen.

"Have a great afternoon, all. I'll check and see if someone would like to give us a tour of the mining sight. Maybe the SPACA group knows of—" My words cut off as the doorbell rang. "Excuse me."

Once I reached the foyer, I pulled open the door. Quint stood on the porch. I tensed while taking in the expression on his face—knitted brow, thin lips, and steely eyes.

"Is Nathan at home? We need to talk."

"Yeah, I'm here. What is it this time?" Nathan circled around me.

I tensed hearing the surliness in his tone. Now was not the time to stir up tempers, especially Quint's. "Come inside. No reason to share with the neighbors." I waved him in, but kept my position between the two men. Anger sometimes escalated into physical action. I knew that much, too. "Let's go into the parlor." I turned and hitched my breath. The guests hadn't moved. Everyone, including Gladys, and Ollie who'd returned from whatever hiding place he'd found, stared at us in silence.

"Okay. Get to it. Are you here to arrest me?" Nathan snapped his words.

"Nathan, please." I rested my hand on his arm. "Why don't you take a seat, and Ollie will get you a glass of water." I shot Ollie a look and gestured to the kitchen with a wave. Pivoting on my heel, I flinched. Quint stood inches from me. The firm gaze and stiff posture were intimidating to say the least.

After an awkward pause, he turned to Nathan. "Why didn't you tell me you and your wife had an argument on the slope? In fact, only steps away from the cliff and minutes before she fell to her death?"

I gasped along with everyone in the room. This wasn't a good sign. Not at all.

CHAPTER SIX

"ALL RIGHT, EVERYONE. MAYBE WE SHOULD let the sheriff talk to Nathan in private," Ollie said.

"Yes, why don't we all sit out in the atrium? Such a bright, sunny day shouldn't be ignored." Gladys motioned the guests out of the parlor then pointed at Ollie. "That includes you, brother. Come along."

Nathan, Quint, and I remained in the room. I didn't have the slightest idea what explanation would come from my cousin, but the sinking feeling in my gut remained.

"Well?" Quint curled his brows. "Skiers nearby heard you, so don't deny it."

Nathan groaned and raked fingers through his hair. "Yes, we argued. We argue like most couples do. What's the crime in that?"

"None at all, until one of you dies soon after. Don't you think that's something to raise suspicion?" Quint shifted his stance.

He widened his stance and tightened his crossed arms even more so in that authoritative pose I'd come to recognize.

"What did you argue about, Nathan?" At once, I got that eye-glare warning from Quint, which I was also used to. I'd stepped over the line and crossed into his territory. "Sorry." I mumbled under my breath but secretly didn't mean the apology. Nathan might be unbearable at times, but I could never desert family at a time like this.

"Small stuff. Like whether coming here was such a good idea." Nathan turned to me and shrugged. "Sorry, Ali. When Izzie suggested we stop in Sierra Pines on our way to L.A, I knew why she wanted to. She's always been jealous of you and your parents."

I didn't doubt him for a moment. That sounded like an Isadora reaction, one of insecurity. "She wanted to flaunt the wedding ring and marriage like saying she beat me to it?" I shook my head but avoided a sarcastic eyeroll.

"She did. And I didn't stop her because, well . . ." He paused and shot a brief, sideways glance at Quint. "I know you won't believe me, but I miss you, cousin. I miss talking like we used to do. I figured this visit would be a pleasant reunion."

My eyes popped. "Seriously?" Our memories weren't exactly warm and fuzzy, at least in my eyes. I puzzled over what line of crazy he was pitching. Maybe he covered up something he didn't want Quint or me to know.

Nathan released a nervous titter. "Well, that hurt. I thought we had a great relationship and plenty of happy memories. Heck, I was thrilled to share my good news with you. Guess I was wrong." His voice hitched as he turned to stare at Quint. "One thing I am sure about is how much I loved Izzie. I could never hurt her."

"Let's move on, okay?" Quint pointed at Nathan. "You argued and then left her?"

Nathan shook his head. "She skied away first, still angry with me."

"But you said your argument was over small stuff?" Quint's eyes grew narrow.

"What can I say? She was in a bad mood."

"Why was she in a bad mood?" Quint fired his questions. "Did something happen earlier to put her in one? Did she mention what upset her?"

Nathan's eyes bulged. "I don't know." He paused to swipe his forehead with the back of one hand. "All I remember is I intended to head back to the lodge. I mean, there was no point in going after her. We would've argued again, and I didn't have the energy to go for round two. Then, I heard the scream." He plopped down in the closest chair and lowered his head into cupped palms.

"You didn't see anyone else in the area? Maybe on your way back to the cliff?" Quint asked.

"No one." He lifted his head. "I was sort of preoccupied at the moment, you know. Not exactly focused on what was around me."

His eyes burned in a way I knew was fueled by anger. Nathan moved into defense mode and was ready to lash out again. I stepped forward. "I think he's told you as much as he can, Quint. Maybe we should take a break and continue the questioning later? Like tomorrow?" *Or never.*

Nagging doubts wormed their way inside me. What if Nathan was hiding details of their argument? Important details. I'd insisted he could never harm Isadora, but if she'd said something that pushed him? Besides his boastful, annoying side, he had a temper. What if . . .? I shook my head. I needed reassurances, and finding evidence was the only way to silence my doubts. Persuading Quint to back off for a while would give me time. In any case, he wouldn't make a move to arrest Nathan unless he had concrete proof.

Quint leveled his gaze at me then at Nathan. "As I said before, don't even think of leaving town until I've solved this case. Got it?" He turned to me and tipped his hat. "Ali."

I waited until I heard the front door slam with a bit more force than needed and then released my breath. "Well, that conversation was certainly tense."

"I'm getting used to it." Nathan managed a half smile. "I think I'll take a walk. Be back in a half-hour or so." He grabbed his coat off the rack and stepped outside.

I shivered as the winter cold seeped through the doorway and into the parlor. Those incidents when I'd witnessed the newlyweds snapping at one another and heard Isadora's almost threatening comments only fueled my doubts. Could she have angered others enough to commit murder? Maybe a crazy person, but not Nathan. Sure, we were cousins and spent a lot of time together, but maybe he had another side to him that I never witnessed. Or could be something that happened recently to change him. "Enough to make him a crazy killer?" I dug my nails into my palms and marched to the parlor sidebar. "Not possible. Nobody moves from sane to insane in a matter of months. Right?" I huffed while gathering any plates, napkins, or cups left behind and then carried them to the kitchen, nearly colliding with Gladys.

"Oh!" I gasped and juggled the teetering cups and plates held in my hands.

"So sorry, Alexis. I was coming in to clean up in the parlor." She held a can of polish in one hand and a linen cloth in the other. "Is everything all right?" She peered around my shoulder.

"I guess so. After spouting off his warning for Nathan to stay in town, Quint left. Then before we could talk about what happened, Nathan hurried outside to take a walk, or so he claimed." I scratched the back of my head. "I'm not sure who to worry about more. They both are on edge."

Gladys clucked her tongue. "And men say women are too emotional. Well, let's not dwell on their moods. Why don't you join Ollie and me in the atrium? I can polish the furniture later."

I grinned.

"What?" Her brows curled while her eyes widened with innocence.

"Did you really plan to polish?"

"Not at all. But you very well knew the answer." She chuckled then cleared her throat.

I wrapped my arm around her shoulders and squeezed. "I love the way you watch over me. Julia would be proud and thankful."

"I certainly hope so." She leaned her head against me before we steered a path outside to the atrium.

Ollie stood in front of Blackbeard's birdcage. In her will, Julia had entrusted her parrot to Ollie. Despite his rocky start to caring for the pet—frequently forgetting to feed him or to cover his cage at night—Ollie had adjusted to the routine, with a little help from me.

"That's a pretty boy. Eat your apple slice." He stroked the back of his head.

"Apple! Apple!" Blackbeard squawked while turning in circles.

My heart warmed. After Julia's passing, the bird spent days without uttering a sound. He mourned like we all did. Thank goodness a lot of tender loving care from us brought Blackbeard back to his former self.

When the warmer months arrived, we would move Blackbeard's cage to the screened-in porch. He loved the fresh air and sounds of nature. For now, the atrium kept him warm and cozy.

I sat on the wicker settee near the back window. Sunlight streamed through the glass. I tucked my feet under my rear end and closed my eyes for a second, letting the rays warm my face. "This is my favorite spot during the winter months."

"Mine too. I feel like I'm visiting the zoo and enjoying nature's beauty behind the glass." Gladys turned her chair to face me and the yard. She tipped her chin. "Like those cardinals. How lovely they are."

I shifted to watch the specks of red flitter from tree to tree. "Peaceful and beautiful." One bird perched on a branch of the rosy teacup dogwood planted in autumn as a tribute to Julia's memory.

"Ah, there's the doorbell. Should be the delivery I've been expecting." Ollie limped toward the kitchen. The uneven gait was a reminder of his stuntman days when a leap off a balcony during the filming of an Errol

Flynn swashbuckler ended with Ollie in traction for a month. "Be back in a minute to clean the bird's cage." He called out then disappeared from the room.

"Huh. What's that all about?" I turned to eye Gladys. She gestured with a dismissive flip of her hand.

"Oh, he's determined to set up his train set by Christmas. My stars. Some men never grow up."

I pressed my lips together to stifle a laugh. "I think it's sweet. And very festive."

Her expression softened into a smile. "I guess you're right. No different than showing our excitement on Christmas morning when we open gifts, is it?"

"Absolutely." I stood and walked to Blackbeard's cage. He ruffled his feathers while I reached in to stroke his head. Soon, his eyes closed. "I got through to my mom this morning." Latching the cage door, I then returned to the settee and sat.

Gladys wiped a hand across her lap to smooth the wrinkles in her dress. "And how did that go?"

"Very well, actually. She offered to fly out here, but I told her we were jumping to conclusions and it was best to stay home. Nathan is innocent of any wrongdoing. Besides, Isadora's death could've been just a very tragic accident, right?" I turned, hoping to see reassurance in Gladys's eyes.

"From what I hear, this wouldn't be the first fall off that cliff." She nodded firmly.

I smiled, but my chin quivered. "Anyway, she offered to tell Aunt Betts. Oh, and I'm ashamed to admit my big mouth blabbed about our financial problems. When she offered to get out the checkbook, I explained my GoFundMe idea. Long story short, Mom is giving Vincent Swallow—he's the producer of their play—a call. With any luck, he'll approve the campaign." I groaned. "She insists if he doesn't, they'll go without pay and give the money to me."

Gladys arched her brows. "But isn't that the same as a loan?"

"I told her." I puffed my cheeks then blew out the air. "Stubborn as usual."

Gladys winked. "Sounds like someone I know."

With lips pursed, I lowered my chin. "Touché."

"Speaking of stubborn, I hope you won't stick your nose into Sheriff Sterling's case. You know he'll be angry if you do."

"Nathan is family, but you're right. I'll try and keep a distance." I rubbed the tip of my nose then held out my finger. "See? Clean as can be." Of course, I didn't admit to the list I'd made. If indeed this incident was murder, I wanted to be prepared. I planned to speak to all those with whom Isadora had come in contact. Nathan had no one fighting for him but me. I refused to sit back while Quint built a case against him. Being on the sidelines as a spectator was too painful. Gladys should know that about me.

"And that's about as much hogwash as I can handle for one day." Gladys smacked her thighs and stood. "Just be careful, Alexis. As Ollie would say, 'the devil doesn't come dressed in a red cape and wear horns.'" She wagged her finger.

I rolled my tongue across the inside of my cheek. "Sound advice, I'm sure." Ollie often spouted words of wisdom. Most of the time, he didn't follow his own advice, but liked to sound important when giving it.

"Oh, and before I forget, would you stop by the town hall for an emergency SPACA meeting this evening? We can use the moral support. Losing Isadora as the MC has turned Florence into a crazy, hysterical drama queen,"

I snorted. "When isn't she a drama queen?"

"In any case, if we don't calm Florence and set her back on track, this year's holiday event will flop."

"True." I walked alongside her and patted her shoulder. "Meeting's at the usual time?"

"Yes, seven o'clock sharp." After announcing dinner would be leftover pot roast, Gladys picked up the can of polish and the linen cloth then headed into the parlor.

THE HUM OF CONVERSATION FILLED THE TOWN HALL ROOM. Chairs squeaked and scraped across the floor as members moved closer to the podium where Florence stood, preparing to speak. Since I'd joined the gang of Sierra Pines's cultural alliance in October, and after our new treasurer straightened out the finances, we'd splurged on comfy chairs to replace the metal folding ones, painted the room a cheery melon shade, and added framed photos of the town to decorate the bare walls. I contributed a redwood plaque engraved with our name—Sierra Pines Arts and Cultural Alliance, which Ollie nailed above the doorway. Sure, we shared the room with other groups, but none of them seemed to mind the plaque or how the name implied ownership. After all, plenty of townsfolk benefited from SPACA's charity projects, like the spectacular holiday event coming up on Christmas Eve.

The gavel pounded, loud enough to stifle the noisy chatter, and all eyes focused on Florence. My gaze strayed for a moment, and I took a head count. Besides the Bellwethers, Florence, and me, Ralph, Owen, Dottie, and Minnie were in attendance. Our team of eight was small but industrious so we accomplished quite a lot. Once more, my attention gravitated to the podium. As if the hint of something wrong put me on alert, my body tensed.

Florence dabbed at her face with a tissue then clutched her agenda program and fanned herself. Her cheeks were beet red and getting redder. She dropped the tissue and gripped the podium. Maybe Gladys was right. Florence looked a mess. If we didn't do something to help get her back on course, our cheerful holiday event would turn into Tim Burton's *Nightmare Before Christmas*.

Gladys nudged my arm and leaned closer to whisper. "See what I mean?"

I held a finger to my lips and gave a slight shake of my head. No point in distracting Florence yet. I wanted to give her a chance to recover. My scowl deepened as Florence started sobbing. Recovery might not be coming. I cleared my throat and raised my hand.

Florence dropped her shoulders, and a quivering smile shaped her lips. "Yes, Ali?"

I stood and walked toward the podium. "If you aren't in any hurry to cover the meeting agenda, I'd like to give everyone an update about the holiday event." What that update would be, I hadn't a clue. However, I raced to think of something as I stepped next to Florence. "Why don't you get a refreshment and take a seat while I talk?" I gave her an encouraging smile.

Florence sniffed. "Thank you."

I waited until she reached the cooler, grabbed a bottle of water, and sat in the back row. Her hand shook a bit as she drank, but she appeared to relax somewhat. I turned to the group. "Good evening. I thought maybe we could cover what we've accomplished so far since our event is little more than a week away. I'll start. I've posted frequent event reminders on the SPACA website. Plenty of folks have commented how excited they are, and several asked if they can donate toys to our Christmas gift giveaway.

If everyone is okay with the idea, I'll comment that as long as the toys are new or slightly used, we'll accept them. Raise your hand if you agree." I nodded then counted all eight of us. "Great. Who wants to go next?"

Dottie raised her hand before anyone had a chance. "Me! I have lots to discuss." She hurried, her short legs pumping, to reach the podium.

I hopped to the side to avoid a near collision. "I'll just . . ." I pointed to the chairs then steered a path to the last row. Gladys had already taken a seat next to Florence. I flanked her side and gave one hand a gentle squeeze.

"Oh my." She sobbed and lowered her voice. "What am I going to do?"

"About what, Florence?" Gladys asked.

"The M.C. job, of course."

This time she screeched, loud enough so all heads turned to stare at us. I sank in my chair and shrugged an apology while Florence continued to babble complaints, ignoring any reproachful stares, including Dottie's.

"Excuse me." Dottie pounded the podium with the gavel. "Everybody gets a turn to speak, but right now, I'm talking."

I gasped. Dottie's tone was surly and her expression sour. Sharp and angry brows peaked while the corners of her lips curled in a menacing frown. This wasn't the Dottie I knew. Sure, she was a braggart at times, but never had she confronted Florence. In fact, from what I observed the past couple of months, Dottie worshipped the SPACA president. What was going on to spark her anger?

"We are a week away from our most important event of the year, and now, we don't have an M.C. because Isadora Lane had to go and die!" Florence's voice hit piercing decibels.

Mouths dropped, eyes popped, and gasps reverberated throughout the room.

"Oh my." Gladys pursed her lips and shook her head.

Florence slapped a hand across her mouth. "I'm so sorry. I don't know what came over me." Her words muffled underneath her fingers.

"I'll take over the M.C. job. I don't mind." Dottie lifted her chin. "Yep, I'll do it. So, don't you worry."

"I had everything in place. A well-known celebrity to host the event who also sings like an angel. I mean, everything was going so well." Florence rested her head on Gladys's shoulder.

"It's okay, Florence. Dottie will take the M.C. spot. And the children's choir can sing without a celebrity. This year will be a true town event with no outsiders performing. Right?" I bit down on my lip, hoping this arrangement would satisfy her.

"I suppose. You can't undo what's happened." Florence closed her eyes and sighed.

Yeah, death didn't have a return policy. I hurdled over my sarcastic and insensitive thought and onto a pleasanter one. I stood and faced the group. "Why don't we cover who's donating what for the refreshments? I hear Lenny promised twenty dozen of assorted bagels and donuts. That's a great start."

Minnie stood and planted her fists on her hips. "Speaking of murder, how about we discuss Isadora first?"

I blinked. "Nobody said anything about murder."

"Guess you haven't heard the scuttlebutt in town, then." Dottie chimed in.

"Absolutely not the case." Gladys wagged her finger.

"Murder?" Florence gasped then snapped her head to the side and glared. "Ali Winston. Are you hiding something about your cousin's dead wife?"

My mouth flapped. What just happened?

Gladys circled in front of me to form a human shield. "Now, Florence, nobody is hiding anything. Sheriff Sterling has the case in hand. Besides, the coroner hasn't finished his report. Whether Miss Lane's death involved hanky-panky, he'll decide. Not up to you or me." Gladys pointed at the alliance members. "Not any of you." Her comments did the trick because mouths clamped shut.

Instead of speculating on the details of Isadora's death, members opened up to share updates on their contributions to the holiday event. Minnie gave the treasurer's report, and Florence did a complete turnaround by adding some encouraging words before ending the meeting.

I was anxious to escape outside. A few lingering stares hinted to me that some members weren't satisfied with the answers Gladys and I had given, especially Minnie. Maybe they sensed my own doubts about Isadora's death. Waiting to hear from the coroner rattled my nerves, and everyone else's it seemed.

"Ollie and I will stay behind to clean up." Gladys paused to wave an arm at Florence. "Besides, she might need a bit more consoling and reassurance."

"You're right. This accident has thrown everyone into a tailspin of emotions. I'll pick up the breakfast order from Bagels and Buns, maybe have a chat with Lenny. He'll know if the town gossip is as serious as Minnie and Dottie implied."

Gladys patted me on the back. "Good luck."

I pulled on my coat, hat, and gloves then rushed out of the room. The SPACA ladies and their comments chipped away at my confidence. If the accident turned out to be murder, Nathan would be the number one suspect. Spouses were always the first ones the authorities looked at, and thanks to me, Quint knew Nathan was at the scene of the crime. How ironic was that? I pictured myself on the stand at Nathan's trial as a witness for the prosecution while the accused wore a dejected look on his face and Aunt Betts, with tears streaming down her cheeks, glared at me. *Et tu, Brute?* I shuddered.

After shoving open the exit door, I skipped down the steps. The wind howled and blew snow flurries sideways. I tugged at the scarf to cover my mouth and nose then faced the winter squall, fighting my way up the block to Bagels and Buns.

Within a few steps, I ran headlong into a solid form that blocked the walk. "Hey, watch where you're—" I raised my head and gasped. "Oh! Hi, *Sheriff*." At once, I stiffened and went into defensive mode. Yesterday's meeting at the B&B was awkward and uncomfortable. He'd left without so much as "have a good evening." Truth told; my feelings were hurt.

"Ali." A smile warmed his expression.

My mood softened. I relaxed and returned the gesture with a chuckle. "Some winter squall, huh?"

He shrugged. "It will pass soon. I hear temps should climb to near fifty tomorrow."

I chewed on my bottom lip. I could be a coward and continue talking about the weather or dive in and ask questions about the investigation. For me, that call wasn't hard. "So, have you found more incriminating evidence to bury my cousin? Or was yesterday's blow to the gut the end of it?" Okay, maybe I hadn't squashed my irritable mood. People came at me, left and right, with their opinions and accusations. Who wouldn't be defensive?

Quint held up his hand. "Woah. Wait a minute. I'm doing my job, as I've told you a million times. I don't care if he's your cousin. I question everyone in an ongoing investigation. Even if the person was my mom, that's what I'd do."

I blinked. "Your mom? That's harsh." Quint's mom had a few rough months after hip surgery. He and his sister, Violet, had nurtured her back to health.

"Seriously, Ali. I was making a point." He removed his hat and raked fingers through his hair.

"Well, Nathan isn't a killer." I skirted around him and marched away. He didn't call after me, and I wouldn't have stopped if he had. Exhaustion drained any energy left in me to defend my opinion, if I even had one to defend. Deep down, I worried. What if I was wrong about Nathan? That nagging doubt left me unsettled as well as defensive.

I stomped up the sidewalk leading to Bagels and Buns then threw open the entrance door. The fragrance of warm, doughy goodness permeated the air. Shelves in glass cases were filled with bagels, every flavor from plain to poppyseed, and donuts—cream sticks, cinnabons, custard-filled, chocolate-covered, butterscotch, and so many more. I groaned. If I worked in this place, I'd gain a hundred more pounds. Gladys's baked goods were bad enough for my so-called diet.

Three customers were ahead of me. I recognized Golda Ewell who lived across the street from the B&B. I assumed the other two ladies must be friends since all three huddled together and whispered like a brood of hens.

"Good evening, Lenny." I smiled and called out to greet him. At once, the three women stopped their chatter and stared at me. "Hi Golda. I see your family is visiting for the holidays."

"Every year. The entire brood. All eight of them in my tiny house." She clucked her tongue.

I grinned, thinking of the hen analogy. "Well, I'm sure that's better than an empty home at Christmas."

"You're right. I should think positive. Even when my grandson breaks a fifty-year-old vase that belonged to my mother." Golda's lips pruned as she clutched her purchases to her chest. With a quick turn, she nodded. "Angie. Brenda. It's been nice chatting with you."

She slipped past me on her way to the door. "Say hello to Gladys and Ollie for me. I hope you're all doing well . . . under the circumstances, I mean."

Circumstances? I frowned.

"Ali, here is your order. A dozen assorted bagels and your special request for two donuts with custard and chocolate filling. Sorry the donuts took me a couple of days to make. My supplier's truck got stuck in Placerville during the storm, which meant I didn't have all the ingredients. Hope your guest isn't too upset." Lenny announced with a shrug.

"I'm sure the donuts will be appreciated, even if a day or two late." As I walked to the checkout counter, Angie and Brenda shot me a nervous smile. My gaze followed them as they hurried out of the shop. "Definitely strange."

"How've you been? Busy as can be with the holidays and festivities, I bet." He smiled and scribbled on his notepad. "Adding this to your account?" He glanced up.

"Yep." I drummed my fingers on the counter. "What was that all about?" I tipped my head toward the doorway.

"Those three? Just typical female gossip." Lenny's brows lifted. "No offense."

"None taken. So, they come here together often?" I shifted the box of breakfast goodies to my other hand.

He shrugged. "Not too often, but whenever they're together, no telling how long the conversation will last. I remember the time I had to ask them to leave because I needed to close the shop." A loud hoot escaped his mouth. "Boy did Golda give me a tongue lashing, claiming she'd never shop here again. She was back the next day, acting as if our squabble never happened. Women, you know?" He shrugged again. "No offense."

I stifled a laugh by pressing my lips together. "Well, you have a good evening, Lenny. Probably see you tomorrow." I waved and exited the shop.

A horn beeped. At the curb sat the Land Rover. Gladys stuck her head out of the passenger window. "Perfect timing, isn't it?" She motioned me to the vehicle.

I slipped into the backseat and buckled up. "Thanks for the lift. That wind is brutal." I pulled off my gloves and blew on cupped hands to thaw the cold.

"Yes. Nothing like a warm and cozy place to come home to. Thank goodness Glenn had no problem installing the furnace," Gladys said.

"I'll drink to that." I snuggled in my seat and tightened the coat collar around my neck.

"Oh! Excellent idea." Gladys clasped her hands. "We'll have hot toddies to warm our insides too."

I laughed. "Sounds wonderful."

As we pulled into the drive, I looked out of the window to view across the street. Golda hugged her grandson and planted a kiss on the top of his head. I smiled. Nothing like the holidays to put spirit into your mood. A messy, crowded house or broken vase didn't really matter.

My phone rang and buzzed when I reached the porch. The name on the screen caused my heart to thump. "Hello?" I motioned for Gladys and Ollie to go ahead inside.

"Miss Winston, how are you this evening."

I gripped the phone tighter. "Hi Meryl. I'm doing well."

"Excellent. I finally have good news. The publisher loved your aunt's journal and would like to make an offer. Fifty thousand for the advance, but I'm sure we can get them to bump that up a few grand. What do you think? Miss Winston? Ali? Are you still there?"

I plopped down on the porch bench and forced myself to breathe. "Yes. Absolutely. Let's make a deal."

CHAPTER SEVEN

THE NEWS HAD BEEN GREAT AND NOT-SO-GREAT. When Meryl mentioned a fifty-thousand-dollar advance for Julia's journal, I pictured all our financial problems vanishing. That bubble of joy burst when I learned advances often aren't delivered until publication. This deal was like that.

I'd spent an hour or so hiding out in Julia's collection room before retiring for the night. I circled to view the priceless memorabilia covering the walls and shelves. Each one whispered a story to me, a cherished snippet of Julia's past. Though many items had a pricey market value, others carried only personal worth. Those, you couldn't put a price on. My heart tore at the very notion of parting with any, but I might not have a choice. Even though Ollie convinced Glenn to divide the cost of our new furnace into three payments, we owed three thousand by the weekend. The second installment was due two months from now, and the third, two months after that. I was grateful, but with only a little over one thousand in our emergency fund, I'd still need that bank loan. At least Glenn installed the furnace right away so we didn't have to freeze.

I squinted at my reflection in the mirror. A few creases on my forehead and the feathered lines around my eyes were hardly noticeable, unless I examined my face up close . . . like now. With my fingers, I stretched the skin to lift my face. "Oh, what's the point?" I groaned. Grabbing the brush, I ran it through my hair. At least I had my figure. At twenty-eight, going on thirty, I looked pretty darn good. "No. Great. I look darn great." I stabbed a finger at the mirror then twirled around to head downstairs. The fragrant smell of bacon was calling to me.

The kitchen was filled with guests and the hum of conversation. I smiled at the warm and cozy scene showing how a B&B should be. Plates and utensils clinked and clattered as everyone made the rounds to dish out choices of scrambled eggs, bacon, sausage, and fresh fruit. A basket of bagels sat in the center of the table, along with an assortment of cream cheese spreads and butter.

I picked a sesame seed bagel from the basket and set it on the plate, next to my portion of fruit and two slices of bacon. No point in being greedy. After sneaking a thick slice of blackberry roly-poly out of the fridge late last night, I was reinforcing my diet this morning. Like that had a chance of working out when Christmas time offered so many delicious desserts. I wrinkled my nose, and in a vulnerable millisecond, I plucked one more slice of bacon off the serving tray then hurried to the table. After all, it was the effort that counted.

I swallowed a bite of pineapple and took a sip of my coffee. "So, what's everyone up to today?"

"I'm planning on a bit of shopping in town, if anyone would like to join me?" Beth shifted her gaze from one end of the table to the other.

"I'll come along." Abby smiled. "I want to check into buying a ski parka. Is Emery and Treadwater Apparel the shop you mentioned, Ali?"

"Yep. Tell Ralph I sent you. He'll give you a discount." I puzzled for a second as I eyed both the counter and the table. "Where are those donuts, Gladys? Didn't someone make a special request? I know Lenny put them in the bag. He apologized for not being able to make them until yesterday. Some sort of glitch in filling his supply of ingredients for custard."

"Oh! I nearly forgot. Those were for . . ." Gladys's eyes widened as she sealed her lips.

"Izzie wasn't much for sweets, but she loved custard and chocolate filled donuts." Nathan rubbed his jaw with a trembling hand.

Gladys dabbed at her mouth. "Oh dear."

"If you'll excuse me." Nathan pushed away from the table and hurried out of the kitchen.

The room fell into an awkward silence until the moose clock in the hall cuckooed nine times. I searched for something, anything to say that might lighten the somber mood, when Gladys let go of a nervous chirp and laughed.

"Did we tell you the story about the moose cuckoo clock? Julia had a real adventure finding that gem." Gladys punched her brother in the arm. "Why don't you give it a go, Ollie? You always have a way with words."

Ollie rubbed his arm and scowled. "I'd agree to tell the story without the bruises, sister dear." He turned to smile at the rest of us. "Now, it started with a trip to Vancouver Canada when our Julia stumbled on a quaint clockmaker's shop."

I carried my dishes to the sink while Ollie went on with the story. My mind wandered to thoughts about Nathan. His emotions seemed genuine. I was convinced he mourned the death of Isadora. So, why ever would he kill her? Yet, somebody might have committed the awful crime. If it was murder, someone cruel and angry enough, and with a strong motive, pushed Isadora off the cliff.

One by one, the guests left the kitchen to get on with their day. I stayed to finish cleaning and loading the dishwasher while Gladys made a list of supplies to reorder and Ollie, with apple slices in hand, went out to the atrium to feed and visit with Blackbeard.

"I should've thought to cancel the donut order, you know." Gladys sighed and wagged her head.

"We all were in shock. No apology necessary." My mood was gloomy, but I managed a smile. Draping the dishtowel on the rack to dry, I nodded. "I'm sure many reminders of Isadora are popping up in Nathan's head. He can be such a goofball at times, but he's strong. He'll get through this." Too bad I lacked the confidence in my words. Nathan was overly emotional and impulsive. Everyone in the acting business was emotional, come to think of it. The question was could he survive losing his wife without falling apart or doing something stupid? On top of that stack of woes, he had to endure Quint's probing questions and, as long as Isadora's cause of death was in question, being looked at as a murder suspect. I gripped the rim of the sink. The coroner's report couldn't arrive soon enough.

"Oh! I hear the doorbell." Gladys left the grocery list on the counter and hurried to the foyer.

A deep, masculine voice echoed from the foyer and made my breath hitch. In seconds, I reached the front of the house to face Quint. When our eyes connected, his expression softened but only for a second or two.

He cleared his throat then motioned with a jerk of the head to the person behind him.

His deputy stepped up to hand him an envelope.

"We have a warrant to search Nathan's room." Quint removed a folded paper and handed it to Gladys rather than me.

I rolled my eyes. "I'll take that, Gladys. Please." I unfolded the signed document and took a deliberately long time studying the contents then gave Quint a curt smile. "Looks all in order. Though you could've at least given us some kind of warning."

"That's the whole point. Why give him notice and a chance to hide something incriminating?" Quint pointed at the steps. "Deputy, go on upstairs and start the search. First door on the right. Isn't that his?" He eyed Gladys who gestured with a slow nod.

"Is this your way of conducting business?" I gritted my teeth as I glared at him.

His eyes widened. "I'm doing a thorough investigation of the case."

I sidestepped to block his path and crossed arms over my chest. "You're sniffing in the wrong spot, Sheriff. However, far be it from me to tell you how to do your job."

He blew air out of his mouth and yanked the hat off his head. "I'm not arguing, Ali. Now, let me pass." He took the stairs two at a time.

I followed fast on his heels to keep up. The deputy had already gone into the bedroom. I winced, hearing Nathan's raised voice.

"I don't care about your pathetic excuse of a warrant. You have no right going through my things," Nathan shouted.

I leaped in front of Quint and into the bedroom. "Nathan, why don't we go down to the library and let these two do their job? I don't think you've seen Julia's and the Bellwethers' massive movie collection."

His shoulders drooped as if he admitted defeat. "Sure. Nothing I can do to stop them."

I wrapped my arm around his shoulders and pulled him out into the hall. I could hear his labored breath. He was angry and probably frightened. "It will be okay. I promise." I squeezed his arm and guided him to the library where we sat on the sofa.

A thick binder rested on the coffee table—an encyclopedia of movie titles belonging to the B&B, organized by genre and the year released. Since Julia's death, Gladys and Ollie had continued adding to the collection, and by now the number reached two-hundred.

Nathan shifted his gaze from floor to ceiling. Numerous shelves covered the wall, each packed tightly with films. Most all of the titles had been transferred from VHS to DVD format, ten years ago. So far, Ollie and Gladys refused the idea of switching those to a digital format.

I cleared my throat. "Impressive, right?"

"Or obsessive." He shrugged then leaned over to flip through pages of the binder.

"I think when you have a passion for something, you tend to want as much of it as you can get." I chewed on the inside of my cheek. "Do you still have your Civil War collection? As I remember, you had over a thousand items, everything from tiny soldier figurines to that Confederate sword."

He closed the binder and rested his head against the sofa. "Point taken. Izzie insisted I sell the lot so we'd have money to buy an expensive bedroom set." He chuckled. "Some French Provincial nonsense with a bed canopy, no less. But she loved it, fancy frills and all."

My breath held as he turned away and sobbed. "Oh, Nathan. I'm so sorry."

"How could I say no to her?" His voice quivered.

"Hey. Why don't we talk about happy times?" I squeezed his hand. "Remember when you and I broke into that abandoned house next to yours on Halloween?"

He sniffed. "Yeah. Tim Bevans, my so-called friend, dared us. We were dressed up as robbers, all in black, along with masks and fake guns."

"Tim knew the police had been watching the place." I shook my head. "He figured you were dumb enough to take the dare."

"We both did, remember?" Nathan eased his mouth into a smile then laughed. "Poor choice of costumes for a break-in. I almost wet myself when the cop pulled out his gun."

"Me too." I threw back my head and laughed. "Aunt Betts didn't speak to you for weeks."

"No. She didn't. I don't know if I would've gotten through those times, if not for you by my side. Thanks." Nathan's voice grew softer. "Ali, I'm a mess. I'm crying one minute, and the next, I'm so angry."

I slid across the sofa and closer to him. After only a moment's hesitation, I lifted my arm to stroke his shoulder. I didn't know how to act, either. Furious, worried, and sad were the emotions that constantly fought for attention.

Heavy footsteps sounded in the hall, drawing me out of my thoughts. I turned my head and discovered Quint standing in the doorway.

"We're done here. Thank you." He tipped his hat then turned to step back into the foyer.

"Wait!" I hurried to catch up with him before he reached the front door. "Quint. Please. Did you, I mean, can you tell me if you found anything? Not that this is a crime investigation because the coroner hasn't given you his report yet. Right? He hasn't, has he?" I wrung my hands.

His expression softened as he cupped my hand in his. "Ali, I promise to let you know when it's safe to do so. As for now . . ." He fixed his gaze on me in silence for a second. "I can't tell you anything else. You have a good day, and I'll talk to you tomorrow."

I wiggled my hand free from his grip without saying goodbye. Instead, I grabbed for the handle and threw open the door. His stubborn resolve infuriated me.

With a long, drawn sigh, he passed through the doorway and down the drive to meet his deputy. I waited until the cruiser pulled away from the curb before shutting the door. I dug knuckles into my temples and rubbed. Not even noon yet, but I was ready for hot tea spiked with brandy.

"Trouble in the romance department, I take it?"

I gasped and twirled around. "Ollie! Please don't sneak up on me like that."

He held up one hand. "Wasn't sneaking. Just a bit of lurking, you might say."

From the corner of my eye I spotted Nathan walking out of the library. He punched buttons on his phone then held the device to his ear. Climbing the stairs, he started a conversation with whoever answered the call.

"Excuse me, Ollie." I widened my steps and picked up the pace to close in the distance between Nathan and me.

"I don't have it. Not yet." He clipped his words.

The surly tone hinted his despondent mood had returned to the angry one I'd witnessed yesterday. I tiptoed up the stairs and, with my head bent, pretended to scroll through my phone, in case he glanced back to catch me snooping.

"I can't help what happened. Look, I'll call you later in the week." He shoved the phone in his pocket and jogged up the remaining steps and into his room.

I paused, studying the closed bedroom door. What didn't he have? Who was he talking to? More questions pummeled my brain and demanded answers. Whatever the call was about, Nathan appeared to have one more problem adding to an already exhausting situation.

I hurried across the hall. As I passed by Beth's open door, I spotted her standing at the window in silence. Her view was exactly like mine with the snowcapped Sierra Mountain range. Maybe taking time to gaze on that scene soothed her like it did for me. I reached my room and lay down on the bed. I set an alarm then closed my eyes, I pictured Julia and me. We were sitting in the parlor, chatting about movies and prop design and reminiscing over family get togethers.

TWENTY MINUTES LATER, MY ALARM CAME TO LIFE with the tune of "Jingle Bells." Energy renewed, I bounced off the bed and ran a brush threw my messy hair. I breathed into a cupped hand and scrunched my nose. "Yuk." After a squirt or two of breath freshener, I was good to go. I rushed down the stairs and shouted while throwing on my coat and hat. "On my way to the bank! Cross your fingers for good news."

Downtown seemed a little less busy than normal for this time of year. Of course, many shoppers could be taking an early lunch. As I drove past the diner, I let off the gas and peered inside. A few tables were occupied, but not enough to explain my theory. I tapped the steering wheel. There had been reports about another storm moving through, but that prediction was for this coming weekend.

I shrugged and picked up speed. Turning right, I slowed to a crawl and searched for an empty parking spot. Once situated, I glanced at my watch. Arriving ten minutes early implied I was a serious business woman ready to play hardball. Or so I hoped. I swallowed the lump in my throat, hiked the strap of my bag over one shoulder, and marched up the sidewalk.

Behind the glass enclosure, Sheryl sat at her desk. I stepped up to the reception counter. "I'm here for my eleven o'clock appointment with the bank manager." I smiled ear to ear and lifted my shoulders.

"Ali! Come on into my office," Sheryl called from the doorway and beckoned me with her hand.

I skirted around a couple of desks and slipped into the office. "Thanks. How are you doing, Sheryl?" I took a seat as she closed the door.

"Good." She nodded. "Well, almost good. The morning's been busier than usual."

"Oh?" I stopped rummaging through my bag and glanced up. "Anything wrong?"

She chuckled. "Heavens no. I mean busy in that some clients wanted to see me immediately without an appointment. Two shop owners." Sheryl's brows knitted. "A drop in holiday business has them worried, but I assured them the bank would work with their situation." She folded her hands and laid them on the desk while leaning forward. "Now, what can I do for you?"

I took a deep breath then explained the need for a new furnace. "We're hoping the bank could give us another loan? Not too much. Maybe, say, five thousand? Or even three thousand would help." As my nerves got to me, the words squeaked out of my mouth.

Sheryl tapped her pen on the table while scrolling through her laptop. She nodded and tapped in unison then, after a few seconds, stopped. "Here's the thing. The B&B has two loans, small ones though, that are past due." She looked up and gave me a grim stare. "One of them was due payment last summer. Did Gladys or Ollie happen to mention this?"

I shook my head. "With Julia passing, lots of things have been overlooked." My heart sank, heavy and hard.

"Ali, I'm sorry, but I can almost guarantee our underwriter won't okay another loan, which means I can't. I wish I could do more to help."

Her eyes grew dull and messaged defeat. With my chin up, I sniffed then stood away from the chair. I didn't want pity, but darned if I could do anything to stop her from dishing it out. "I'll pay those overdue loans as quickly as I can, Sheryl. I promise. Anyway, I do have other options to pay for the furnace, so don't you worry about me." I shook her hand then hurried out before I broke down with some serious, uncontrollable sobbing.

I took my time returning home, weaving up and down side streets, and once through the Sierra Pines Park where kids were building a snow fort. My shoulders sagged. "Oh, to be that young again with no worries about loans or murder or anything to bring Christmas spirit down." I circled back out of the park and continued on Englewood Boulevard to reach the B&B.

I parked in the drive and sat while drumming the steering wheel with my thumbs and staring at the front door. I hated giving the Bellwethers bad news. What I hated even more was accepting a loan from my parents. Defeat was a hard pill to swallow. My only hope was for the GoFundMe idea I'd suggested. Maybe the producer would pull through and give his approval. What I hoped for was a Christmas miracle because otherwise, I might lose the B&B. I shuddered and pushed open the car door. "Put a smile on your face, Winston. Nobody likes a gloomy grouch during the holidays."

Stepping into the foyer, I shrugged off my coat to hang on the rack. The shuffle of footsteps echoed down the hall. I turned to face Gladys who was armed with a feather duster, rag, and glass cleaner. I shifted my shoulders along with a slight headshake. "No loan."

"Oh, Alexis. I'm so sorry." She rubbed my back. "We'll find another way. At least we have until the weekend to come up with the first payment." Her eyes brightened. "Say! If you like, I can get Ollie to try for a postponement. He can be annoyingly persuasive when he puts his mind to it."

A smile reached my lips. "Let's wait. I haven't heard from my parents. The campaign idea to raise money would certainly help." I pushed for optimism in my tone, but my mood wasn't exactly doing cartwheels. "In the meantime, I'll busy myself with tasks I do have control over."

"Like the new classic movie theme for our guest rooms?" Gladys clapped her hands. "Ollie and have so many movies to suggest. We just need to narrow down the list."

"Sure. Planning the B&B makeover is certainly in our control." I pressed my lips together to keep from blurting out my real agenda. I intended to make a trip to the ski lodge this afternoon. I'd asked myself who might want to harm Isadora the most. The first ones who came to my mind were Tabitha and Kyle. Both had engaged in arguments with Isadora on that tragic day. Kyle had a reputation for being a hothead and flying off the handle, though I had a difficult time picturing him as a murderer. And I doubted Tabitha could be so thin-skinned that she'd kill Isadora over something like bad-mouthing the resort. Tahoe Pine had been doing a fantastic business since she took over. Then again, what motivated anyone to commit such an act? I'd bet most folks had secrets that were dark and damaging if revealed. Those secrets could be lethal triggers. In any case, I needed a place to start, and those two were worth investigating.

I checked my watch. "I need to make a quick trip to the ski lodge to speak with Owen about rental equipment."

Gladys tipped her chin and wagged a finger. "Don't go nosing into business you shouldn't."

"Me?" I laid a hand over my chest. "Never."

"Um, hmm. Well, just be careful." Gladys swiped the feather duster over the foyer table.

"Always." I ran up to my room to change into warmer, more comfortable clothes while I thought about my plan. I needed to approach Tabitha and Kyle in a cautious manner. Firing questions at them about their arguments with Isadora or where they'd been right before the femme fatale plummeted to her death would seem like an ambush. They'd clam up and order me banned from the resort. So, I'd start with polite topics like how business was going, their plans for the holidays, and then casually mention how Isadora's death has made everyone worried. From there, I'd wing it. My digging would hit a nerve at some point, but I was desperate to do something to help Nathan.

The drive took less time than usual as traffic remained light. Rain pinged the windshield with heavy drops when I neared the resort. Flipping on the wipers, I slowed and entered the resort drive. With most of the lot empty, I chose a spot in the front row and next to a familiar red sports car. I mumbled under my breath. The vanity plate read, "Cool Steele" and fit Kyle's huge ego. Exiting my vehicle, I pulled on the hood of my coat then circled around the sporty car and peeked inside the window. All was neat and tidy, but with one exception. I put my face against the glass and squinted at the stack of papers on the backseat. Scribbling covered the top sheet. Isadora Lane and a phone number next to it were written in blue ink. "Now, what in the heck could that mean?"

"Is there something I can do to help you?"

I jumped back and slapped a hand over my mouth to keep from screaming. Twirling around, I faced an older gentleman with a face scary enough to bring me to my knees. Bushy brows, deep wrinkles, and peppered gray hair that spiked in all directions were more reasons to make anyone tremble. He was the groundskeeper who'd worked at the resort forever. "Mr. Farley. You nearly frightened the ghost out of me." I cleared my throat and lifted both hands, palms up. "Sorry. I thought I heard crying inside and worried someone, maybe a baby or puppy needed help." Like he'd buy that excuse. I held my breath and waited.

"Well, babies and puppies are vulnerable little creatures." He leaned to peek around my shoulder. "Everything okay?"

I licked my bottom lip. "Um, yeah. No baby or puppy needs rescuing." I pointed at the lodge. "I was on my way to visit your boss. Is Tabitha working?"

"*Harrumph.* When isn't she working? You'll find her in the lodge somewhere, I'd imagine. Have a good day." He tipped his cap and shuffled across the parking lot.

The rain fell harder. Getting soaked, I hurried to the lodge. Once inside, I took a moment to regain my calm. I puzzled over what I'd discovered inside Kyle's car. Why would he have her name and number? Had she made an appointment for a ski lesson? Not likely. Isadora insisted she skied like a pro. No lessons for her, but then the conversation, or argument, she'd had with Kyle would make more sense. *Perfectly capable of skiing* and then his response, *it's not that easy* implied the spat was about skiing and nothing more. "Who argues about ski lessons?" I muttered and shook my head. It was yet another question I could ask him.

Nearing the ski rental kiosk, I spotted Owen chatting with a lady. He held up a bright pink pair of skis and nodded with enthusiasm. I grinned at the tall, handsome man with dark hair and a dimple in his chin. His smile was engaging and those deep blue eyes sparkled when he laughed. No wonder Ralph was so in love. And that was only the surface attraction. Owen had a heart big enough to love a hundred Ralphs but he only had eyes for his soulmate.

I scanned the rest of the lodge, searching for signs of Kyle or Tabitha, and stopped when I spotted the ski instructor lounging in a chair close to the fireplace. With quick strides, I maneuvered my way around tables and furniture to reach him. A tiny gasp bubbled from my lips as I studied the wrapped ankle. "Woah. What happened to you?" I remembered the tumble Beth had mentioned the day of Isadora's fall and how Kyle had limped.

Kyle narrowed his eyes, and a scowl downturned his lips. "What do you think it looks like? I fell and sprained my ankle of all things. According to that quack doctor, I shouldn't ski for several weeks. That's some serious green I'd be losing." He winced as he rested the wrapped ankle on an ottoman. "With rest and some serious pain killers I'll be back on the slopes in a week. Just you watch me."

I clenched the strap of my bag and, with a quick nod, moved to sit next to him. It was not my place to argue how foolish he sounded. "I'm so very sorry. Skiing is your lifeline, I'd imagine."

"Stating the obvious." He rolled his eyes. "I don't want your pity, so why don't you go find someone else to bother?"

I did a mental count to ten then smiled. "I do know you're too much of an expert to take a fall while skiing. So, what happened? Working at home? Slipped off the roof? Car ran into you?" I kept the underlying surly tone out of my voice and wore an expression of what I hoped conveyed real concern.

"None of those." He glared. "A clumsy, inexperienced client—much like yourself—fell into me, and I lost control, rolled down the hill, and hit a tree. Satisfied?"

"Ouch. Guess you're lucky it's only a sprain." I winced at both his story and the sarcastic jab. "Come to think of it, Beth mentioned you had a tumble. That was the day Isadora fell to her death, wasn't it?"

He sipped from his mug, looking over the rim at me with a steely glare. "It was. What's your point?"

I recognized the defensive tone and switched gears. "So, any special plans for the holidays?"

He sighed and pointed to his ankle. "Not in the mood, as you can guess."

"Hmm, yeah. Bummer." I gazed side to side. "Business seems good at least. You get some sort of pay, don't you? Like worker's comp or something."

"I do, now if you'll excuse me." He leaned back in the chair and closed his eyes.

"Oh, of course. Just one more question?" I braced myself for his reaction.

His one eye squinted open. "Guess I can't stop you."

"What exactly did you and Isadora argue about that day at the ski lift?"

"None of your business, Miss Winston."

"Well, everyone in town is worried about her death, some even speculating it could have been murder. Let's hope that isn't the case. You have a good day." I didn't wait for a response because the beet-red face and bulging eyes gave me a hint anything after this point would not be pleasant. I sprinted across the lobby and straight into someone coming the other way.

"Oh! I'm so sorry. I didn't watch where I was going." I hiccupped and tried to take gulps of air to slow my heartbeat.

"No harm done. Is there something I can help you with?"

I looked up to see the familiar forest green t-shirt and the logo of the resort worn by a young woman. The name Kristin Mulvane was embroidered on top. "Yes. Maybe you can. Where do I inquire about accidents that occur on the premises? Do you keep a record of those?"

Kristin's lips pressed flat. "Are you from an insurance company? If so, you'll need to speak with the representative of ours."

"Oh! No, I'm, a, I'm an investigator following up on events that happened before and after Isadora Lane's accident." I worried how easy fabricating these lies became.

"I thought the Placerville sheriff's department was handling the investigation." Her eyes narrowed more and hinted at suspicion.

I pulled out my phone. "I'd like to take down some notes, if you don't mind." I punched in a few keys and brought up my notes app. I smiled and nodded. "Now, was there anything out of the ordinary that happened that day? Any other reports, for instance? I heard that your ski instructor had a fall. Did that have anything to do with Miss Lane's accident?"

Kristin's mouth fell open. "No, of course not. Kyle reported an injury, claimed he fell while getting off the ski lift. Not the first time I've heard that story."

I chewed on the inside of my cheek. "I heard the fall was caused by one of his clients."

She shook her head. "No. There would've been another report filed, if that was the case. I should know since I work in HR."

I tapped a few more keys on my phone then glanced up. "I don't suppose I could take a look at those records?"

Kristin pulled back her shoulders and lifted her chin. "No, you cannot. Company policy and HIPA rules apply. If you want to follow up, you'll need to speak with the resort manager, Tabitha Wells."

Which of course was my next stop. "Is she available?" I tipped my chin in the direction of the office behind Kristin.

"She's in a meeting and won't be finished until four or so." She snapped her words and walked away before I could say more.

"Well, I guess we're done here." I slipped my phone into the bag and headed for the exit. I had lots to puzzle over. Kyle lied about his accident for some reason. If a client caused his tumble, maybe he or she begged him not to tell. Maybe the client didn't have insurance and couldn't afford to pay Kyle's medical costs. I moaned. No doubt, I was reaching. Kyle lied either to me or to HR. An image of the ski instructor shoving Isadora over the cliff forced its way inside my head. I shivered at the thought taking over. Maybe I had found a new murder suspect for Quint to investigate.

CHAPTER EIGHT

I SNUGGLED IN THE PARLOR WING CHAIR and flipped through pages of the book contract Meryl had emailed me. The crackle of wood burning in the fireplace and the toasty warmth blanketing the air threatened to put me to sleep. That added to the boring legal jargon I struggled to understand.

"You're groaning again." Gladys broke the silence with her comment. She sat across from me next to the window. Needles clicked in a smooth, constant rhythm but at a frenzied pace as she knitted the sweater for Ollie. She swore an oath to finish the garment by Christmas morning, no matter what.

"I know." I laid the contract on the end table next to my chair. "Maybe I should get our lawyer to look it over. I really can't make sense of all this legal jargon."

Gladys glance up and wrinkled her brow. "Sal Fenworthy is vacationing up north with family during the holidays. I thought I told you."

"I'm in no hurry to sign. Meryl even suggested I have a lawyer go through the details. After the first of the year would be soon enough to turn in the contract, I guess. Besides, I won't receive the advance until publication." I took a sip of my tea and scowled. "I'll be right back." I held up my cup. "Would you like a warm up, too?"

Gladys rubbed her chest. "No, dear. I've had way too much caffeine. I'm feeling a bit of heartburn."

"How about some of your antacid tablets then?" I stood and waited.

"I'll be fine." She smiled and winked. "Already popped a couple after breakfast."

I chuckled and turned to face the kitchen doorway when the doorbell chimed. Today's tune was "Joy to the World." Ollie was a genius with electronics. He'd somehow managed to program the doorbell to play various holiday tunes. Every morning, the song would change and every evening we invited the guests to predict what tomorrow's choice would be. Something fun and traditional to do, we decided.

"I'll get that." I redirected my steps to the foyer and opened the door. "Florence?" I hopped sideways as she stampeded into the house like a woman on a fervent mission.

"You must stop her!" She huffed and threw up her arms. "I can't do the job myself. She's a sly cookie, I tell you. Knows exactly how to execute the DD maneuver."

I blinked. "DD maneuver?" I followed her frantic steps into the parlor.

"Deflect and destroy. She gets me off track and then goes in for the kill to accomplish her mission." Florence plopped down in my comfy wing chair.

I took a seat on the sofa and rested both hands in my lap. Lifting my shoulders, I gave a slight head shake. "Florence Greeley, I haven't the slightest idea what you mean. DD maneuver? Sly cookie? Who do we need to stop? And for what?" Those were enough questions to start.

"Dottie has gone bonkers. She's insane with the notion of being the MC for our holiday event. I mean, what in all the heavens has gotten into her?" Florence stood once more and paced the room, her heels clicking and cheeks puffing.

I glowered at Gladys. She'd shrunk in her seat and remained quiet, as if to become invisible. *Coward.* That meant I was on my own. "Ah, Florence? Florence. Would you stop pacing for a second?" I snapped my fingers until she finally faced me. "Okay, don't you remember the other night? Dottie offered to step in as MC and you said yes. Well, sort of." Come to think of it, Florence had been too hot and bothered to pay attention to what anyone said, especially Dottie.

Florence's eyes popped. "Why on earth would I agree to such a crazy idea? Dottie has social anxiety. She will never get through the program without having a panic attack. Why does she think this time would be any different?" She wiped a hand across her brow. "Oh, my word. This is my worst nightmare." Her finger jabbed my chest. "Or my second worst. Isadora Lane and her dramatic end is my undoing."

She resumed pacing and my gaze followed, shifting back and forth until I reached out to grab her arm. "Florence, stop." Once she faced me, I cringed. The wild-eyed, jaw-dropping expression sent chills through me. I gulped air and calmed myself. "Why don't you just tell her she can't. I'm sure she'll listen to you."

A frantic headshake messed her perfect hairdo. She blew a stray curl out of her eye. "Once she's made up her mind, she won't hear a word of reason. Not from me."

My arms hung to my sides. I let out a long, low sigh. "Fine. I'll talk to her."

"Perfect." Florence clapped her hands.

I scowled. Bright eyes and a beaming smile transformed her mood from gloomy to pure joy. Talk about maneuvers. I fell for her CF tactic. The charm 'em and fool 'em had been my downfall.

She gathered her bag and headed for the entrance. "Don't forget practice for the Christmas program is this evening, and that would be the perfect opportunity to speak with Dottie, don't you think?" She threw open the door and heaved her chest. "My, what a beautiful day. You should get outside and enjoy the sunshine." With a wave of one hand, Florence disappeared through the doorway.

I glared at the closed door then turned as Gladys stood up from her hiding place. "You could've jumped into the conversation at any point and saved me from her CF attack."

Gladys scratched her forehead. "CF? Whatever are you talking about?"

"Oh, never mind. What's done is done. She charmed and fooled me, and I now have the obligation of telling Dottie the bad news." I plopped down in the chair and pouted.

Gladys approached. She tapped my shoulder. "Did you think for one second that I wouldn't help you? We'll both talk to Dottie. A force of two is much better than one." She winked.

Glancing up, I wrinkled my nose. "Sorry. Too many problems fill our plates, at the moment. I'm having a difficult time juggling." I patted her hand. "And look at you. You are my rock, Gladys."

"Oh, hush. You give me too much credit." Gladys blushed then cleared her throat. "Sorry to say I do know of another problem that adds to our growing list. Minnie is concerned about the lack of enthusiasm for our event."

I leaned forward. "Really? How so?"

"Compared to previous years, shop owners and others aren't donating as much." She dropped her chin.

"Hmm." I rapped the end table with my knuckles. "Maybe we should give the merchants a pep talk, help them rediscover their charitable side. What do you think?"

"I think the effort would be a waste of time. The owners are griping how business has taken a nosedive. Sales are half what's normal during the holidays." Gladys gathered her knitting and slid everything into a cupboard.

"Strange. I wonder what's caused the slump?" I replayed my trip to the bank—the sparse foot traffic and Sheryl's comment about the merchants' worries. "Well, at least we might have success with Dottie." I stood, gripping my tea cup once more.

"We can only hope." Gladys walked to the kitchen.

I followed close behind, consumed by thoughts of grouchy shop owners, poor sales, and Dottie's stage fright. Our town's stack of problems came with an even taller stack of questions. This was real life and not like a movie or a novel that resolved with a neat and tidy ending. How and when we'd get some answers was anybody's guess.

As noon approached, I shoved the contract in the desk drawer. Consumed by defeat, I opted to have a pleasant lunch with Ollie and Gladys. A scrumptious toasted BLT made with home-baked rye bread and a side dish of Gladys's loaded potato salad trumped complicated legal jargon, any day.

I'd suggested eating in the atrium. Sunlight bathed the room, making it a warm and cozy retreat. Blackbeard kept us company as he hopped in his cage and chattered on about apples. I sat back in the wicker chair and munched on my BLT.

"It's odd how he has her name and number when he didn't know her." Gladys unfolded a napkin and covered her lap.

"Kyle worries me." I nodded. "But if I'm to be fair, Isadora might have arranged a ski lesson, and he wrote down the information for that reason."

"Hogwash." Ollie threw up his arms. "She didn't seem the type to ask for help. Not from what you've told us about her."

I chewed on my fingernail. Ollie was right. Besides, I'd already dismissed the idea of Isadora arranging a ski lesson. Mentioning it now was my way of hearing what the Bellwethers thought, and I got my answer. "Well, whatever his reason for writing down her name and number, I won't know more unless I ask him."

"Alexis Winston, you'll do no such thing." Gladys shook her finger. "From what you've told us, Kyle Steele sounds like a dangerous man. Questioning him once was risky enough."

I set my empty plate and glass aside. "I suppose I could tell Quint what I discovered about Kyle."

"Yes. Let the sheriff handle the questioning." Gladys dabbed her lips with the napkin then folded it neatly.

"I don't know if that's such a wise idea." Ollie limped over to the cage and held out a piece of apple to Blackbeard. "Quint might get angry to find out you've been asking folks questions."

The doorbell rang, and I popped out of my seat. "I'll see who's here." I grabbed my dishes and hurried out of the room. No point in exhausting the topic of my snooping. I knew the risk and took the chance because I cared. Quint had to understand, or he didn't really know me.

I set the dishes in the sink and continued on to the foyer. Since this morning, I constructed the conversation I'd have with Dottie at the rehearsal. With Gladys's help, we covered every possible reaction and how to respond. The most important goal was to avoid offending her. Dottie might come off as bossy at times, but underneath, she was vulnerable and easily hurt. I hated the idea of destroying her confidence.

I lifted my shoulders and smiled before opening the door. "Oh!" My jaw dropped and the scowl from a moment ago threatened to surface again. "If you're looking for Nathan, he isn't available right now."

One arm came from behind Quint's back. He held a bouquet of white lilies and blue delphinium. "I'm here to see you, Ali, and to apologize." He pushed the flowers into my hands. "I hope you'll forgive me for being such a jerk."

"A jerk about what?" I set the bouquet on the front stand without looking away. I refused to make this easy. He needed to say the words.

He let out a nervous laugh and stroked his chin. "Figured you'd make me grovel a bit. Okay, I apologize for the way I've been acting toward you about this case."

I opened my mouth, but then he held up his finger.

"I admit I was a fool, and you deserve better." His eyes brightened. "Forgive me?"

I threw up my hands. "I don't blame you for doing your job. I do, however, expect you to understand my position. Nathan is family and he needs me. I can't help being defensive, even if my behavior looks like I'm challenging you."

"Yeah." His shoulders sagged. "I'm ashamed for not understanding."

"Good. Then we're fine." I stood on tiptoe to kiss him. Now would be the time to let him know about Kyle, but then again, why should I ruin the moment? I backed away and groaned. "There's something I need to tell you." Taking a deep breath, I dove into yesterday's confrontation with Kyle and what I'd learned. Though Quint's face tensed and his body grew rigid, I gave him credit for not blowing up at me.

"I can't lecture you or warn you anymore. You'll do what you think is best." Quint suddenly grabbed both my hands. "Just like you telling me not to worry, but I will. I don't want you getting hurt."

"I realize." My voice trembled. "Seriously, maybe we should talk about something else. Anything." I tugged at his arm. "Come sit in the parlor with me."

Quint shook his head. "I'm due back at the station to go over a case, and I need to check on Mom first." He twirled me around and hugged me. "Why don't I take you out to dinner and dancing tomorrow evening?"

I wrapped my arms around him and sighed. "Sounds wonderful."

Nathan stood at the top of the stairs. He was on his phone again. Shaking his head, he rubbed a hand along one side of his neck.

I pulled away from Quint and smiled. "How about seven? And let's go someplace away from Sierra Pines. I need a change of atmosphere."

"Sure. I'll make reservations. How about the Mountain View Inn? You always tell me how much you like that place."

"I do. See you tomorrow then." I closed the door then turned to face the stairs. Nathan had disappeared. I scratched behind one ear and walked down the hall. His behavior was strange. Could the call be with the same person as yesterday? He acted upset both then and now. Maybe the talk was with his agent about issues over a commercial deal, and nothing more serious than that. In any case, I felt uneasy. His emotions were all over the place. The possibility he could do something rash and impulsive concerned me more than anything.

"PEOPLE! EVERYONE NEEDS TO BE QUIET SO YOU CAN HEAR ME." Florence clapped her hands. After the volume dwindled to silence, the SPACA president nodded and cleared her throat. "Children, please take your places on stage. Gladys, if you'd be so kind?" She gestured to the piano.

Gladys volunteered to fill in until Florence could find a veteran accompanist, as she so bluntly put it.

I lingered near the theater entrance, hundreds of feet from Florence's watchful eye, and engaged in whispered conversation with Ralph and Owen while keeping my gaze on the stage. Front row and center stood a curly-haired girl with a shining smile. "Sophie is an angel. You're so lucky to have her in your lives." I watched and listened to the young people sing, "Away in the Manger." My heart filled with warmth. Despite the tragedy of death bringing its suggestion of murder and the plummeting holiday sales, the town and its people had kept the holiday spirit.

"She's a blessing and gives us pure joy." Owen beamed with pleasure, his smile reaching ear to ear.

Ralph wrapped his arm around Owen's shoulders and squeezed. "Sophie is the best thing that's happened to us since coming to Sierra Pines."

"Well, we're all happy to have you as town neighbors." I went in for a group hug. "Boy, am I overloaded with sappy emotion."

"You're all so adorable." Florence clutched her throat. "Makes me teary-eyed. But how about we try the song one more time? No such thing as too much practice, is there?"

An echo of groans passed through both the choir and the parents. I choked back a laugh. "Leave it to Florence. She's never satisfied."

"Amen to that." Ralph waved his arm and whistled to get Sophie's attention. "Florence will have to do without a star performer. Sophie has last-minute touches to make on her science project, which happens to be due tomorrow." He sighed. "I worry my bad habit of procrastination has rubbed off on her."

"Nonsense. She was like that from the moment she came to live with us." Owen glanced at me. "Aren't most children procrastinators? Especially right before the holidays. Who assigns projects at such a time?"

"Don't look at me. I'm not a parent, and I've never procrastinated. Putting things off makes me nervous." I shrugged.

"You're making excuses for her, Owen." Ralph winked at me. "He's such a softy. Good thing he has me to keep the ship tight."

"Stop being so righteous." Owen pursed his lips. "Besides, one parent in the family needs to be the softy."

As several children followed Sophie's lead and left the stage, Florence threw up her arms in what looked like a gesture of defeat. "Practice appears to be over. See you all next Monday evening, unless something else comes up to ruin our plans." Florence grumbled under her breath and approached a group of our SPACA members huddled in a corner.

"Might as well join them." I pointed. "Care to come along?"

Sophie approached and hopped up and down. "Hi, Ali. Did you hear me? I think I'm the loudest in the choir." She giggled and grabbed Owen's hand. "We need to hurry home and finish my project, right?"

"*You* need to finish your project, Miss Sophie." Ralph poked her belly with his finger, but a smile burst on his face. "Of course, if you run into any problems, I'm certain Owen will be right at your side to assist."

Owen mumbled under his breath then hugged Sophie to his side. "Don't you worry. I'm a genius when it comes to sciency stuff. You're sure to win first prize."

Sophie drew her lips into a puzzled frown. "There are no prizes, Owen."

"Grades are like prizes, you know. And your project will get an A. Wait and see." Owen turned. "We'll head out to the car, if you need a minute."

"No, that's okay. You all go on. I'm going to say my goodbyes and leave." I searched the theater once more. "I don't see Dottie anywhere. So, Gladys and I will have to save our talk for the next time."

I waved goodbye and then approached the SPACA group, which now included several others. Many of them were shop owners. I tensed. All those scowls couldn't be a good sign.

"I tell you, something strange is going on." Margie, owner of the Taffy House, wagged a finger. "Almost like Sierra Pines is under some dark spell."

I reared back my head and blinked. Superstitions and spells?

"My sales have dropped more than fifty percent in the past week. I don't know how much longer I can survive." Meeka heaved her ample chest and pushed a loose curl of black hair from her face.

"Might be hokey to think, but who says a town can't be cursed? Especially when events take a sudden turn for the worse and that happens right after someone new comes to town." Bonita turned her head slowly.

I shivered. Cold, steely eyes penetrated right through me. I guessed where this conversation was headed and couldn't stop it.

"Curses are total hogwash." Ollie stepped between Bonita and me. "I imagine folks have enough trinkets. Your Gems and Baubles is the last place I'd shop for Christmas gifts."

"Ollie! No need to be disrespectful and mean," Gladys said.

"Isn't he suspected of murdering his wife? What if that turns out to be true?" Margie's eyes widened.

"My cousin is not a killer!" As heat traveled through me, I snapped. "In fact, unless the coroner comes out to say otherwise, Isadora's death was an accident." I pointed a finger at Bonita. "Like Ollie said, curses are hogwash."

With weary-eyed stares, most everyone walked away. Only Florence, the Bellwethers and I remained.

Gladys stood close and patted my arm. "I don't think they care what you say, dear. They are frightened and worried. Desperate people have desperate thoughts."

Florence glanced around her. "Never mind all that. Where's Dottie? How can we tell her she won't be the MC, if she's not here?"

We? I rolled my eyes. "Maybe she had an emergency of some sort. Or a last-minute order to fill at Boxes and Bows. Of course, you'd think she'd call to let us know." Dottie was punctual and meticulous in her actions.

"Absolutely. This behavior is inexcusable." Florence huffed.

Not exactly my point, but putting off the awkward conversation we needed to have didn't make me happy either. "Why don't you try calling her?"

As if on cue, Florence's phone rang. She scowled at the screen then brought the device to her ear. "Hello, Minnie. Where are you? And have you seen Dottie? I swear, the lack of commitment from some members is concerting. We need to set some rules. I—" Florence dropped her jaw. "She hung up on me. What nerve."

"I'm here, Florence. Couldn't find a parking spot any closer than two blocks away. Good thing the weather is mild. Oh! Hi Ollie. How are you?" She stopped and fluttered her eyelashes while dipping her chin. "You look very nice this evening."

Ollie flushed tomato red and grumbled words under his breath as he tugged at his collar.

"Anyway . . ." Minnie cleared her throat and pursed her lips. "We have a problem."

"We? What do you mean we have a problem?" Florence clutched her throat. "Please don't tell me there's another issue with the Christmas event? I can't handle anything else to go wrong."

Minnie pulled papers from her backpack and shoved them at Florence. "Take a look."

Inching closer, I looked over Florence's shoulder to get a peek. Lots of numbers and dates detailed SPACA's financial history. Near the bottom of the column, one amount was circled in red. "What's that?" I pointed a finger then glanced up at Minnie.

"Yes, what am I supposed to make of this?" Florence waved the paper.

"Oh, for goodness sakes." Minnie groaned. "What you can make of it is there's money missing from our funds." She paced the room. "I thought maybe I'd had a senior moment and already deposited what we collected from the Placerville charity event and the ticket sales. Or maybe one of our other members had put the money in, though that would've been unusual. I mean, we had everything locked up in the safe box. I saw for myself just yesterday morning." She paused to face us, and a quivering sigh escaped her lips. "When I found the box empty, I got online and checked our bank balance. No deposit was made yesterday or this morning. None at all." Her shoulders dropped. "I'm a failure. Should've never volunteered to be treasurer. Hip hop class takes too much out of me, you know."

"Oh my." As Florence let go, the papers floated to the floor. She fanned her face with both hands. "Oh my, oh my, oh my. It's happening again."

My stomach rolled. I knew, like everyone in the room, Florence referred to the one who stole money from SPACA last fall. However, that greedy thief was long gone and locked behind bars. Who could have taken money this time? I shuddered. Maybe Bonita and Margie were right. The town was cursed.

"That's not all." Minnie's voice trembled. She stuck a hand in her backpack once again to retrieve a crumbled note. "An I.O.U was left in the safe box. For two thousand and thirty-nine dollars and fifty cents. The exact amount we collected yesterday."

A unified collection of gasps echoed throughout the theater. A tiny hunch tickled my brain, and then grew. "Florence, would you call Dottie? Right now, please." I wasn't sure why I thought of her, other than because she was the only member who hadn't shown up this evening.

Without comment, Florence pressed a couple of buttons then held out the phone. "I put the call on speaker."

The ringtone repeated several times until voicemail picked up. "You've reached Dottie Sample, owner of Boxes and Bows and SPACA's event coordinator. If this is Florence calling, I know what you planned to do, you back stabber. Thanks a whole bunch, Miss High and Mighty.

And for anyone else, just leave your name and number. *Adios* and *despedida, amigos.*"

Florence tapped her foot with a frantic, loud beat until the beep prompted a message. "Now, listen here, Dottie Sample . . ." She paused for more toe-tapping beats. "You need to call me, and I mean right this minute. We are in a crisis and, well—just call!" She stabbed another button then pocketed her phone while darting her gaze at all of us. "What in blazes does *despedida* mean? Dottie and her Spanish blathering. Always showing off."

"It means forever. She said goodbye and forever." My voice trailed into a whisper. Grim faces accompanied the silence in the room as if everyone had processed Dottie's message and come to a worrisome conclusion. At least I did. What if Dottie took the two thousand and thirty-nine dollars and fifty cents? Goosepimples covered my arms as I reached an even darker, though wild and farfetched, conclusion. What if the real reason she left town had nothing to do with Florence? What if Dottie was on the run because she killed Isadora?

CHAPTER NINE

I PULLED THE BACON, SPINACH, AND CHEESE quiche pie from the oven and set it on the counter to cool a bit. I turned to Gladys who placed freshly baked biscuits in a bread basket. "Have you talked to Florence since last night?"

Gladys shook her head. "She won't answer her phone. Maybe I'll drop by her place later after breakfast cleanup."

"I thought she'd faint after Bonita spilled what we'd all been thinking." I poured juice into the pitcher and placed it on the table.

"Yes. Hearing the idea out loud gave me the willies." She shook her upper body. "To think Dottie could be a murderer? Not in my wildest nightmare would I guess such a thing."

"Most likely she's not. I mean, I know it looks bad, the timing and all." I flipped open the lids of boxes filled with bagels and donuts from Lenny's shop, then set out tubs of cream cheese and butter. "Dottie was fed up with the way Florence had been treating her, or I should say ignoring her. Finding out she'd lose the MC job must've pushed her over the edge."

Steps pattered down the hall and grew louder as guests entered the kitchen. I smiled at the group. "Morning, everyone. I have great news!" I motioned toward the counter. "First, come load up your plates. The special of the day is quiche pie. Gladys's secret recipe."

Murmurs of thank you passed down the line as plates and serving ware clinked and rattled. Animated chatter carried on through the meal. While the last pot of coffee brewed, I smiled and stood. "I'm happy to say we have a guide who's agreed to take us through the mining sight. Plus, as an added treat, Clive Schumacher is eager to tell us stories about his grandfather, Thomas Schumacher, and those first mining days. Who's on board to come along this morning?" I counted heads. All but Nathan wanted to take part.

"Sorry. I'm not feeling so hot. I'd better spend the morning in my room, catch up on some reading or something else relaxing." He shrugged, grabbed a bagel to go, and left the room.

I smacked my thighs and lifted my chin. "Fine. The six of us it is. How about meeting in the foyer in twenty minutes?" Just enough time for me to check on Nathan. Somehow, I couldn't stop myself from acting the part of his older cousin. Although at this point, I worried my caring gesture was doing more harm than good. He should have the time to grieve without me butting in.

"It's for you." Gladys tapped me on the shoulder.

I turned and spotted the house phone in her hand. A frown on her face prompted my own. "Who is it?" I mouthed the words, but she only shrugged. "Hello?"

"Yes, this is Gerald Spalding. I have a reservation at your B&B scheduled for this weekend, but something's come up and I need to cancel." The words tumbled out in choppy rhythm.

"Oh, yes, I, um, I understand, Mr. Spalding." I grabbed for the reservation ledger stored in the kitchen. "Unfortunately, I can't refund your deposit, and there's a cancellation fee."

"That's fine. Thanks for your help."

"Wait. Would you like to reschedule? We have a Valentine's Day package deal you might want to take advantage of. I can—"

"I'll let you know, after I discuss the idea with my wife. Good day."

I flinched at the rather abrupt click to end the call. Sitting down at the table, I scratched my chin then looked up at Gladys. "That was totally weird."

"Is it bad news?" Gladys nestled in a chair next to me.

"A cancellation, but that isn't the weird part." I drummed my fingers on the table surface. "Not sure how to explain, just got a feeling something's not right. Oh, well." I glanced at my watch. Not enough time left to speak with Nathan, but I figured that might be for the best. I shifted my gaze toward the hall. Voices hummed and carried from the foyer.

"Seems your group of tourists are anxious to visit the mine." Gladys chuckled and patted my hand. "I'll have a hot lunch ready for you when you return. Homemade bean and ham soup with a loaf of sourdough bread."

I licked my lips. "Sounds yummy. Thanks, Gladys. See you in a few hours." I stepped toward the hall, excited for our excursion. In all the times I'd visited Sierra Pines, not once had my trip included a stop at the mine, though Julia and the Bellwethers had offered plenty of stories about the gold rush days.

All five guests congregated at the door, bundled in coats, hats, and gloves. I smiled. "Looks like everyone is ready."

Abby raised a hand. "Are we walking? We can't all fit in your SUV."

"No, we can't. That's why I've booked a rental for this morning." I held up the keys. "A suburban with nine seat capacity."

I maneuvered the rental down Englewood and into town. Within minutes, Clive's hardware store came into view. The panoramic white-framed window, bordered with red garland for the holidays displayed gift-wrapped boxes and plenty of items to entice shoppers who'd hope-fully include Schumacher's when making their holiday purchases.

Clive was waiting at the door, a grin plastered to his face and eyes wild with excitement. "Welcome! Come on in folks and gather around the pot-belly stove, which just happened to belong to my grandfather, Thomas Schumacher. He was one of the original settlers in Sierra Pines, you know."

I covered my mouth with a gloved hand to suppress the laugh. Clive mentioned his family history every time I visited the store—his pioneer grandfather and the dangerous journey across the country, hauling the stove as well as the cash register from back east. I imagined he shared that tale, among others, with anyone who'd listen. I checked my watch. "Our guide, Eli Preston, is meeting us here in a half hour, but, in the meantime, we are all anxious to hear one of your stories about the min-ing days, Mr. Schumacher."

With a dramatic arm wave, Clive bowed and cleared his throat. "As a young man in his twenties, my granddad traveled from Chicago to what's now Sierra Pines by wagon with his brother, my great uncle Zeke." He settled in his chair and motioned for us to take our seats. "Unfortunately, Uncle Zeke came down with pneumonia on the way and died passing through Nevada. He almost made it. They were only a few hundred miles from their destination."

I straightened in my seat with renewed interest. I'd never heard about Uncle Zeke.

"Thomas was hiking through the woods that day gold was discovered. He and another settler, James Kellogg, came to what looked like a cave. They figured the spot was a good place to rest. Of course, they'd heard about gold discovered at Sutter's Mill. Everybody in California had." Clive scooted forward in his chair. He shook his finger. "But my dad swears that Thomas and James weren't thinking about gold that day. No sir. They were searching for game. Times were hard, and if you didn't bag a deer or rabbit or some other animal, you might not have food on the table. Winter was approaching and they were getting anxious." Clive stood and paced the floor.

"Then how did they find gold, Mr. Schumacher?" Faith poised her pen in one hand while holding her notepad in the other.

"I'm getting to it." Clive nodded and sat back in his chair. "According to the story my granddad told, James was gathering up dirt to help clean his dish. People used all sorts of materials to wash out their utensils, you see. They'd add a bit of water from their canteen and scrub away." He shook his head. "Sorry, I get sidetracked. Anyway, James happened to notice some shiny flecks in the dirt. Before you know it, he's yelling that there's gold. Of course, they sent a sample to the Sacramento office to have it tested. James turned out to be right."

"How fascinating." Faith scribbled away in her notepad.

"Problem was, news spread like the dickens, and folks were anxious to get their share." Clive shook his head. "Gun fights were common and tempers flared. In trying to protect their discovery, James and my granddad patrolled the sight with rifles at their sides. One night, while James was taking his turn to watch, a gun fired and hit him in the chest. He died the next day."

"Oh! How awful." Beth clutched her throat.

"Yep. Granddad hired several men to guard the sight, ones with experience. Nobody messed with their claim after that. Eventually, when matters calmed down, he sold shares to those who had interest. Much more civilized approach. Sad that someone had to die first."

"Thank you for the story, Mr. Schumacher. Your granddad was a very brave man." As the door creaked open, I shifted my gaze. A man walked into the shop. I recognized Eli Preston from his bright red beard and thin, lanky build. People swore his legs took up more than half his height.

"He was wise, too, and kept a level head which helped." Clive groaned while rising from his seat. "Darn weather makes my bones ache. You all have a good time on your tour."

Everyone chimed in to give thanks as they pulled on their hats and gloves then moved toward the door to follow Eli.

Within fifteen minutes, we reached the entrance to the mining sight. A gap between the pines about six-feet wide showed the way into woods. Tuffs of grass nearly a foot tall grew in spots across the dirt trail, hinting at neglect and lack of visitors. I guessed we were probably the first in months.

"You play tour guide very often, Mr. Preston?" I walked alongside him while the rest of our group followed.

He scratched his beard. "Hmm, let me think . . ." His head tilted. "Maybe five times in the past year?" He slapped his thigh. "Hip replacement the summer before last makes hiking painful."

My eyes widened and I stopped to stare. "Oh, Mr. Preston. I'm sorry. You shouldn't be doing this, and it's all my fault." I slipped my phone out of my coat pocket. "Let me make a call and see if—"

"Stop, now." He laid his hand over mine. "If I didn't feel up to the hike, I would've said no. Besides, I'm not a man to just sit in a rocker, waiting to die." He picked up the pace and called over his shoulder. "Watch around the next bend, folks. Lots of prickle bushes have taken over and grow close to the path."

I dropped my shoulders in defeat. No point in arguing whether he should be hiking. "Red hair and a stubborn streak must go hand in hand." I bent my chin and kept my voice low.

"Don't forget a quick temper. I got that too." Eli threw back his head and let go of a bold, full-bellied laugh. "Might have a bum hip, but my ears are working just fine."

Heat rose to my cheeks and I winced. "Sorry."

"I'm sure his feelings aren't bruised." Faith leaned closer. "My husband was just like him. Stubborn, hot tempered, but with a fine sense of humor."

I relaxed. "Thanks, Faith. Oh, look! There's the mining sight." I pointed at the clearing several feet ahead.

Chiseled rock formed a tower-like structure that rose from the flat ground. A tiny, thin stream snaked along one side and disappeared beyond the clearing. Pines outlined the area, forming a natural perimeter that both hid and protected the mining sight. I imagined Thomas and James standing vigil with no way to see what was coming through the woods. A rustling, a twig snapping, or maybe the cry of a startled bird would be their only warning. I shivered. It would be easy enough for an intruder to hide behind a tree and fire a shot to kill James.

"Holy smokes!" Eli jumped back with a lopsided gait. He glanced back at me and gave a slight shake of his head. "Might be best to tell the others to stay put."

What now? I hesitated for a second before giving the order. "Everyone, please wait here. I'll be right back."

"Why? I thought we came to see the gold rush sight," Beth said.

"Our guide must have a good reason. Just be a minute, and then we'll go on with the tour." I clenched my fists while concern rippled through me. Taking a deep breath, I marched up to Eli. "What's wrong? You sounded upset."

He held out a steady arm to point to the ground in front of him. "Plenty to get upset about."

I gasped, then slapped a hand over my mouth to keep from screaming or gagging. A body lay on the ground with a blood-stained rock next to the head. Dozens of paper bills scattered around her and made a slight crackling sound as they stirred in the wind. A few feet away, a leather satchel gaped open like a mouth with its contents spilled, leaving a trail of even more money. However, my gaze fixed mostly on the person who lay dead just a few feet away from me. The tidy auburn-tinted perm was messed and one muscular arm lay in a crooked angle. Poor Dottie Sample. She had a plan to leave town. I was sure of that. Sadly, and thanks to a tragic turn of fate, she didn't get very far.

"Oh, wow. Who is she?" Beth peeked around me while handling my arm in a deathlike grip.

I winced and pried her fingers loose. Seeing how the others had inched forward, despite my warning, I moaned. "Dottie Sample. She owns, *owned*, Boxes and Bows and was the SPACA event coordinator." The words stumbled out in a strained and awkward voice. A zillion thoughts ran through my head. Had Dottie been murdered? Did she trip and hit her head in the fall? Why did she bring a duffle bag of money to this sight? I feared taking the questions any further or connecting dots when I didn't know much yet—other than the fact Dottie had obviously met with an untimely death.

"This here's Eli Preston. We're here at the Schumacher gold mining sight." He raked fingers through his hair then lifted his head to stare at the sky. "I'm calling to report a dead body . . . Yes, sir. I recognize her. It's Dottie Sample . . . Yep. We'll be waiting. Bye."

Eli and I stared at one another without speaking. If I had to guess, his thoughts ventured where mine did, not a pleasant place to be.

"Sheriff will be here soon." With narrowed eyes, Eli scanned the area.

Like he waited for someone to burst through the woods, I thought.

At once, I held out the car keys to Eli. "No point in any of you hanging around. Will you drive the guests back to the B&B, Eli? Maybe we can save the tour for another day if you're willing."

"I'll stay behind to keep you company." Beth approached and squeezed my hand.

"Thanks. That would be nice." I smiled.

As they disappeared down the path, a siren screamed in the distance. Within minutes, rapid footfall moved through the woods and the murmur of voices grew louder. Quint Sterling, his team of deputies, and the Placerville coroner came into the clearing.

I crossed my arms tightly over my chest. "Quint." I nodded.

He pushed back his hat. "Ali. Seems we're doing this dance again."

"What dance?" I shifted my feet.

"The one where you happen to be at a crime scene with a dead body."

I blinked. "Total coincidence."

"I'd certainly hope so." He squatted to take a closer look while one team member snapped photos and the coroner pulled tools from his case.

I scowled and tapped my foot. "What's that supposed to mean? I'm not the killer."

Quint twisted his head to look up. His brow arched. "Here we go again. Who says this is a murder?"

My mouth gaped. "Well, I mean—look at her!" I waved an arm then let it drop, limp at my side. "Have you heard anything about Isadora's death?" I tipped my chin in the direction of the coroner.

Quint gripped his thighs and pushed off to stand. "Nope. He'll be done with the report in another day or so. Waiting for the lab results."

"Labs sure take long enough." I grumbled and kicked at the ground, scattering dirt. On the inside, though, I was panicked.

A long, dragged-out breath escaped his mouth. "Why don't you and your guest—what's your name?" He stared at Beth.

"Beth Rawlings, meet Sheriff Quint Sterling," I said.

"Great. I'll be a few minutes. After I have a chat with the coroner, I'll want to ask you some questions. Maybe you won't mind waiting?"

"Sure." I nodded. "We'll just be over . . ." I searched around me then pointed. "Sitting on that bench." Without another word, I paced, slow and deliberate, to the other side of the clearing.

"He seems nice." Beth hurried to walk alongside me.

I scrunched my nose. "He can be. When he's on a case, his professional demeanor is . . ." I searched for adjectives that wouldn't sound so critical. "He gets intense. All business and little time for social niceties." Rude, condescending, bossy—those were the ones I refused to say aloud. Thinking them was bad enough.

I sat on the bench and Beth next to me. "So, the coroner is very thorough, which means we might have to wait more than a few minutes." I shifted and tucked one leg under my rear. "What's your story, Beth?"

She blinked and pulled back her head. "What do you mean?"

"Sorry. That was abrupt. How about what do you do back in Ohio besides skiing?" I unfolded my legs, pulled one knee to my chest, and rested my chin.

She chuckled and her shoulders relaxed. "I work at a major department store. I had a few days of vacation left, and since I love to ski . . ." She shrugged and raised her hands, palms facing up. "Here I am. A really nice, relaxing getaway."

I grunted and shot a glimpse at Dottie. "Maybe not so relaxing."

"I'm sure this is unusual, right?" Her lips parted into a wide smile. "Plenty to enjoy, though. The people are friendly. Fresh, mountain air is great. The skiing is spectacular." She threw up her arms. "I'm still glad I came."

I rolled my chin side to side on my knee. "Well, I'm glad you're glad."

"Okay, ladies. Looks like the coroner is finished and ready to take off." Quint walked toward us.

I watched the team of deputies carry poor Dottie on a gurney. Once they disappeared down the path, I turned. "Any information you can share?" I dropped my feet to the ground and gripped the edge of the bench.

Quint shook his head. "I can't. Now, I have a couple of questions." He plucked his pen and pad out of one pocket.

"There's nothing much I can tell you. We approached the mining sight, then Eli discovered Dottie." Somehow, I couldn't say body. That seemed too impersonal, like she wasn't anyone I knew.

"Eli Preston." He nodded. "I'll speak with him later."

He tapped his pen against the notepad. The irritating sound reminded me of a bird pecking on a window. I bit down on my thumbnail.

"Did you hear any unusual sounds as you were walking the trail?"

"You mean like a scream? Or someone shouting?" Beth interjected as she scooted to the edge of her seat. "I didn't. Did you, Ali?"

"No unusual sounds. Nothing but mother nature's creatures." I stood. "Are we done? Because I'm getting hungry, and Beth probably is too."

"Right. Sorry for keeping you. Um . . ." He held up one finger. "You need a ride back to town, don't you?"

I rocked back on my heels. "Unless we're walking, a ride would be nice."

He clicked his tongue then grinned. "Straight to the point, as always. Okay, let's get out of here."

Riding west in Quint's cruiser, I sat in the passenger seat and stared out the window rather than carry on a conversation. I couldn't erase the image of Dottie. It was haunting and sent shivers up and down my back. Quint's refusal to share details only fueled my imagination. I pieced together everything—Dottie's phone message, the likelihood she stole the money from SPACA funds, and her unexpected death. I shifted in my seat while my stomach rolled. The rational side of me insisted this wasn't an accident, and my gut obviously agreed.

"Here we are." Quint shifted his cruiser into park, letting the engine idle.

"Thanks for the lift." I grabbed hold of the door handle when he reached for my arm.

"Would you hang back a minute? I'd like to speak with you alone." He turned to Beth. "Take care, Beth."

"Sure. You too." After a long pause, she opened the door to get out.

I waited as Beth walked up the drive then shifted my gaze. Quint's brow knitted, deepening the lines in his forehead. He attempted a smile but the effort didn't reach his eyes. "You're worried, aren't you? You think Dottie's death wasn't an accident."

He pulled off his hat and rubbed the top of his head. "You need to be careful. Promise me."

"What the heck, Quint." I threw up my arms. "You can't even say it out loud. Swear it isn't murder and I'll believe you."

His expression softened. "We still on for dinner? I'll pick you up at around five."

"Oh, for the love of . . ." I smacked the dashboard with the flat of my hand. "You are exhausting, you know that? Fine. I'll be ready. You owe me that dinner after nearly driving me crazy."

He leaned over to give me a quick peck on the cheek. "Always aim to please."

"Uh, huh." I muttered while exiting the car and, without looking back, hurried to enter the house. I should know Quint's methods by now. He never speculated, or at least never to me. He believed speculations or guesses were nothing unless backed by evidence. And when I asked questions, it wasn't what he said. It was what he didn't say. Silence hinted at plenty.

I closed the front door then pulled back the window curtain to peek outside. The cruiser was gone and no other cars were in sight. *Evidence.* What if the coroner's reports on the two women proved foul play? Worse yet, what if he found some similarities that connected the two? I tensed, rubbing both my arms to ward off a chill. A murderer might be out there who was watching and waiting and willing to kill again.

CHAPTER TEN

$\mathbf{T}$HE MOUNTAIN VIEW INN WAS BUILT in the early nineteen-hundreds. After the gold rush boom settled and people began spending money or investing more wisely, businesses sprouted up and towns grew. The inn was a joint venture among two men and one woman who'd become wealthy without discovering gold. The men opened a hardware store that sold mining equipment. Sales burst at the seams as dreamy-eyed prospectors flooded the store. The woman went a different direction and provided miners with other needs. The Blue Hawk Saloon's main floor offered plenty of liquor and gambling, while the upstairs was reserved for more personal entertainment. The owner made lots of money, more than she knew what to do with. As the story goes, the two hardware store owners happened to stop in the bar, and a conversation among the three led to their collaboration to build a restaurant near Lake Tahoe. The partners aimed high and planned a spectacular venue, so unique that customers would travel as far as a hundred miles to eat there.

I walked alongside Quint, arm in arm, as we followed the host to our table. My gaze captured the rustic details of the room. Light fixtures made of massive antlers hung from the ceiling. Everything from rifles, knives, and bear traps, stuffed and mounted game, photos of hunters, prospectors, pioneer families posing in front of log cabins, and so many other cherished items decorated the redwood planked walls. A whole history of northern California was found right here in this inn and in these treasured items.

I scooted to bring the chair closer to the table and rested my arms. "Thanks for the suggestion. I needed to get out and away from the B&B for some fun."

Quint reached across the table with one hand, palm up, until I placed mine in his. "I think we both needed time together that didn't involve my investigation."

"Eh, eh. Don't even mention the word." I smiled and took in a deep breath. "I'm going to sit back, enjoy the bluegrass and country tunes while waiting to order a thick steak, medium well, and a loaded baked potato with lots of sour cream and butter. Doesn't get better than that. Right?"

Quint chuckled. "Absolutely. Now . . ." He picked up the menu. His eyes narrowed as his head shifted up and down ever so slightly. "Let's see how much a steak dinner will set me back." He glanced up. "We may have to split the bill. I don't make much on a sheriff's salary, you know." He waited a second or two then winked.

"Seriously, you are such a child at times." I glared but then a smile popped out.

The server appeared with his smart pad poised. "Are we ready to order?"

"We certainly are." I straightened in my seat and pointed at a place on the menu. After stating my dinner choice, I relaxed in my chair while Quint spoke. An upbeat tune by Sheryl Crow played and my hands tapped to keep time with the rhythm when loud voices from a nearby table caused me to stop and turn. I tensed and stifled a gasp. Tabitha sat not more than twenty feet from us. At the table with her were three men in suits, stylish and pricey which hinted to me they were business-men. Obviously, I couldn't hear the conversation because everyone in the place was talking and laughing. However, whatever was discussed, those matters didn't seem to go well for Tabitha. She looked ready to cry. Throwing up her arms, she finally stomped off and disappeared through the restroom doorway.

"Ali. Did you hear me?" Quint poked my arm.

"Hmm?" I blinked. "Oh! Sorry. I was daydreaming about things."

"What things?" Quint's gaze fixed on me as he sipped his water.

I shoved a stray curl behind my ear, stalling for time to pluck a topic out of my head that didn't involve the deaths of Isadora and Dottie, or about how only seconds ago I witnessed Tabitha having an emotional conversation with three well-groomed men whom I didn't recognize. "The B&B. Yeah." I wagged my head and stuck out my lower lip. "Finances are a mess. We had to replace the furnace, which drained our emergency fund. I have drafty windows that obviously add to my heating and cooling bill. My plans to create a new theme and website for the business will probably be put on hold because . . ." I lifted my shoulders and sighed. "Money. It's always about money."

He tilted his head. "Money can be essential."

"In running a business, always." I grabbed a napkin and blotted the ring of sweat left by my glass then scooted my chair away from the table. "I need to visit the restroom. Be right back."

Clutching my bag to my side, I avoided eye-contact because his powerful observation skills could always tell when I lied—something about a facial tic or the way I brushed my hair back. I wasn't going to wait and find out. Instead, I hurried away from the table, acting like this was an urgent mission.

There'd be plenty of opportunity to question Tabitha later. Plus, she could always lie about her meeting with the three suits. On the other hand, now was my only chance to hear what those men were talking about. I unzipped my bag as I neared their table, and, in one smooth move, I let go of the strap. Contents scattered and rolled across the floor. "Good grief. What a klutzy thing to do." I stooped to gather the spilled items, inching closer to hear any bits of conversation.

"I tell you he'll turn down the offer. Little to no profit."

"Stiletto has room for small investments, but this ski resort worries me."

"I still can't figure out why you pushed so hard and so fast. You sure you don't have a thing for the Wells woman?"

"Hah! Too uptight for my taste. Say, are you coming over this weekend? Barbecue ribs and plenty of sides. Becky got a great deal from Sal's Meat Market."

The conversation had shifted and my knees ached from squatting down. Besides, I'd picked up everything but a balled-up napkin and a tater tot dropped on the floor. Standing, I adjusted my skirt and walked back to our table. I ignored Quint's pointed stare that arrowed through me. "That was awkward and embarrassing. Ooo! Breadsticks." I grabbed one from the basket.

"I bet. Didn't you say you had to visit the restroom?" With the tip of one thumb, he traced his bottom lip.

"Um." I held up one finger and chewed on a bite of breadstick, a slow and deliberate gesture. "I thought I did, but then after my clumsy accident, I realized I didn't." I rolled my tongue along the inside of my mouth. "Do I have sesame seeds stuck between my teeth?" I leaned in and gave him a toothy grin.

"Nope. No seeds." He slid the bread basket my way.

In perfect timing, the server delivered our meals. I relaxed and sniffed at the savory smells of grilled meat and garlic butter. Devouring food left little time for conversation, especially any probing questions Quint might have, which was a relief. The quiet allowed me to sift through what I'd overheard. The words Stiletto and investments piqued my interest. I recognized the company name from conversations at the regional business group to which I belonged. Stiletto Investments bought up companies that were struggling or had gone bankrupt. The question in my mind was what did Stiletto have to do with Tabitha Wells and the resort? Morton Enterprise owned Tahoe Pine. Had the business been sold to Stiletto recently? If so, that was news to me. I hadn't heard a peep that the resort was in financial trouble. In fact, word around town was Tabitha frequently found unique and clever ways to lure guests. She was Morton's golden girl of profit. None of what the three suits said made sense. I pushed my plate to the side and finished my drink. I reminded myself that whatever problem Tabitha and the Stiletto group were involved in had no connection to Isadora's death. I shouldn't waste effort by snooping into the matter. Then again, what other leads did I have?

"Hey, Martinez. Any news?"

Quint's voice brought me out of my thoughts. I studied his face and the wrinkled brow of concern before he turned sideways in his chair.

"Tonight? What about the other case?" He glimpsed my way then lowered his chin. "Call the Uber service and get a statement from the driver. Ask why he dropped her off and left. Maybe she said something to explain. Okay? I'll drop by the office on my way home in a couple of hours."

I folded my hands in front of me and rested them on the table. "So? What was that about?" I officially ended our "no talking about business" by asking the question. Or maybe he did by making that call.

He sucked in air and then let it out. "The coroner is emailing me his report on Isadora's death later this evening."

"Uh huh, good. What was that you said about an Uber driver?"

"Ali." He leaned back in his chair.

"No. You don't get to clam up. You made the call right in front of me. I deserve to know." Crossing my arms tightly, I glared.

"Dottie got to the mining site in an Uber, then told the driver not to wait."

His lips tightened as he looked away. I wouldn't get another word out of him.

As if our server sensed the tension, he slid the bill on the table. "Whenever you're ready."

At once, he cleared distance from us and moved on to the next customers who, ironically, were the three suits. Tabitha wasn't with them. I glanced from one end of the restaurant to the other but saw no sign of her.

"Is anything wrong?"

I started at the sound of Quint's voice. Wide-eyed, I shook my head and shrugged. "Nothing. I thought I spotted someone I knew. Guess I was mistaken."

"Hmm. Well, if you're ready?" He clipped money to the bill and set it under the centerpiece, then stood and circled around to pull out my chair.

"Thank you. I loved the dinner and the company." Underneath that statement was the worry churning in my stomach. I was anxious to talk with Tabitha. Maybe I'd get the answers needed to put my mind at ease. If I dug deeper, I might discover a more credible reason that pushed Tabitha Wells far enough to commit murder.

We pulled into the drive. Lights shown in the parlor windows and a rear view of Gladys's gray hair. More than likely she was knitting again. I grinned. The sweater for Ollie was a labor of love.

Quint leaned over to plant a kiss on my cheek then whispered in my ear. "I think I like you, Ali Winston. Like you a lot."

I pulled back to stare at him. "I certainly hope so, after buying me a pricey steak dinner on your measly salary." In the next second, I burst out laughing. Despite all the troubling events surrounding me, I could count on these moments to lift my spirits. I snuggled against his arm and tickled his chin. "Will you call later to let me know what the coroner has to say?"

"Absolutely won't."

I scooted away and glowered at him. "Why not? Nathan has practically been branded a killer by you and all of Sierra Pines. Whether his wife had a horrible accident or was murdered, he should know about it."

"Trust me, he will be the first one I call, if it turns out to be an accident." He tweaked my nose. "So, calm down, will you?"

"And if it's murder?" My voice barely registered above a whisper.

"Then the investigation into her death continues and nothing comes out until we're done."

I groaned. "You are a stubborn and exasperating man."

"Ali, I'm just doing—"

"Your job. Yeah, I'm reading that message loud and clear." I chewed on my lip and instantly scooted over to kiss him. "Good thing I still like you. A lot." I pushed open the door and called over my shoulder. "Good evening, Sheriff. Call me tomorrow, if you're not too busy."

I shut the car door and jogged up the sidewalk. After a quick wave, I stepped inside the house. As the saying went, I was barking up the wrong tree. However, Quint wasn't my only source of information. Being a former researcher on the television series sharpened my own style of investigative skills. The job also saddled me with intense curiosity to learn the truth. Deputy Martinez was married to Minnie's great granddaughter, Charlene. And Charlene worked at Lucinda's beauty salon where town gossip was the main topic of conversation. "Guess it's time to make an appointment to see my hair stylist." I hung my coat on the rack then walked across the foyer and into the parlor, expecting to find Gladys. The room was empty. "Where did you go?" I muttered and retraced my steps.

A soft murmur of voices came from across the hall, followed by a loud cry. Hitching my breath, I hurried past the stairway and into the library. My steps skidded to a halt and the air eased from my lungs.

Gladys and Ollie sat on the sofa, facing the big screen TV. "Can you believe the nerve of her? Such a conniving woman. And poor Margo Channing is so trusting." Gladys clucked her tongue.

"Makes for great entertainment, don't you think?" Ollie let go of a throaty laugh that wouldn't quit. "Reminds me of Rita Hayworth in *Gilda*. She sure knew how to use her feminine wiles. Boy, the men she fooled."

"They deserved every trick she pulled." Gladys sniffed. "Those despicable men were entirely different from Margo. She was sweet and kind and—"

"Jealous and suspicious of anyone who she thought was after her movie roles," Ollie finished.

"Glad to see you two are having fun." I plopped in a chair next to the sofa and grinned. "What are we watching?"

"Remember when I said Anne Baxter's character in *All About Eve* reminded me of Isadora?" She waved an arm at the screen. "Here's the proof. The more I see—and we are only halfway through the movie—the more I think of Isadora."

As if she realized the implication of her words, Gladys's eyes widened. "Oh my. I'm speaking ill of the dead." She lifted her chin to stare at the ceiling. "Please forgive me."

"I'm sure there's no real harm done, Gladys." I grabbed for a handful of popcorn from the bowl sitting on the coffee table. I settled in my chair and focused on the movie. After a few minutes of watching Eve Harrington's behavior, the well-rehearsed flattery and attentiveness she gave Margo, I sort of understood Gladys's claim. Yes, Isadora schemed to get what she wanted and saved her flattery for those who had whatever she was after. All others mostly experienced her venom and cruelty.

After an hour, I grew tired and barely kept my eyes open to see the end of the movie. When in the final moments, a young ingenue treated the now famous Eve Harrington in the same way Eve had done with Margo, a glimmer of an idea perked me up. If Isadora was murdered, maybe the act wasn't impulsive and provoked out of anger. Maybe it was premeditated, a well thought out plan to get rid of her and make it appear as an accident. I squirmed in my seat as the credits rolled across the screen. Premeditated took time and she'd only been in town for two days. The only ones who knew she and Nathan were coming to Sierra Pines were me and staff at Tahoe Pine Ski Resort; staff like Tabitha and maybe Kyle. I tugged at the hem of my shirt then excused myself. After thanking the Bellwethers for the entertainment, I left the library and stopped in the foyer. The hum of voices sounded from outside. What about employees who took reservation requests? They could be suspects, too. I walked to the front door and the voices grew louder. However, none of the resort staff really knew Isadora. The only ones who had a past with her were Nathan and me. I shivered. But I hadn't killed her. "Maybe not premeditated. Yeah, let's not go down that path." I pulled the window curtain back. A dozen or so carolers stood on the front sidewalk. I opened the door and greeted them as they sang "God Rest Ye Merry Gentlemen" in perfect harmony.

"Oh, how sweet." As she moved alongside me, Gladys squeezed my arm. "Nothing like a Christmas carol to brighten one's holiday cheer."

My worrisome thoughts dwindled away and a sense of comforting warmth filled my insides. I wrapped my arm around her waist. "Just perfect."

"Look! There's Ralph. He's standing next to Owen and Sophie." Gladys waved.

"Saint Genesius! What's the point of a new furnace? You're letting all the heat out." Ollie limped across the foyer to join us.

"Oh, hush, Ollie. We're listening to the carolers." Gladys pointed outside.

Another holiday tune carried through the night. I took in a deep breath. The air was cool, and clouds formed puffy shadows across the sky. A light snowfall covered the ground and tree branches like a layer of white frosting. I laughed as Sophie stuck out her tongue to catch a snowflake. Nice as it was, within a few minutes, the magical scene came to a close. The carolers sang the last notes of "Jingle Bells" then bid us good evening and moved on to the next house.

Gladys sighed. "I do love this time of year. The holidays are full of joy. If only horrible things didn't happen to try and ruin the mood."

"*Humph.* Look at you. I thought I was the grumpy one, always complaining." Ollie rubbed his sister's shoulders then pulled her close for a hug. "You're the one who cheers up everybody. Please don't stop now."

She hugged him back. "Don't worry. I have plenty of cheerful spirit to share."

"Much as I enjoy this touching scene, I'm tired and heading off to bed." I turned and made my way to the stairs. "Love you guys. Don't ever change."

"We love you too, dear," Gladys said.

In case any guests were sleeping, I tiptoed down the hall. It was past ten. The day and all that happened wore me down. I was dog-tired, and at this point, my brain couldn't put more than two thoughts together.

Reaching the end of the hall, I heard faint whimpers and sobs coming from Beth's room. I raised my fist, ready to knock, but then hesitated. What if she needed a private moment? Maybe she'd resent the interruption and tell me to butt out.

I pivoted on my heel to walk away. "None of my business, right?" I grimaced and swung around to knock. "Beth? It's me, Ali. Are you okay?" I rested my ear against the door. The sobbing stopped, but no other sound replaced it. I rubbed the back of my neck, growing anxious. "Beth?"

The door eased open. "I'm fine." She sniffed and shrugged. "Boyfriend problems is all. You know how it is."

"Yeah. I actually do." My gaze dropped and I spotted the cell phone held against her thigh as her fingers clenched and unclenched. "Well, as long as you're okay."

"I am. Good night, Ali. Thanks for checking on me."

The door inched closed. I lingered to make sure there'd be no more crying. Instead, the sound of running water met my ear. I climbed the stairs to the third floor. On impulse, I stopped in front of Julia's collection room then entered. I scanned the rows of framed photos hung on the walls. My gaze stopped. I walked closer to study a black and white candid shot at the far end, top row. Julia stood next to Anne Baxter, the actress who would play Eve Harrington a few years later. This shot was taken on the set of *The Razor's Edge,* a nineteen-forty-six production where Baxter played an alcoholic and Julia worked as the prop designer. A few months later, Julia quit Hollywood and escaped to Sierra Pines. She took care of her ailing mother, my great, great aunt Viola, who died soon after.

I traced my finger along the image of Baxter. She would've been in her early twenties, a mere ingenue in the business. Yet, in this photo her eyes shown with the pain and experience of someone much older. Maybe she transformed to fit the movie role, and this expression of sadness was part of an act.

I closed my eyes for a second. Fear threaded its way through me. If what happened to Isadora, and maybe to Dottie, was foul play, a killer might be walking among us—someone who had the skills to put on an act of innocence. I rubbed my arms to get rid of the sudden chill in me and hurried out of the collection room. Once in my bedroom with the door locked, I relaxed. Slipping out of my clothes, I crawled into bed. The image and voice of Nathan played in my head—his smirk of a smile and boastful words, and the way he could charm me with that pitiful, teary-eyed act to help him get out of trouble. Was that what he was doing now? Was he charming me with an act? I squeezed my eyes shut and yanked the covers up to my chin. Within a few minutes, my mind wandered and the images of Nathan vanished. Instead, I heard Margo Channing speak, as if her warning was met only for me. *Fasten your seatbelts. It's going to be a bumpy night.*

CHAPTER ELEVEN

"THANK YOU, CHARLENE. I'LL SEE YOU AT ELEVEN." I pressed the end call button and tossed my phone on the bed. Before long, I should know all the details of the coroner's report on Isadora's death. My hairdresser spilled gossip with every breath she took, as if her life depended on it. Lucky for me, one of her sources was her husband, Deputy Mike Martinez.

After a hardy breakfast and a last-minute check on the well-being of our guests—yesterday's trauma at the mining sight was bound to put anyone into a funk, myself included—I grabbed my coat and powered down the walkway to the Land Rover. Blinding sunlight glared through the windshield. I pulled down the visor and backed out of the drive. On the way to town, I rehearsed my mental list of questions to ask Charlene. I'd start out with the easy stuff like how business was going, had she finished her gift shopping, and was Mikey Junior excited for Christmas. Then, I'd mention poor Dottie's unfortunate demise and how strange it was for two deaths in one week to happen. I'd add a comment about Nathan and his depression over losing Isadora.

"If that approach doesn't work, I might as well give up." I turned into the parking area reserved for Lucinda's customers then shifted into park and killed the engine. Glancing side to side, I took count of the vehicles in the reserved area. Only two, and one of them was Lucinda's, which meant one other customer was getting her hair done. *Great.* I'd have Charlene to myself. I stepped up to the door and pulled it open. The smell of ammonia stung my nostrils. Several candles placed around the shop burned with lavender and lemon verbena scents—Lucinda's attempt to mask the more unpleasant odor of hair coloring.

I waved at Charlene who stood next to the coffee maker, sipping from a mug. The cute, curvy frame and waist-length blonde hair caused eyes to turn, but her being married to a law enforcer kept those oglers at a distance.

Lucinda leaned over her customer at the sink, rinsing out shampoo. She was Charlene's opposite with that short, spikey black hair and a frame as skinny as a flagpole.

Both ladies glanced up and greeted me as I hung up my coat. "Beautiful, sunny morning, isn't it?" I started with the most popular pleasantry, then steered a path to Charlene's chair.

"Coffee? Chocolate éclair?" Charlene asked.

I shook my head. "Had enough coffee and breakfast to last the day."

She laughed. "What was I thinking? B&B breakfast and Gladys Bellwether mean plenty of food at the table. Right?" She pulled scissors out of the drawer and a plastic apron from the rack. Her fingers ran through my hair. "Just a cut and style, today? Though you could use a few highlights to brighten things up."

Coloring meant more time with Charlene. "Sure. Let's do both." I settled in my chair as she tied the apron strings around my neck then ran to the back room to mix colors. When she returned, I was ready to chat. "So, how's business? Lots of customers, I bet. Everyone getting hair done for the holidays."

"Oh my, you can't imagine how busy." Charlene rambled on about who came into the shop, how each had a story to tell. "I tell you, it's crazy out there."

That was the perfect lead-in. I twisted my mouth into a frown. "Sure is. I mean, poor Dottie Sample. Such a tragic death. And so soon after Isadora Lane falling off that cliff."

Charlene tore off several sheets of aluminum foil. "What a tragedy. Nothing Sierra Pines hasn't experienced before, though." She brushed coloring on a section of hair then wrapped it in foil. "Only two months ago, can you believe it?"

She referred to the tragedy that happened in late October, soon after I arrived in Sierra Pines. I shuddered at the reminder. "But two deaths less than a week apart? And my poor cousin Nathan. He's depressed and heart-broken. I mean, to be on your honeymoon?"

"I can't imagine." Charlene paused. She licked her bottom lip and tapped a well-manicured fingernail on the container of coloring. "You know, my hubby is a deputy, working for the Placerville sheriff's department." She nodded then leaned closer and lowered her voice. "He lets me know what's going on in the office."

"Oh? Is that so?" A tingling sensation sparked my insides. This could be the moment I'd learn if Isadora's death was a murder.

She snorted. "Of course, all that work talk is his way of boasting. He thinks he's more important in what he does. I never say what I think. I let him blather on, every evening at the dinner table, and you know why?" She straightened her shoulders. "I don't plan to spend the rest of my days coloring and cutting hair. No sir. I plan to be a writer. I already worked out the details of a detective novel, and Mike's stories are like research. I can use plenty of those to make my story more realistic. You know what I mean?"

She yanked at another section of hair, and I winced. "So, what's Mike been telling you? Anything interesting?"

"Oh! Yeah, that's where I was going with this. He says . . ." She glanced toward the back of the shop.

I followed her direction and spotted Lucinda chatting with her customer.

"Mike says he overheard his boss—you know Quint Sterling, right? Surprised he hasn't told you already. Anyway, Mike heard him talking to the coroner. Turns out that actress your cousin married? She was murdered." Her eyes grew wide. "Bruises found on her neck were dark purple, which means they were put there right before she fell. That's what the coroner says. And she had cuts on her wrists, like she'd been in a tussle with someone. Her killer, obviously." She gave her chin a firm nod.

My stomach rolled. Even though I expected this outcome, the news didn't disturb me any less, or worry me. I had plenty to worry about. We all did.

Charlene tapped me on the arm. "There's more. Kind of like a clue the department is keeping secret, which I shouldn't be telling you, but what the hey." She chuckled. "The coroner found brown wool fibers on her body. Mike says they hope that tiny detail will help them solve the case."

I frowned. Why would brown-colored wool fibers help them find Isadora's killer? Sounded flimsy to me. I imagined lots of folks wore brown wool coats, gloves or scarves, which would make it difficult to narrow down to one suspect. "All that is very interesting. Thanks for sharing Charlene. And I'll be the first to buy your book when it comes out. Autographed, of course."

Charlene beamed ear to ear and blushed. "Why thank you, Ali. Now, let's put you under the dryer for a bit before washing out this coloring."

I settled in the chair and listened to the dryer hum. The sound was soothing, and if my head stopped reeling with all I'd learned, it would put me to sleep. The seeds of a new plan sprouted in my brain. That meant another conversation with Quint. I'd spill the details of what Charlene had told me, even though I'd feel a bit guilty in ratting out Deputy Martinez. Afterward, Quint had to tell me if there was more to the case. Or at least I hoped he would. The plan was worth a try, no matter what.

An hour later, I said goodbye to Charlene and Lucinda. I had one more stop to make before heading home. Meeka's Mementos was a five-minute walk from the salon, so I left my car parked and hoofed it to the shop. I had gifts to buy for Gladys and Ollie. I'd spent several weeks searching for the perfect choice but with no luck. Funny how the older people got, the less they really needed or wanted. Every time I asked for suggestions, I got the same answer. *You don't need to buy me anything. Your company at Christmas is enough to make me happy.*

Reaching the next block, I crossed the street. Bells strapped to horses jingled as a large, six-passenger carriage passed by. Several arms lifted to wave at me. I waved in return. "Merry Christmas!"

"Why Merry Christmas to you too, Alexis."

Startled, I twirled around to face Florence. She was bundled in a white, ankle-length wool coat with scarf, hat, and gloves to match. The scarf covered the bottom half of her face, leaving only her dark eyes staring at me. She was the perfect image of a talking snowman. "Florence. You look toasty warm."

She brushed the front of her coat with those gloved hands. "People my age should be extra careful. Flu and colds are so common." She lifted her scarf-covered chin. "I pride myself on being extremely healthy. I haven't caught a cold in ten years. If not for Minnie Short sneezing all over me the winter before, my record would be closer to fifteen."

I fastened the top button of my coat and tightened my scarf. "The weather is a bit breezy and chilly today."

"Getting a chill has nothing to do with catching a cold. Didn't your doctor tell you?"

I sighed in exasperation. "Yes, I seem to recall that information. Anyway, what are you doing in town?"

"Shopping for gifts." She lifted the bags in her hands. "Of course, I'm multi-tasking, too. Checking on shop owners to drum up last-minute donations."

"Kind of late to approach them, isn't it?" I frowned.

"Last-minute is better than nothing at all." She dropped her shoulders and groaned. "With Dottie gone, I've got twice as much to do. On top of that burden, your precious sheriff refuses to give back the money our fine, upstanding SPACA member stole. Such hogwash. He says it's part of the investigation."

"That's too bad. I'm sure people in town will understand." I struggled to offer encouraging words. "At least we have the entertainment portion prepared. The children's choir sounds beautiful."

"Yes, I suppose so." Florence hefted her bags to her sides. "No matter. We do the best we can. Now, if you'll excuse me, I have plenty of shops left to visit."

I opened and shut my mouth as she marched off without saying a proper goodbye. "Huh. That was rude." I finished my walk to Meeka's and stepped inside.

Meeka stood on a ladder at the front window. She pointed in the direction I'd just come from. "What was that all about?"

"Oh, you mean my Florence moment." I unwrapped the scarf from my neck and grinned. "You know how she can be."

The dimples in Meeka's cheeks deepened as she laughed. Dressed in a bright turquoise blue frock and chunky jewelry, she brightened the room.

"Oh, yeah. I do." She handed me bags of snowflakes and glitter. "Would you lay those on the table next to you?" She gathered her scissors and glue gun and descended the ladder.

I admired the window display. "You always do such a nice job decorating. Maybe you could come to the B&B? Our windows could use your festive touch." I winked.

"Uh, huh." She planted closed fists on her hips. "You know I would if I had the time."

I chuckled. "Kidding." I surveyed the shelves with holiday gift ideas on display. "However, I do need your help." I held up one hand as she opened her mouth. "Not window displays. I need suggestions for what to buy Gladys and Ollie." I picked up a porcelain figurine of an angel then returned it to the shelf. Turning, I faced her, quiet and waiting.

Meeka tapped her lip with one finger. "Let's see." She twisted side to side then walked up and down the aisles. "Cookware? No, I'm sure Gladys has plenty. Garden tools? Books?" Her head popped from behind a shelf. "How about sister and brother coffee mugs?"

I shook my head and moaned. "No. They have all those things." I planted my rear end on the window ledge. "It's hopeless."

"Nothing's hopeless, Ali." Meeka marched with determined steps to the front of the store. She unlocked a glass case and pulled out several items. "What if you have two of these engraved? Something personal is always appreciated, don't you think?"

I approached to examine the display of items, some made of silver and others of brass, and a range of sizes to choose from. I picked up a bookmark. "Gladys would like this, I think. And . . ." My hand swiped across the glass counter, pausing to touch each item. "This." I handed her a pirate's nautical telescope made of brass. "Ollie would love it." I pictured the item on his bedroom shelf, alongside the musket used during his stuntman days as a double for Errol Flynn and the autographed photo from the swashbuckler movie *The Sea Hawk.*

"Perfect choices." Meeka set them aside and pulled out an order form. "Now, tell me what you want engraved on each."

I blinked. "Are you sure there's enough time to get them done before Christmas?"

"Absolutely." She gave her chin a firm nod. "I'll expedite the order and pay for the extra cost of shipping. My gift to you."

"No, I couldn't let you—"

Her hand covered mine. "Stop. You've done me plenty of favors and so much good for the town. I insist. So . . .?" She tapped her pen on the order form.

I composed words for both of the gifts, thanked Meeka, and exited the shop, pleased with my purchases and excited for Christmas morning when Gladys and Ollie would open them. Plus, with the information I received from Charlene, I was armed and ready to fire questions at Quint, the next time we talked. Right now, I had other leads to follow. Stiletto Investments was worth googling. I wanted to make sure they had officially bought Tahoe Pine Ski Resort. Of course, learning more about the details of the scene at Mountain View Inn could only be done via a face-to-face meeting with Tabitha Wells, which meant another trip to the resort. I sighed. It seemed I'd been spending more time on the road than tending to business and enjoying the comforts of the B&B.

Stepping into the foyer, I hung my coat and slipped out of my boots. The drive and front walk hadn't been shoveled. Odd, since Ollie was always on top of such tasks. "Gladys? Ollie?" I called out as I walked across the hall.

"In here, dear." Gladys shouted from the kitchen.

I entered the room and chuckled at the sight. A dusting of flour covered Gladys from head to chest, while the rest of the spill coated the floor. "Trying out a new recipe?" I grabbed a dust pan and broom.

Gladys clucked her tongue and shook out her apron. "My goodness. One minute I was struggling to open this bag, and before I knew it, flour burst out everywhere. Such a mess."

I pressed my lips together and nodded. "We'll have it cleaned up in no time."

I swept flour into the pan as Gladys wiped the floor and table clean with a damp rag. "By the way, have you seen Ollie?"

"He went next door to speak with Mr. Thorsby. He's hoping to borrow his snow blower. Seems ours is on the fritz. Always something breaking." She leaned back and threw up her arms. "This won't do. After my baking, I'll have to bring out the mop and clean this the right way."

"Say, you'll never guess what I learned at the beauty salon." Nothing like gossip and town news to distract her from kitchen disasters.

Gladys plopped in the chair. "Really? I could use a good story to cheer me up."

"Sorry. This one isn't the cheerful, pick-me-up you'd hope for." I sat and shared the details of Charlene's report on Isadora's death.

"Another homicide in Sierra Pines? What are the odds?" Gladys folded and laid the rag in her lap. "Does Quint know you know?" Her brow shifted.

"Not yet. I don't imagine he'll be too pleased with Martinez." I traced the edge of the table with my finger. "Or with me."

"Well, I don't feel sorry for Martinez. He should keep his mouth shut when it comes to an investigation and not make it a topic at the dinner table." She stood and walked to the sink. "As for you, maybe don't mention it to Quint?"

"If I'm going to learn more, I have to ask him questions." I stood. "I'll take the chance and hope he doesn't hate me for interfering . . . again."

"You do what you think is best, dear." Gladys removed another bag of flour from the pantry. "Now, let's see if I can manage this one."

I handed her a pair of scissors then shoulder-shrugged. "Maybe this will help."

She pursed her lips. "The easy way out, but I'll take it. So, what are your plans for this afternoon?"

"A trip to the ski lodge, for one." I grabbed a bottle of vegetable juice and a plastic container of leftover quinoa from the fridge. "First, I need to surf the internet for some information on Stiletto Investments."

Gladys handed me a fork. "Have fun and stay out of trouble. I'll be in here for the next hour or two, if you need me."

"Will do! Thanks, Gladys." I hiked up the stairs to my room. It took little more than a half hour, and I found the information on Stiletto and its purchase of Tahoe Pine from Morton Enterprise, dated December first. I imagined being under new ownership meant every employee was hustling to prove their value to the business, especially the resort manager, Tabitha Wells.

I sipped the last of my vegetable juice and set the container aside. More curious than ever to speak with Tabitha, I turned off the laptop and hurried down the stairs. Passing by Nathan's room, I got a quick peek of him sitting in his chair, or more like slouching. Gladys had mentioned this morning that she was concerned. He hadn't left his room the whole time the rest of us were at the mining sight and discovering Dottie's body. In fact, he hadn't gone out for dinner while Quint and I had ours at the Mountain View Inn. Guilt weighted down my shoulders. I should be paying more attention to his wellbeing. Instead of coming out of his depression, he seemed to get worse. Of course, all those accusatory looks from the other guests and rumors in town didn't exactly make him feel welcome. I had hoped he would stand his ground and defend himself. If I was suspected of murder, I'd be shouting my innocence from the Sierra mountain tops.

"Looks like I'll have to do that shouting for him and find the real killer." I popped in the kitchen to announce I was leaving. Gladys stood at the sink, wringing out the mop. "Well, that floor has never looked shinier."

She turned. "It needed a good cleaning anyway. Are you headed to the resort?"

"Yes. I should be back in a couple hours." I scratched behind one ear. "Say, if you don't mind, would you invite Nathan to dine with us this evening? I'm worried about him."

"The same thought crossed my mind. Both the worry and the dinner invitation." She nodded. "What's one of his favorite dishes?"

I tapped my lip. "Hmm. Aunt Betts always fixed him country-fried chicken and mashed potatoes when he needed cheering up. Oh, and broccoli. He loves broccoli."

"Huh. You came up with that one quick enough. You know him well."

I shrugged. "Despite my gripes and groans, Nathan and I had some good times together. Okay, I'll be back in time to help fix dinner." I waved over my shoulder as I walked to the door. Feeling like the inspector, Hercules Poirot or the amateur sleuth Mrs. Marple on the hunt for clues, I was energized. Whether brave or foolish, I didn't care. Sometimes, a person had to take that leap to get results, especially when a friend was in trouble.

Forty some minutes later, I pulled into the resort parking lot and scanned the area for any sign of Mr. Farley, the grumpy groundskeeper. He had a way of sneaking up on a body, which I hoped to avoid this time around. After a near collision with a deer leaping out of the woods and onto Lincoln highway, my nerves were frazzled. Maybe I'd let down my guard during the last visit to the lodge. In that instance, my preoccupation with the contents of Kyle's car didn't help. I couldn't afford the risk of Farley snooping after my snooping. If he asked too many questions, I might crack and spill everything I knew about the murder and my plan to interrogate Tabitha.

As I exited my vehicle, I spotted Farley fixing a window near the far end of the building. Relieved, I hefted my bag strap over one shoulder, locked the vehicle, and walked to the lodge entrance. Guests mingled near the fireplace, chatting and sipping from steaming mugs while skiers, bundled in their gear, trekked from the rental kiosk to the rear exit. I paused at the door and shifted my gaze to a section of windows next to Tahoe Eats and Beverages. Gold letters etched on glass read Office of the Manager. Tabitha sat at her desk with a phone plastered to one ear. In the next second, she tossed the device to one side and paced the floor.

I took a deep breath. "Not Ready to Make Nice" by the Dixie Chicks played over the intercom. I wasn't about to play nice either. I was a woman on a mission. I'd take advantage of Tabitha's distracted mood and crack her tough exterior to get the information I wanted.

"Can I help you?"

Kristin from HR came out of nowhere and blocked my path, only a dozen steps from the office doorway. I groaned. Those squinty eyes and pursed lips hinted in a big way that I was not welcome. Widening my stance, I planted fists on hips. "I'm here to see Tabitha. Now, if you don't mind." I sidestepped to get around her, but she imitated my move, keeping us nose to nose.

"Do you have an appointment?"

"Nope. Don't need one." In seconds, I hopped to the left then leaped forward to land on the other side of her. "Thanks for the concern, but I got this." I waved before pulling open the office door and stepping inside.

"Excuse me?" Tabitha stopped her pacing and glared. "I don't remember scheduling a meeting with you."

"Yes, but this is urgent." I sat in a chair and crossed my legs. "How's your day going? I noticed you talking on the phone a moment ago and you seemed upset."

She gathered up the papers scattered across her desk and stuffed them in a folder. "I don't know what you mean, and I don't have time to waste on empty babble." She picked up her coat and bag then walked to the doorway. "I have a meeting."

"Speaking of babble, I saw you at the Mountain View Inn last night. Dinner and a conversation with three sharp-looking men in suits, right?"

Tabitha twisted around to face me. She tossed her coat to the side then dragged herself behind the desk and sank into her chair. "Stiletto Investments."

I nodded. "They bought the resort a month ago."

"And announced there would be a twenty percent cut in staff." She scoffed. "Talk about pressure. Everyone is in competition to stay ahead of the game and keep their jobs."

"Is that what your conversation with the three men was about? Keeping your job?" I was pleased but surprised she offered to talk. I just had to keep up the momentum with questions.

"Not exactly." She chewed on a fingernail then pointed at me. "You know what it takes to run a business successfully. Promo strategies, advertising, new ideas to make the business grow, and you can never stop." She smacked her hand on the desk.

I jerked at the sound. "Well, I've only been running the B&B a couple of months."

"Great! A fresh start to get things right. Lucky you. I, on the other hand, inherited a financial nightmare. The previous owner had no business savvy, I tell you."

At once, I realized what she'd done. She totally derailed the conversation and away from my question. "About that meeting with the Stiletto group?" I raised my brow.

She leaned back in her chair. "I have big plans, but big means I need money." Her eyes brightened and the tempo of her words raced. "Picture a play area for kids with trampolines and an arcade full of the latest games. A luxury spa for the grownups and one of those alpine coasters." She nodded at me. "That coaster would be a gold mine. It's the rage in Europe, you know." She scooted forward in her seat. "People ride the rails on sled-like cars. I mean, even if you don't ski, that alpine coaster would be fun for the whole family, don't you think?"

I cleared my throat, not sure what to say. Up until now, Tabitha's eyes and her voice hinted at pure elation. All of that disappeared as if she suddenly caught up to the ending of her story. "What you're really saying is the Stiletto group refuses to give you the money." I shook my head. "I'm so sorry, Tabitha." My mission to interrogate a murder suspect deflated along with my enthusiasm. Instead, all I wanted to do was console her. We business women had to stick together.

She lifted her chin and sniffed. "Not your problem. So, if we're done, I really do have a meeting." Clutching the folder to her chest, she then pointed at the door. "Thanks for stopping by. Next time, please make an appointment. I'm a busy manager with a very tight schedule."

It looked like the warm heart-to-heart talk was over. I shrugged. "See you around." I left the office and walked toward the exit. Buttoning my coat, I pushed open the door. Powdery snow carried by a blast of wind sprayed my face. Chin to chest, I hurried to the parked Land Rover. I considered all the details Tabitha had shared. Her plans sounded grandiose, but those additions would certainly attract guests. All kinds and ages. I wondered why the Stiletto group turned her down. Sliding into the driver's seat, I frowned. I was getting off track. I should be searching for a reasonable motive as to why Tabitha would murder Isadora. I could hear Quint's stern voice telling me what to do. "I should collect the evidence and stop leading with my emotions." I smacked the steering wheel. "Think, Ali. Tabitha is on the edge of possibly losing her job. She's scheduled a meeting with Stiletto to pitch her ideas, and her mood is tense. Even a tiny push, such as Isadora's threat to badmouth the resort, could make her lose control, right?" I shifted into gear and drove out of the parking lot. "What if Tabitha went out on the slopes to find Isadora and beg her not to carry out that threat? Things didn't go as planned. Isadora spewed out one of her sarcastic lines, and, in a flash of anger, Tabitha pushed her off of the cliff." I whistled. "Scary thought, Winston, but totally believable."

CHAPTER TWELVE

I MADE THE TRIP HOME IN RECORD TIME—no animal collisions or road construction. I rewound my gruesome scenario between Tabitha and Isadora, playing the scene again and again. Each time, the possibility became more probability. I'd made a case for both motive and opportunity. Now all I needed was concrete evidence to prove Tabitha had been at the cliff and confronted Isadora. Quint's voice interrupted my thoughts again. "Yeah, I should admit my scenario is too easy. A neat and tidy package isn't a good fit. Murder is messy."

My watch read four o'clock. I hurried inside and headed to the kitchen to help Gladys make dinner. The warm, doughy smell of baked rolls wafted through the air. I sniffed. With a drawn-out moan, I picked up my pace to reach the counter. "I am famished." Before Gladys could smack my hand away, I grabbed a roll and took a generous bite. "Thank you." I mumbled the words with a full mouth.

Gladys tied an apron around my waist. "You're here to help make dinner, remember?" She winked.

"Food is energy." I patted my stomach. "Now, I'm fueled and ready. How about I make a broccoli cheese casserole while you start the chicken?" I wasn't exactly Rachel Ray in the kitchen, but my broccoli casserole brought plenty of compliments. I pulled ingredients out of the fridge and cupboard. "Did Nathan give you a hard time about the invitation?"

Gladys clucked her tongue. "That man is stubborn."

"I'm sure you wore him down. After all, it takes one to know one." I winked.

"Darn right it does. He caved after five minutes. My argument and persuasive nature are unbeatable." She coated the chicken pieces in egg and bread crumbs. "He'll bring his appetite and sit at the table. Guaranteed."

I skirted around the topic for as long as I could manage, talking about the other guests, the Christmas event, the meager holiday sales, and Ollie's headache over fixing the snow blower.

Gladys slapped the dishrag against her thigh. "When are you going to tell me about your visit to the resort?"

"I figured I'd wait until you asked because I knew you would." I tipped my head and pointed a finger at her.

"Smarty." She tossed the dishrag in the sink then sat in a chair. "Spill."

I gave her a quick rundown of Tabitha's agenda and how Stiletto rejected her proposal. "What do you think?"

"Meaning?" Her brow arched like a question mark.

I shoved the casserole in the oven. "Meaning, could that be reason enough to believe Tabitha would commit murder after Isadora threatened to send out scathing comments across social media about the resort?"

Gladys swiped a stray curl from her forehead. "Anything is possible, dear, but is it reasonable to think Tabitha would kill Isadora? I'm not so sure."

I flopped in a chair next to her and sighed. "Me neither. I'm grasping for any foothold, Gladys. The idea that my cousin would turn so evil and kill his wife?" I shook my head. "I'm struggling with every fiber of my body to accept that. There has to be another answer."

She reached across the table and patted my hand. "Don't worry. I'm sure everything will turn out okay."

I read the confidence in her tone but her eyes registered a flicker of doubt. If Quint found solid proof that Nathan was the killer, I had to accept that, whether I wanted to or not. I stood and checked my watch. "The timer should go off in forty minutes. Would you mind taking the casserole out of the oven? I want to give Mom and Dad a call, ask them if the go-fund-me idea is working and how Aunt Betts took the news about Isadora."

She nodded. "I'm sorry Glenn won't give you more time. Ollie says Glenn's business is in a slump. He has bills to pay."

"Are you kidding? I'm grateful he's willing to put me on a payment plan. Not every merchant is so understanding." I stepped toward the hall. "I'll be down to help set the table. And come to think of it, I'll stop by

Nathan's room on my way. No point in giving him a chance to back out of dinner. Of course, who can resist dining with three fabulous people like us?" I laughed.

As I climbed the stairs, my teasing mood sobered. Making the phone call to my parents caused me a fierce level of anxiety. If they had bad news to report about the fund raising, I had no choice but to accept their loan, unless I sold some items from Julia's collection. My heart sank and guilt waved through me. That idea seemed like a betrayal to Julia.

Backed into a corner with no way out, I envisioned a for sale sign in the front yard while the Bellwethers and I packed our belongings with tear-filled eyes. I gave my head a firm shake. "Stop being so melodramatic, Winston. There's no shame in borrowing from your parents. Adult children do it all the time." I pepped up my mood with each word and marched down the second-floor hallway. Taking the stairs to the attic two at a time, I pulled my shoulders straight. With a split second's hesitation, I stabbed the call button then sat on my bed, waiting for someone to pick up. I glimpsed my reflection in the mirror—creased brow, thinned lips . . . and was my left eye twitching? I groaned. "Get a grip."

"Hello, Ali. So good to hear from you. How are you and Nathan doing?"

Mom's cheerful lilt put me somewhat at ease. "Hi, Mom. I'm still sane and holding things together. Nathan, on the other hand, is depressed and frustrated. Quint hasn't been easy on him, which makes things worse." I gripped the phone tighter.

"That's such a shame. Your aunt took the news hard. Difficult as it is to believe, she had a soft spot for Isadora. As for Nathan, she called and spoke with him. I suppose Kinsey keeps her busy so she won't have time to worry as much."

"Yeah, let's hope. Any news from your producer?" I held my breath.

"Oh yes. Before you burst a blood vessel waiting to hear, your funding idea is trending along. The play is a wonderful success, a full house every night. Nearly four thousand dollars have been raised so far. Vincent was very excited about the whole idea. He happens to be a lover of B&Bs."

Good thing I was sitting. Relief channeled through me, and my body felt like a limp noodle—one less problem to worry about. "That's—I'm so grateful. Thank you, Mom." I gulped air and willed myself to calm down.

"I remember you said how the first payment on the furnace is due tomorrow. So, I've deposited the four thousand in your PayPal account."

Tears blurred my eyes. "Well, I'm happy and so very grateful. Tell Mr. Swallow I plan on repaying his kindness somehow." My voice quivered.

"Sweetie. That's not at all necessary. Family takes care of each other, and that family reaches to those in the theater. Otherwise, we'd never survive the hard times." She paused a few seconds. "Now, not that Nathan and the B&B isn't enough, but something else is bothering you. I can hear something in your voice."

I sighed. "I haven't told you everything that's been going on in Sierra Pines." I explained the news about Isadora's death being classified as murder, and the death of Dottie Sample. "The coroner hasn't finished his report on Dottie's death, but I have a queasy feeling in my gut hers was murder, too." I raked fingers through my hair. Her death hit me hard because, despite her faults, I truly liked Dottie. "There's more. I think Quint's become certain Nathan killed Isadora."

"Sweetie, carrying around that amount of stress and worry is too unhealthy. Maybe I can make flight arrangements for Dad and me to come out there. Let's see . . . Oh! There are two seats available on a flight leaving tomorrow. We could be together for Christmas. Wouldn't that be nice?"

"Mom." I gripped the phone and my breath hitched. "You and Dad have the play. You can't just leave. Besides, we already discussed me coming home for New Year's." Arguing with Willa Winston when she wanted something had been a work in progress. Most of the time, I'd lose, but this battle was one I had to win. "To change the subject, I wanted to ask about Isadora and Nathan."

"Like what?"

"Like their marriage. I got the impression Isadora was angrier than usual. She snapped at Nathan and had a shouting match with both the manager and ski instructor at the resort. I thought maybe since you talk to Aunt Betts most every day, she might have said something."

"Ali, where are going with this? You don't think Nathan—"

"No! If anything, I'm trying to find ways to prove he didn't have anything to do with what happened." A groan rumbled in my throat. "What I'm asking is did she have any troubles in her life, personal or professional? For all we know, someone had a beef with Isadora."

Her breath rattled. "I want to be truthful, sweetheart. I'm afraid Nathan and Isadora were arguing more than getting along. Your hunch is right, though. Isadora was mean and vindictive toward most everyone."

I clutched the phone in a white-knuckled grip. "Oh? How so?"

"Your aunt Betts is a proud woman and would never tell me about any issues with the newlyweds, but I got the sense she was troubled. No wonder their problems didn't take long to go public. While dining at a restaurant, an argument broke out between Nathan and Isadora. It escalated until the owner asked them to leave. Nathan grew angry. He smashed his glass then stormed out, leaving Isadora behind."

I tensed. Nathan losing his temper in such a way wasn't a small thing when it came to a murder investigation. "Maybe what you heard was exaggerated. You know how people like to embellish when it comes to gossip."

"Nope. Every detail is true."

"How can you be so sure?"

"Because your dad and I were there."

I gasped. "Do you know what they argued about?"

"We couldn't hear every word, that is, until right before Nathan left the restaurant. Isadora shouted a warning that she wouldn't let him ruin her career, even if it meant leaving him."

I scratched the back of my neck. I'd overheard Isadora say something similar to Nathan that afternoon in their bedroom. She must have been extremely worried about her career, but why? "Mom, did you hear anything else about Isadora? Like whether she'd lost a role in a play or was fired from a job? That could explain her mood."

"None that I know of. Then again, I tend to avoid reading or listening to most anything involving her. You can understand."

I sure did. "Thanks, Mom. You've been a big help. Text me Mr. Swallow's address. I want to send him flowers, at least."

I ended the call, and, almost immediately, the phone dinged with Mom's text. Prompt as usual. I jotted down Swallow's address then searched online for florists and picked one that would deliver to New York the next day. After ordering, I checked my watch. I had time to shower before dinner. I'd gathered a ton of information today and was bursting to tell, or admittedly to boast, about my accomplishments to one person. The question was whether he'd blow a fuse or welcome my contribution. Either way, I planned to share.

I stepped toward the shower when a shout from downstairs stopped me.

"Ali! You have a visitor."

Gladys's voice echoed up the stairway.

"That figures." I sighed and pulled on my jeans and sweater. Tromping down the stairs, I reached the foyer to find Quint standing at the door. I grinned. "Hey there, Sheriff. You look kind of handsome in that uniform."

"Only kind of?" He squinted his eyes then brushed off the top of his hat. "Guess I'll need to work on that image a bit more."

I walked closer and gave him a peck on the cheek. "It's the person wearing the uniform that I'm attracted to. So, don't change a thing."

"Yes, Ma'am." He spoke in a throaty growl.

"What brings you here? Don't you have sheriff things to keep you busy?" I teased as I took his hand and led him into the parlor.

"I took an early dinner break and thought I'd stop by for a few minutes." He sat next to me and wrapped one arm around my shoulder. "Besides, it's painfully hard not seeing you for so long."

I scoffed. "It's been less than twenty-four hours."

"But like a lifetime to me."

He blinked with those puppy-dog eyes. I squeezed his chin with my fingers and thumb then kissed him lightly on the lips. "Sappy, but I'll take what I can get."

"Now, what have you been up to today?" He leaned against the sofa and spread his arms to rest along the back then stared at the ceiling.

At once, I was on alert. He knew something. Someone must have snitched on my whereabouts, either my visit in town or at the resort. I shrugged. "Nothing much. Got my hair done. Did some Christmas shopping. How about you? Anything new you'd like to share?" I could be as coy as Eve Harrington or Margo Channing.

"Darn it, Ali." He dropped his arms and twisted around to face me. "Why did you go to the resort and question Tabitha Wells? After I spotted her at the Mountain View Inn, I knew you couldn't resist talking to her."

"What? You saw her too? Why didn't you say something?"

"I could ask you the same thing." He tipped his head. "Now, why don't you share what you learned? I'm keeping an open mind."

I rolled my eyes. At least he was curious rather than angry. "I would've gotten around to it." I relayed the details of the conversation with Tabitha and my research on Stiletto.

"Stiletto." He nodded. "As soon as I found out Morton sold the resort to them, I had Martinez dig for details, and he learned what you did."

"Huh. Speaking of Martinez there's something else you should know. His wife Charlene told me all about the coroner's report and how he's classified Isadora's death a homicide."

Quint's eyes bulged and his face reddened.

"Please don't shoot the messenger. Me or Charlene. You might want to speak with your deputy though. Tell him loose lips sink ships or something equally effective." I bit down on my tongue to keep from laughing. "Sorry. I don't mean to take this lightly."

"Oh, believe me. I'm taking this very seriously. Martinez has been told before. Don't talk about our business outside of the office, and that includes to his wife. She's a sweet lady but can't keep her trap shut."

"Quint! That's not at all nice." To be honest, I felt a twinge of guilt. Outing Martinez and his wife wasn't nice either. I fiddled with a button on my sweater. Since I'd already gone that far, I might as well take it to the finish line. "Charlene also told me about the clue your department is keeping a secret. The brown wool fibers?"

His frown deepened and a few choice words slipped from his mouth. "That man is seriously in for a reprimand. I trust you'll keep quiet about that information? At least until the coroner has finished Dottie's report."

"Ah hah!" I stabbed my finger at his chest. "The wool fibers were found on her too, weren't they? Don't lie. I can always tell when you do."

"Not exactly. Brown-colored fibers were found on the rock, along with traces of her blood."

"Which would lead us to believe whoever killed Isadora also killed Dottie." I rubbed my hands together. "Now all we need to figure out is who owns a brown wool coat or gloves or scarf or some other clothing item."

Quint's lips thinned as he glared. "First of all, quit saying we or us. This case isn't yours. It belongs to the sheriff's department. More specifically, to me. And second, the coroner hasn't determined if Dottie Sample was murdered. So, stop saying that too. Got it?"

"Geesh." I threw up my arms. "Don't be so touchy, Sheriff. Open mind, remember?"

He raked fingers through his hair. "Right. I do appreciate your efforts. But . . ." He held up one finger.

"I know. You're afraid I'll put myself in a dangerous situation like before." I grasped his hand and pulled it down. "I promise that won't happen. I've learned a lot from the last time. I know when to walk away, or run if I have to. Besides, shouldn't the townsfolk be warned if there's a killer lurking close by? Better to be on alert and prepared." I nodded.

"Maybe you're right, but stirring up panic is a risk. You know it could happen, Ali. Think about some of the people in this town."

I considered Florence and her overly dramatic behavior, Minnie who loved being a vigilante and taking out the bad guys, and Clive whose motto was to shoot first and ask questions later, but he couldn't hit a target from ten feet because his eyesight was that poor. Yeah, Quint was right. Panic would explode. "Okay, I see your point. How about just between you and me? Do you think Dottie was murdered?"

Quint stuffed a stick of gum in his mouth and slowly chewed. "The position of the wound on the back of her head suggests something." He placed fingers behind my head, near the base. "If she stumbled, fell backwards, and hit her head on the rock, the wound wouldn't be this far down but it is." He moved his finger up my skull then stopped midway. "Here. This most likely would be the point of impact if it happened by accident." He dropped his hand and shrugged. "At least that's what the coroner claims."

My body went all tingly from the touch of his hand on my hair. "I see. Well, in that case, I guess our cozy little town has a killer with a healthy appetite for murder." I slouched in my seat, feeling sick. The scary situation had become too real.

He shook his head. "Not going there yet. Not until—"

"You have enough evidence to prove it." I finished and relaxed my breath. "Thank you for being honest. I know you don't like spilling details of a case."

"You're getting pretty clever with your ways of wearing me down." He tweaked my nose. "Try and stay out of danger, okay?" His eyes darkened and his voice grew serious.

My lips quivered as I attempted to smile. "That won't happen if you hurry up and find Isadora's killer."

He stood. "In that case, I better be on my way. Can't catch the bad guys sitting here talking to you." He wrapped both arms around my waist and kissed the top of my head.

"Indeed, you can't." I chuckled. "Before you go, would you like some dessert to top off your dinner? Gladys baked cherry cobbler. I can grab a to-go bag from the kitchen."

He rubbed his stomach and groaned. "Thanks. I'm tempted, but I'll pass. Got to keep my trim figure." He laughed. "Anyway, I'll talk to you tomorrow."

I walked him to the door and watched as he drove away. Our talk hadn't been the explosion I worried about, but a thought hit me during the conversation, one I kept to myself. Brown wool fiber found on both bodies was more than a connection between the two deaths. I slowly came to realize this bit of information was the evidence Quint needed to identify the killer.

My heart pounded as I turned to the coat rack next to the front door. I shuffled through the collection of outerwear and pulled out an item from underneath one coat. My hand shook. I couldn't tear my gaze away from the brown wool scarf embroidered with the letters NG. "Too simple. Too convenient." I shook my head and quickly placed the scarf underneath the coat. After all, fibers from his scarf could've gotten on Isadora days before.

"Ali! Dinner will be ready in ten minutes. Why don't you stop by Nathan's room and bring him down?" Gladys called out from the kitchen.

"Be right there." I clenched my fists and marched up the stairs. How was I supposed to keep those suspicious thoughts running through my head from showing on my face? I knocked on the door and worked my lips into a smile. At least, I could manage that. Impatient, I rapped on the door again—still no answer. I wanted to ask him direct questions. No more hiding behind his grief or sad stories of how happy they were or how much he loved her. Now was the time for straight answers.

"Nathan? Please come out. Gladys has a scrumptious dinner on the table. All your favorites." I leaned my ear against the door but heard nothing. Easing the doorknob, I opened the door and gasped. "What the heck?"

I turned on my heel and ran downstairs. Churning with a mix of anger and worry, I burst into the kitchen. Gladys and Ollie sat at the table. Plates of chicken, broccoli casserole, and cheesy potatoes sat in the center. "Have either of you seen Nathan in the past hour or so? He's not in his room." I chewed on my lower lip and waited for one of them to say something.

Gladys's forehead creased. "I heard music coming from his room when I passed by to put away linens in the closest. That would've been less than an hour ago."

Ollie lifted his glass to take a drink. "Maybe he left in the Uber car that was idling out front."

"What?" I frowned.

"Yep. It pulled up in front of the house about forty minutes ago. It had one of those beacon lights on the windshield. You know the kind the local Uber drivers use? Anyway, I had to store some supplies in the garage. When I came back out, the car was gone."

My mind raced. If he'd left, why didn't he tell one of us? He knew we were supposed to dine together. "I'm giving the local Uber service a call. Maybe Nathan phoned them for a ride." I left them and sprinted across the hall and upstairs to grab my phone. If he left, he hadn't taken his coat and that incriminating scarf. I grumbled under my breath. "What is going on, Nathan?"

I called the service and someone answered on the first ring. "Hi, I'm trying to track down one of your drivers. He would've picked up a customer at the Sierra Pines B&B about an hour ago."

"Can't give out that information, Ma'am."

The gravelly voice was short and to the point. I clenched my jaw. "There's a person missing and he might be in serious danger, if you don't give me that information."

"I still can't. There's privacy laws in place, you know."

I groaned. It was time to bluff. "Sheriff Sterling is a close friend of mine. Maybe I'll give him a call and suggest he pay you a visit. Could be time for an inspection, right? Of course, I'd sure hate to see you shut down." I held my breath as the sound of paper shuffling carried over the phone.

"Someone called for a pick up at the Sierra Pines B&B and was dropped off at Tahoe Pine Ski Resort a half hour ago. Does that satisfy your curiosity? Now, I've got a legitimate business to run."

I winced as the call ended with a *clunk*. Why would he go to the resort? My imagination reeled. Dangerous plots popped into my head, spiking my fear. I pictured Nathan jumping off the cliff where Isadora plummeted to her death. Or worse, maybe he was planning another murder. "Stop, Ali. This isn't helping." I skipped down the two flights of stairs and landed in the foyer. Grabbing my coat off the coat rack, I turned at the sound of footsteps.

"Now, where do you think you're going?" Gladys planted fists on hips. "Dinner. Remember?"

"No time, Gladys." I shoved my arms into coat sleeves. "I'll explain when I get home."

Gladys shook her head. "Maybe you should call Quint to handle whatever you're about to do."

"Don't worry. I got this." Or at least I hoped so. I waved goodbye and stepped outside. That queasy feeling in my gut urged me to hurry because I sensed something was wrong. Whether Nathan was guilty of murder or not, in my heart it didn't matter. I had to help him. "Or stop him from doing something stupid." I pressed the pedal to the floor and headed east.

CHAPTER THIRTEEN

I SPRINTED ACROSS THE PARKING LOT AND into the lodge. Scanning for any sign of Nathan, I paused as I recognized Kyle by the food counter.

He was dressed for outdoors—parka, hat, gloves, boots. Downing his drink, he stepped toward the back exit.

I caught up to him and grabbed hold of his arm. "Hey. Sorry." I lifted my hand and slowly dropped it to my side. That scowl and rigid posture warned me to go easy. I pointed. "Aren't you supposed to be resting that sprained ankle?"

"My problem. Not yours. Now, what do you want?"

"Have you seen my cousin Nathan Goyer in the past hour or so? He, um, left the B&B and, ah, we were supposed to meet up for dinner." I shrugged. "I was worried."

He grunted. "Just like a woman. Always hovering. Why can't you— never mind. Yeah, I watched him come inside. He rented some skis before heading out to the slopes. That was about an hour ago. So, you can stop looking so desperate. He's fine."

I skipped over his last comment and the pity look he gave me. "Thanks. You can go, now."

"Whatever. Like I need your permission." He smacked the door with both gloved hands to exit the building.

"Wait!" A sudden idea came to me.

Kyle threw up his arms and turned. "What now?"

"I don't suppose there's a snowmobile available to rent?" I twisted my mouth into a stiff smile.

"I suppose not. All of them are rented. A group of reckless college students on winter break decided to celebrate the end of the semester. With any luck, they'll bring the vehicles back undamaged. We already had to take one in for repairs. That's been almost a week ago. So, no snowmobile for you." He wagged his finger in my face then hurried outside.

"Fine. I have options." I muttered and pushed on to plan B. In spite of Kyle's lecture on women who stalked men, I refused to quit. I stopped by the kiosk and rented skis and snow apparel. With a quick hello and goodbye to Owen, I steered outside, pulled on all the gear, and then hopped into the first available ski lift car. Panic drove my heartbeat to hammer at full speed. I drummed fingers on my thighs. I couldn't stop the worry from escalating. Sure, my imagination pushed the scariest scenarios to play in my head. And the only solution was to find Nathan and see with my eyes he was not in danger nor causing trouble.

The cable squeaked as the lift came to a stop. I stared down the steep slope and trembled at the intimidating scene. Reminding myself I'd done this before, I pushed off and schussed down the hill. Keeping the poles close to my sides and my upper half leaning forward, I picked up speed. The wind whistled in my ears, and the cold air took my breath away. Several skiers were ahead of me. I studied each one to find the familiar red parka.

Off to the far right and downhill, I spotted Nathan. I slalomed toward him in an attempt to catch up. Hopefully, I'd get his attention. I surprised myself with a quick maneuver to gain several yards ahead of him. Circling around, I dragged my poles to slow to a stop then dropped them to the ground. I waved both arms.

He took a sharp right, avoiding a collision. Dropping his ski poles, he then threw off his goggles and hat. At once, his eyes grew wide as he hitched his breath. "Ali? What are you doing here?"

My heartbeat evened. "We were worried when you didn't come down to dinner." I warned myself to tread slowly. "You could've told us you were coming here and saved me the trip." I lifted both arms, palms facing skyward, and shrugged. "But here I am."

A frown creased his brow. "Wait. How did you know I came to the resort?"

I cringed. "Yeah, about that." I explained how Ollie's information led me to call the Uber service. "With everything that's happened, I guess I overreacted. Sorry. So . . . you just had the urge to go skiing?"

He rubbed his jaw. "I needed some fresh air. Being cooped up in the B&B makes me stir crazy. No offense."

"None taken."

"And I apologize for not letting you know. And for missing dinner. Maybe there's some leftovers when I get back?" He smiled.

"Sure. Gladys made plenty." I bent down and picked up the poles, debating whether to ask the one question I needed an answer to more than any other. "Say, I forgot to mention that Ollie found a brown wool scarf with the letters NG lying in the yard. Is that yours?" No harm in tweaking the facts a bit. I steadied my gaze on his face and any reaction that might tell me something more.

He blinked for a brief second but then shook his head. "That's strange. I haven't worn it since the day we arrived. For the holidays, I packed this one." He fingered the layer of green knit covering his neck. "Red and green. More festive, don't you think? Though it makes me look like a Christmas tree decoration." He chuckled.

"Kinda does. Well, since I can see you're okay, I'll leave you be. Dinner will be keeping warm in the oven for you when you return. Bye Nathan." I pushed off down the slope. His explanation made sense. I couldn't deny or confirm the scarf had been hanging on the rack for the past several days. I only saw him wear it the day they arrived. What if someone borrowed it? Of course, he could be lying to cover up. "Darn it, Ali. Whose side are you on?" I mumbled into my parka. Yeah, I was on the side of getting justice for Isadora and Dottie, though the answer might turn out to be disappointing and hurtful.

I approached the grove of pines and flashed back to the day we found Isadora. I shuddered. On impulse, I directed my skis toward the opening leading to the cliff. Why I did, I wasn't sure. Maybe searching for clues, anything to detour my train of thought. I stopped at the clearing and viewed the area. Footprints, most likely left by Quint and his team, were barely visible, covered by the last snowfall. I trudged over to the edge of the cliff and looked down. At once, I felt foolish for thinking Nathan came here to kill himself. However depressed and sad he was right now, the cousin I grew up with would never take his life. I had to believe in him, no matter how many clues or pieces of evidence Quint found that made Nathan look guilty.

I turned away and stepped across the clearing, nearer the tree line. With my gaze focused on the ground, I searched for anything Quint's team might have missed, though the possibility seemed unlikely. The tree line was straight, as if someone had purposefully measured and planted pine saplings in a row and evenly spaced. I stuck my poles and traveled along the line then stopped at one tree that stood out from the others. The trunk was gouged, scraped of its bark. I pictured mule deer that would pass through and rub their antlers to help shed the velvet covering and to mark their territory before mating season. That was one explanation. Leaning closer, I fingered the bruised trunk. Pulling off my glove, I picked at the tiny flecks of purple. Paint, I guessed, which obviously was not left by an animal. Glancing around, I spotted faint tracks. They ran along the tree line and exited the other side of the pines. I knew that led to one of the snowmobile trails.

I blew warm air on my fingertips then shoved my hand inside the glove. Were the damaged tree and tracks here the day we discovered Isadora's body? Had Quint and his team found that evidence? I didn't think so. At least, I couldn't recall seeing the tracks or the trunk's bruised spot. I rubbed my arms to ward off the chill running through me. "Seriously, Ali. How could you notice anything, after the shock of seeing Isadora's body?"

The sun dipped into the horizon, warning me I had less than thirty minutes of daylight left. I finished my trip down the hill and back into the lodge. Slipping out of my ski gear, I handed everything back to Owen. "Thanks."

"You're so welcome, Ali." Owen smiled as he handed me my coat. "Come visit more often. I can always use a friendly conversation with one of my favorite people." He winked.

"I promise." I tapped my watch. "Right now, I better hurry back to the B&B before Gladys locks me out. See you soon."

I jogged to my parked vehicle and warmed up the engine. Turning on the wipers to dust off the light coating of snow, I peered out of the windshield as Nathan got inside a waiting Uber. He'd probably beat me back to the B&B. I knew most car service drivers used a heavy foot on the gas pedal.

I drove across the parking lot toward the exit and stopped. A snow plow idled and blocked my path. Mr. Farley sat behind the wheel. I beeped my horn and he raised his head to glare at me. With a slight nod, he revved up the engine and shifted into gear. Moving at turtle-speed, the plow steered toward the rear end of the lot. I shrugged. "Good evening to you too, Mr. Farley."

The last rays of sunlight melted, swallowed up by the pine trees, and the sky blushed deep shades of purple and orange. My shoulders ached from the workout on the slopes, and fatigue caught up to me. I had more than a half hour's drive to reach home. Punching the buttons on the stereo, I tuned in to a classic rock station and dialed up the volume. The sound of Lynyrd Skynyrd's "What's Your Name?" filled the speakers and guaranteed to keep me awake. I drummed my fingers on the steering wheel and belted out the chorus. I refused to let negative thoughts get to me. Nathan had to be innocent. I only had to believe in him.

Pulling into the B&B's drive, I pressed the remote to open the garage door. With another snowfall and below freezing temperatures on the way, sheltering the Land Rover seemed wise.

Ollie stood off to the side of the drive with his arms resting on the snow blower handle. He nodded as I idled past and parked alongside his truck.

Gathering my bag and phone, I exited the vehicle. "You got it running, huh?" I nodded at the machine.

He patted the handle. "Yes, indeedy. Just needed some minor adjustments. We'll get a few more years out of old Walter B."

"Walter B?" I leaned my head to one side.

"Walter Brennan." He waited a few seconds then sighed. "He was a true pioneer in our history and in the movie industry. I'll excuse you for not knowing, though. You're way too young."

"But why name the snow blower—" I shook my head. "Never mind. Did you notice if Nathan returned?"

"He did. Marched right inside without so much as a word. Seemed preoccupied."

"Thanks, Ollie." I stepped through the doorway leading to the screened porch.

Gladys sat in the wicker settee, sipping from her mug. A book lay open in her lap. "Dinner's keeping warm in the oven."

I chewed on my lip as I pulled off my coat and gloves. She looked tired. Her eyes drooped at the corners and her shoulders sagged. "You okay?"

"I'm fine. Just taking a break before game night. Despite all that's happened lately, most of the guests are eager to participate in a round of movie trivia." She pulled her shoulders straight and smirked. "Those poor souls don't have a chance against Ollie and me."

I laughed. "Right you are." I sat next to her and patted her hand. "Seriously, I have a feeling something is bothering you. Fess up, Gladys."

Her lips narrowed. She reached inside her pocket and pulled out her phone. She tapped the screen and handed the device to me. "Look at our Facebook page. I warn you. What you'll find is disturbing."

I skimmed through several comments. "Criminals? Unsafe?" I looked up. "What in the world?"

Gladys nodded. "There's more, I'm afraid. While you were gone, I received two phone calls. Both were to cancel reservations. I couldn't imagine why, but then one of them—Elenore O'Toole who was supposed to arrive next week with her sister—said she'd never feel comfortable staying in a place that allows criminals as guests." She scowled. "I knew something was off. So, I got on Facebook to find those comments."

I stared at the phone screen again, struggling to make sense of it all. "Okay." I set the phone on her lap and stood to pace the room. "Business has dropped in Sierra Pines. I wonder if the cancellations have more to do with that?" I stopped and sat down once more.

Gladys scrunched her face, deepening the wrinkles. "It's much worse, dear. I called Florence to find out if she'd read those comments. Well, just so happens she got an earful from Mayor Simpson. He received a call from a friend who lives in Placerville who told him damaging comments about our town are popping up on websites everywhere. Yelp and TripAdvisor to name a couple. Even on the Sierra Pine's webpage. Florence was beside herself with worry. The mayor was furious and demanded that Florence, as SPACA's president, should do something because those comments on social media are the reason people aren't visiting and shopping in Sierra Pines." Gladys huffed and threw up her arms. "How much more can we take? This is the second internet sabotage incident in a matter of months."

I knew she was referring to the scandalous comments attacking SPACA this past fall. She was right to worry. Now that bad press was spreading to include our businesses, Sierra Pines could end up the ghost town that Florence always feared.

My stomach churned. The survival of Sierra Pines depended on every shop owner doing well. Plus, we all cared about each other. That sense of community was the very essence of small-town life. When one of us was hurting, we all came together to help. "We need to do something." I tapped my lip. "Call a SPACA meeting. Or even bigger, call all the mer-chants for a town meeting. There has to be a solution."

"I did do something." Gladys wiggled her nose. "I hope you don't mind, but I couldn't wait for you to get home. I called Sheriff Sterling."

I lifted my brow. "Why?"

"I called to ask him for a favor and he agreed." She lifted her chin. "Those horrible comments about our B&B and the town popping up all of a sudden certainly raise my suspicions." She leaned forward and wagged her finger. "I'm telling you there are whatchamacallits creating mischief on the internet, and they mean to destroy us."

"You mean hackers?"

"Maybe Russian bots!" She smacked the book resting in her lap with the flat of her palm. "How about them?"

I rolled my eyes but didn't comment. In taking my crash course on using the internet, Gladys was still a work-in-progress, though I had to give her credit for trying. "So, what did you ask Quint to do?"

"We need Jerry Mackelroy." She grinned.

"Jerry who?" I glanced at my watch. If game night started on time, we'd be lucky. "Gladys, can we please move this story along?"

"Sorry, dear. I'm trying. Jerry Mackelroy is a second or third cousin of Ollie's. On his mother's side, I think."

"Gladys." I weighted my voice with a stern tone.

"Yes. Not important. Jerry is a computer guy who works for the Sacramento police. He's an expert and will figure out who's causing all this internet sabotage."

"And you asked Quint to call the Sacramento authorities and request Jerry's help." I scratched behind one ear. More than likely, a few unpleas-ant comments on social media wouldn't be enough to convince Quint to investigate.

"I recognize that look. You think I'm being foolish." A heavy breath escaped her lips.

I squeezed her arm. "No. Not at all. I just—I'm surprised Quint agreed."

"The mayor might have something to do with that decision." She stood and held the empty mug in one hand while hugging the book to her chest. "He's even more persuasive than me." She grinned.

No surprise to me that after giving Florence an earful of gripes, the mayor moved on to Quint. "If this problem turns out to be some hacker's scheme, let's hope Ollie's cousin is as great as you claim. In the meantime, we have game night to get ready."

I followed Gladys as she led the way into the kitchen. After scarfing down my dinner, I helped prepare appetizers and drinks. This evening's menu included bacon and cream cheese roll-ups, jalapeno poppers, assorted raw vegetables with ranch dressing dip, and Gladys's special apple cinnamon punch, minus the vodka. We wanted to keep minds alert during the game.

"Have to give the competition a fair chance." Gladys laughed.

"We wouldn't have it any other way." Ollie chimed in as he walked into the kitchen and grabbed a bacon and cream cheese roll-up off the tray. As he reached for seconds, Gladys smacked his hand.

"Save some for the guests, will you?" She clucked her tongue. "Bottomless pit."

Ollie rubbed his stomach. "Or a healthy appetite. Say, did Mr. Goyer say anything when he passed through the house?"

I took the tray out of Gladys's hands. "Yes, I meant to ask the same thing."

"He returned?" A puzzled frown etched her forehead. "I was so caught up in my reading, I must've missed him."

"Which means he didn't say a word to you either." Ollie snatched a popper from the warming dish before Gladys could react. He winked. "Your poppers are impossible to resist."

When Ollie came in for a hug, Gladys twisted out of reach and ignored giving him a response. "Ali, you never told us where you went earlier this evening. Does it have something to do with Nathan?"

I led the way out of the kitchen and into the parlor with the Bellwether siblings close behind. "I made a call to the local Uber service and found out where Nathan went." Once I explained how my trip to the resort had gone, and what I'd found near the murder sight, both Ollie and Gladys grew silent, which was not the reaction I expected. "Guys? What do you think?"

Gladys cleared her throat and shifted her gaze to Ollie for a brief moment. "I, that is Ollie and I, think you should take a step back, or maybe several steps come to think of it, and let the sheriff do his job."

I set the tray on the serving board and pushed air from my lungs. Turning on my heel, I walked across the room to sit down. "Quint told you to say that, didn't he?" Anxious, I rolled my neck back and forth and attempted to relax. He wasn't my boss, and making sure Nathan was not in danger should be my business.

"Alexis." Gladys's tone was soft. "We worry about you. Poking around might spark anger in Isadora's killer. What if he, or she, comes after you next?"

I studied her face. Her eyes misted and chin quivered. "Look, I'm Julia's niece. That fierce determination to do what's right and get justice is in my DNA too. Asking me to quit and back away is like telling me to stop breathing. I can't. I won't." I shook my head. "Besides, our B&B's reputation is in jeopardy too. Nobody will want to stay at a place with murder attached to it."

"We tried, sister. Now, let Ali do what she must," Ollie said.

"But—" Gladys protested.

"Could we ever stop Julia?" Ollie interrupted.

Gladys plopped in a chair and lowered her chin. "You're right. Doesn't mean I won't stop trying."

"And that's okay. Your persistence shows you care." I smiled. The Bellwethers loved me like family. With Mom and Dad living on the other side of the country, Ollie and Gladys stepped up to take over the role as my surrogate parents. Even if they sometimes overwhelmed and smothered me with caring, I appreciated every gesture.

Footsteps pounded down the stairs and across the hall, bringing a halt to our conversation. Smiles and laughter followed as five of our guests entered the parlor. No surprise, Nathan was the only one who declined this evening's invitation. Faith Ritter and Abby Lewis mentioned they made every attempt to comfort him, inviting him to dinner or a movie at the town theater, even including him in their conversations. A twinge of sadness crept inside me. It was hard knowing what to say to someone who's lost a loved one. "Sorry for your loss" felt like an empty sentiment.

Beth rubbed her hands together and squealed with excitement. "This will be so much fun! I love movie trivia."

"I hope you feel the same way after we win." Ollie slapped his leg, and a peal of laughter filled the room. He shuffled the cards and dealt out four stacks then nodded at everyone. "Pair up, ladies and gent. Let the game begin."

"Help yourselves to some snacks, first. There are plenty to go around." Gladys gestured to the serving board.

Abby and Beth formed a team. With the Bellwethers and the Smiths already coupled, that left Faith and me. I linked arms with her, and we got in line to fill our plates.

"I'm afraid I don't know much about movies. In fact, if you put my knowledge of pop culture to the test, I'd score a zero," Faith said.

I poked her arm. "But you write such wonderful books about our history."

"I guess you're right. Everyone has his own expertise."

"Exactly. And don't worry. I've got the movie trivia covered." I winked.

"Oh!" Her eyes widened. "I should've remembered. Is there anyone in your family who isn't in the business?"

I tapped my lip. "Hmm. Let me think." I snapped my fingers. "Uncle Theo. He's in real estate. Then again, his office is in L.A. and plenty of his customers are in the acting profession, but I don't think that counts."

"Well, I'm relieved you reminded me. I won't feel so bad when I can't think of an answer." Faith chose several roll ups and a few vegetables along with dip. "I'll pass on the poppers. Acid reflux is a problem at my age."

Gladys clapped her hands. "If everyone is ready, let's get started. Beth and Abby, why don't you take your turn first?"

"What female actress starred in the silent movie, *Birth of a Nation*, and had a sister who was also an actress?" Beth read the card then leaned to whisper in Abby's ear. Clearing her throat, she nodded. "This one's too easy. Lillian Gish starred in the movie. Her younger sister was Dorothy Gish."

Gladys frowned. "That's quite impressive. Let's see if you can keep it up."

The game went on for an hour or more. Tension and excitement sparked the air as the Bellwethers and Beth's team fought neck and neck to gain the lead. The Smiths trailed close behind, but never caught up. I tried my best to avoid putting Faith and me in last place. If Willa and Robert learned about it, the embarrassment would be too much.

At a little after nine, Ollie blew his game whistle. "Time! The top scorers are in a tie: Gladys and me versus Beth and Abby. Ali and Faith earned second place and the Smiths a respectable third place score."

With an exasperating breath, Beth stood. Her face flushed beet red. "This was such fun. Thank you." She wagged a finger at Gladys. "However, if I'm still here next Friday, I'd like a rematch."

"Absolutely. We enjoy the competition." Gladys smiled. She gathered the cards and handed them to Ollie who placed everything inside the box. "Have a good night, everyone."

I helped Gladys and Ollie to carry trays and the empty pitcher to the kitchen. "You know, I think you met your match in movie trivia."

"Beth and Abby were certainly impressive. For a moment there, I was afraid we'd lose." Gladys wrapped leftovers and placed them in the fridge.

"Not me. It's all in here." Ollie pointed to his head. "Decades of trivia." He bent to look inside the fridge.

"I guess no one could beat your appetite either." Gladys scolded him with an edgy tone.

I loaded the dishwasher then stretched my arms. Every inch of my body cried for rest. "I'm heading off to bed. Night."

I reached the foyer when my pocket buzzed and jingled. I pulled out my phone and smiled at the face lighting the screen. "Kind of late, isn't it?" I teased while taking a seat on the foyer bench.

"I'm working overtime this evening and wanted to hear your voice." Quint answered. "But if you're busy—"

"No. I'm turning in for the night. Actually, I'm glad you called. Gladys told me about Jerry the computer genius who's going to help find the hacker out to destroy Sierra Pines. I must say I'm surprised."

"You don't agree?" A soft whistle traveled across the receiver. "Talk about switching roles."

"Not true. You always tell me you go by concrete, foolproof evidence to convince you. A few critical comments on social media hardly seem enough to rattle you. Could this have something to do with the mayor?" Leaning against the wall, I crossed my ankles. The urge to poke fun at him was too much to resist. He hated any politics interfering with his job. Mayor Simson tried his patience and pushed those buttons.

A low and drawn out moan came from the other end of my phone.

"Okay, I'm sorry. Why don't we change the topic of conversation? I have news."

"You went to the resort, chasing after Nathan. Yeah, I heard from Owen who called to tell me he was concerned about your frenzied state of mind." Quint cleared his throat. "Ali."

"Would you let me finish?" I broke in before he launched into a lecture.

"I wasn't going to say what you think. I was going to thank you."

I scowled and held out the phone to stare at the screen. What was he up to? "Thank me?"

"Yes, thank you for not getting yourself killed going after someone who could be a murderer." He snapped but kept the volume down. "For your safety and for your employees and guests, I should tell you the coroner finished his report. We've classified Dottie Sample's death as a homicide."

Even though I'd come to that conclusion on my own, hearing the words about Dottie was a punch to the gut. I pulled back my shoulders and gritted my teeth to keep from shivering. "Thanks, but as for our safety, if you're implying Nathan is the killer . . ."

"I'm not implying—look, everyone in town should be aware and worried, until the killer is caught. No matter who that person is." His voice grew louder and on edge.

"Fine. Speaking of homicide and suspects, I discovered some interesting evidence at the crime scene."

"Ali, that's not your job."

"It might be important to the case, but if you're not interested . . ." I paused, picturing the tense muscles of his face. I could almost hear his teeth grinding. Let him ask, I thought.

"Fine. What do you think you discovered that my team hasn't already?"

With detail, I explained the damage to the tree, the purple paint chips, and the snowmobile tracks. I also mentioned that when I found him, Nathan was nowhere near the crime scene. "He needed some fresh air to clear his head. He's been trapped in the B&B for the past week. Thanks to all the accusing eyes from townsfolk, he feels uncomfortable going into town. I don't blame him for wanting to get away from here."

"Yes, my team found and collected that evidence the morning after Isadora's incident."

"You never told me."

"There are many things I don't share with you. As for Nathan, I can't help how the folks in town feel or treat him. My job is to follow any lead and find who killed Isadora. You have to understand that the spouse is suspect in most every murder case."

I nodded even though he couldn't see me. If I were Quint or any other law enforcement agent, I'd think the same way. Too bad this was personal for me. I rubbed my face with one hand. "Well, I'm in desperate need of sleep. Talk to you tomorrow?"

"Absolutely. Night, Ali."

"Night." I heard a click to end the call and then dropped the phone in my lap. Until he arrested Isadora and Dottie's killer, Nathan would remain a suspect under his radar. Nothing I could do or say would convince him otherwise. I couldn't bring myself to tell the Bellwethers about Dottie. She'd been a close friend of Gladys's for decades. I'd wait until morning, after what I hoped would be a good night's sleep.

I pushed through my exhaustion and trudged up the stairs. Reaching the first floor, I paused to glance at Nathan's door. Maybe it was too late to bother him, but I'd sleep better knowing he was safe in his room. Raising my arm, I knocked. "Nathan? I don't mean to wake you if you're trying to sleep . . . I wanted to apologize for following you to the resort today. I worry about you. That's all." I placed my ear against the door to listen. "Nathan?"

"Yeah, it's fine. Night, Ali"

I bit down on my lip. His words warbled in a sleepy tone. "Sorry I woke you. See you tomorrow."

I turned toward the hallway and glanced down. A small piece of paper lay near his door. Puzzled, I picked it up and studied the words scribbled in a familiar handwriting. *Call Dewhurst about life insurance policy. Follow up with call to Ace of Spades.* I twisted the ring on my finger as I searched my memory. I gasped then slapped a hand over my mouth. Tiptoeing away, I heaved my chest to breathe. Ace of Spades owned several casinos in Las Vegas. One of our previous guests lived in the gambling city and managed one of those casinos. He'd offered me a personal invitation to stop by if I ever visited. I probably wouldn't. I didn't care for gambling, but Nathan did. That tiny detail concerned me. I remembered how he played online and bet plenty. Was he in debt? Is that why he wrote a note to call Ace of Spades? A shiver trailed down my spine. The life insurance policy had to be Isadora's. Of course, Nathan would contact Dewhurst. I climbed the stairs to reach the attic. "That's reasonable, isn't it? Your spouse dies and you let the insurance company know. It's what people do." I tried convincing myself there was nothing unusual or suspicious about the note. However, the voice in my head that always played devil's advocate hollered for attention. I climbed into bed and pulled the covers up to my neck. I argued and defended him at every turn, even when I had my doubts, but I truly believed in his innocence. Right now, I felt like a fool because cashing in on an insurance policy was a common motive for murder.

CHAPTER FOURTEEN

A SOFT KNOCK ON MY DOOR STIRRED me out of my sleep. "Yes?" I rubbed drool off my chin and grabbed for a tissue. "Who is it?"

"Me. Of course." Gladys said. "Who else would be outside your bedroom door?"

I grinned. "Oh, I don't know. Maybe I have a secret lover."

The door creaked open and she peeked around the edge. Her eyes narrowed as she wagged a finger. "Don't tease about such a thing. I came up here to ask if you want me to keep breakfast warm." She hitched one fist to her hip and winked. "Or maybe you want to stay and wait for that secret lover."

I tossed my pillow across the room, but Gladys ducked behind the door in time. "Give me five minutes to get dressed."

I stretched my arms and yawned. Awakening later than usual, I felt rejuvenated and ready to take on any challenge. Too bad the last thoughts I had while lying awake in bed last night stirred up my doubts about Nathan. I shoved both legs into my pants and buttoned up my flannel shirt. Rushing downstairs, I patted my shirt pocket to find the note tucked inside. I intended to confront Nathan and demand answers about the insurance and Ace of Spades, whatever helped to give me peace of mind.

As I reached the foyer, voices echoed from the library. I peeked in to see Gladys and Ollie huddled over in front of the wall shelf filled with movies. Without disturbing them, I took a path to the kitchen. The coffeemaker bubbled as it finished perking what I imagined was the third pot of the day. I poured a mug full and stared out the window. The rosy teacup dogwood stood in the middle of the yard with snow coating its branches. A redwood plaque engraved with Julia's name was nestled near the trunk's base. A twinge of sadness grew inside me. I sighed then turned away from the window. Only two months passed since her death. I missed her talks and warm smile that always gave me comfort.

I opened the oven door and pulled out the rack. Sausage croissant roll-ups filled one pan, and a casserole dish contained a spinach souffle. As with every morning, a bowl of fruit sat on the refrigerator shelf. I loaded my plate with healthy portions of souffle and fruit then headed for the atrium. I needed quiet. Blackbeard's company suited me. He didn't care if I contributed to his conversation.

Windows bathed in sunlight left the atrium toasty warm. I snuggled in a chair next to Blackbeard's cage. I laughed as he hopped across the cage floor and pecked at the bars, begging for attention, or, most likely, a bite of my breakfast. I rose from my seat. "Here, you greedy bird." Holding a slice of orange, I slipped my fingers through the bars. He grasped the tidbit with his beak and hopped to the other side of the cage.

Once more, I settled in the chair and enjoyed my breakfast and quiet time. Finishing the last crumbs of souffle, I stood and let out a sigh. The atrium was a quiet, sunny, and cozy retreat. I hated to leave. "Sad to say, I have things to do, Blackbeard." I dropped the last piece of fruit in his cage. "But you enjoy your morning and breakfast. Take a nap. Stay warm in the sunlight. I envy you, pretty bird."

Gathering my plate and mug, I entered the kitchen, poured a coffee refill, then headed to the library.

The Bellwethers were in the same spot in front of the movie shelf. Stacked on the floor next to Ollie was a pile of DVDs and alongside that were several VHS tapes.

"Morning, all. I'd ask what is happening here, but I think I can guess." I laughed while searching for an empty seat. More stacks of movies sat on the sofa, two chairs, and the coffee table.

Gladys wiped her brow and grinned. Bright eyes completed her cheery expression. "The shipment of DVDs we've been expecting arrived late yesterday."

Ollie pulled more VHS tapes off the shelves. "We decided to donate these to charity. Maybe the retirement home will enjoy them."

"Do you need my help? I could grab the footstool from the kitchen and reach those on the top shelf."

Ollie shook his head and pointed to the floor where the stool leaned against the wall. "Got it covered."

I sat and cradled my coffee mug. "Would you mind multi-tasking by giving me your opinion about something?"

"Of course, dear. What is it?" Gladys dusted the bottom shelves.

I slipped the paper out of my pocket. "I found this on the floor next to Nathan's room." I read the note aloud then looked up. "What do you think?"

"Oh my. That's not good, is it?" Gladys bit down on her lip. "I remember our guest George Wells from Las Vegas. He manages one of those casinos owned by Ace of Spades, right?" Her eyes widened. "Do you think Nathan has gambling debts?"

I slumped my shoulders. "I do. And I worry about the insurance reference."

"Motive to murder. Insurance payout is a big one." Ollie shoved DVDs on the shelf.

I cringed. He was right, of course. I wanted to deny it, find a way to dismiss the notion. "I'm going to confront Nathan and ask him about the note."

"Hogwash. Why bother? If he's guilty, he'll lie to get around your questions." Ollie stabbed a finger in my direction then quickly sent me an apologetic smile. "Sorry. I know he's your cousin, but wouldn't it be wiser to give Quint the note and let him deal with this?"

I groaned. Downing the rest of my coffee, I set the mug on the end table. "Point taken. For my own peace of mind, though, I'll confront Nathan, first. I'm curious to hear what he says."

Like diving into cold water, I worried how to tell them the news I'd been avoiding. "I talked to Quint last night. The coroner confirmed Dottie's death was murder."

Gladys frowned, then gave Ollie a quick glance. "We expected as much."

"He thought we should know." I pressed my lips together. They'd taken the news well.

"You mean in case Nathan is the killer?" Ollie nodded. "You know what happened the last time. We'll defend ourselves if needed." He reached for his baseball bat and swung.

"Ollie, dear. Don't wave that around so near the movie collection. You might break something," Gladys said.

I ignored his accusation and leaned back in my chair. "Now, what's next? Any news about our social media bandit?"

Gladys sat next to me. "Oh yes. I got a call from Minnie early this morning. She griped how Sheriff Sterling still refuses to release the money Dottie stole from SPACA. He claims the money is evidence in an ongoing investigation. Of course, Florence blew a gasket and accused Dottie and the sheriff for ruining Christmas."

"Oh, boy. This is a mess." My insides churned and threatened to heave the souffle and fruit breakfast I enjoyed. Too much tragedy happened in the past week. On top of the two murders, our town's business was failing miserably. Now, if the Christmas event was in trouble, what would all of this do to people's spirit? I felt like we were living a version of *How the Grinch Stole Christmas* but with the added gruesome details of murder. I shivered and rubbed my arms. "Did Minnie share any good news?"

"Yes. The sheriff promised he'd release the money soon. In the meantime, Florence is calling for a SPACA meeting this afternoon and has invited a few of the shop owners for their input. According to Minnie, with limited funds, we must decide which charities are most in need. Those will receive a donation. We've already prepared gift baskets for the needy families and presents for the children at the orphanage. Unfortunately, some charities will have to do without help from us this year." She sighed and threw up her arms. "We can only do so much."

I stood. "Ollie, let's hope your cousin is as smart as you claim. If all those damaging comments are the work of a hacker, he has to find him or her, and quick."

"Don't worry. He's a prodigy of Silicon Valley and one of the top people in the field," Ollie said. "No one in the internet world can hide from Jerry."

"Good." I turned to Gladys. "What time is the SPACA meeting?"

"At noon. Florence asks us to be prompt. She has a hair appointment at Lucinda's scheduled for two o'clock." Gladys pursed her lips into a scowl.

"Do or die, a woman's hair care takes priority in life." I couldn't help but mock the idea. "You want to meet in the kitchen fifteen minutes beforehand? I'll drive."

Ollie stuck up his thumb while Gladys nodded. Both returned their efforts to the stacks of movies.

That was my cue to leave. I wasn't a computer genius like Jerry, but at least I could make some changes to our B&B website, like renaming our guest rooms and giving them a movie theme, just as Gladys and I had discussed. She and Ollie gave me their list of favorite movies, ones that either Julia acted in or worked on as prop designer. With three hours until the SPACA meeting, I could accomplish a lot. Anything too challenging would be handed off to a hired expert.

I returned to the atrium to work. "Let's start with my favorite. Guest room number one will now be named *Notorious*." With furious energy, my fingers tapped across the keyboard, and soon, I was lost in the world of cinema.

THE POUNDING OF FLORENCE'S GAVEL RESONATED throughout the theater. Due to a double booking, we moved the meeting's location from the town hall to the empty theater. Last I heard, the Committee to Beautify Sierra Pines had carried out a successful campaign, and the new ordinance passed. Now, they were on a mission to collect funds for the new signage, displaying a uniform logo and color. Every business owner must comply, which also meant each had to chip in a percentage of the cost and to hang their own sign. No surprise, many of them complained, but the majority agreed. Even the B&B would receive one. Personally, I was glad. Our existing sign showed plenty of wear.

"I imagine everyone has heard about the horrific tragedy put upon our dear town." Florence sniffed and dabbed her eyes with a handkerchief.

I pressed my lips together. Adding dramatic overkill to any situation or problem was Florence's signature trademark.

"Oh, please. Enough with the theatrics." Gladys muttered under her breath as she rolled her eyes.

"Well, we are in the appropriate place for it." I joked, keeping my voice to a whisper.

"Even though the damage has cost us huge losses in our business, not to mention dampening our holiday spirit, we must stop whoever is doing this before Sierra Pines becomes a ghost town."

And there it was. Her go-to, worst-case scenario. I wondered if she expected the town to vanish into thin air, like some magical spell cast on us. I waved my hand.

Florence pointed her gavel. "Ali, you have a suggestion, I hope?"

"I do." I stood and cleared my throat. "Fight fire with fire. Or, in this case, we amp up positive publicity in any way we can. Personally, I spent the morning polishing the B&B website by adding some new features and perks to attract guests. Why not do the same for our town Facebook page and our own individual websites? We give people an incentive to write positive comments about us."

Clive Schumacher sat in the third row, alongside the two other merchants invited to the meeting. He cleared his throat and raised his hand. "Some of us older folks don't have a website. Word of mouth is my way of getting business. What are we supposed to do? I can't deal with those new contraptions. I don't even have a mail whatchamacallit. People call me on the phone or stop by the store. That's the way it's always been done. See no reason to change now." He crossed his arms over his chest.

"He's right, Ali. You can't spruce up a website if you don't have one. That issue needs to be addressed," Florence said.

"I'm not finished. What if we make video clips where merchants can give folks a peek inside their shops and talk up their merchandise? Then we upload the videos to the town website. You don't need to be tech savvy or have social media. Some of us who carry smart phones can visit each shop to film. I'll gladly volunteer to be one." I glanced around at the members and guests. A glimmer of interest livened their expressions. A few nodded or gave me a thumbs-up sign.

"Fine. It's settled. Please make a show of hands if you have a smart phone and are willing to participate in Ali's idea." Florence pointed her finger at each of the raised arms.

A half dozen members volunteered. I smiled. That many should be enough to get the filming done before Christmas and loaded onto our social media sites.

"Now, how many businesses does Sierra Pines have? We should make a list." Florence flipped the pages of her handbook and mumbled. Within a minute or two, she laid the book on the podium. "I count thirty-four shops. That number also includes Ali's B&B."

Ralph and Owen leaned into each other and whispered. With a firm nod, Ralph raised his hand. "If you haven't added it to the list, we should include Tahoe Pine."

Florence pulled back her shoulders and sniffed. "Of course, though from what I gather, Tabitha Wells has been dishing out enough perks and deal incentives to keep business hopping. The resort will go unscathed from all this internet drama, no doubt."

Gladys cupped her mouth with one hand and whispered in my ear. "Not so sure about that."

I muttered in agreement. Tabitha hid her troubles well.

Florence barked orders, assigning each of the seven volunteers five or six places to visit. "Owen, I suppose you'll want to take the resort since you're there most every day."

"Let me film the resort video." I interrupted before glancing at Owen, pouncing on the opportunity to question Tabitha once more. "If you don't mind. Besides, you're busy with the rental kiosk, right?"

He shrugged. "Sure. Business has been hectic, and I barely have time for a bathroom break. Thanks, Ali."

Florence pounded her gavel once more to announce the end of the meeting. "Oh, good. I have a half hour to spare before my appointment at Lucinda's." She fanned her flushed face. "Maybe I'll stop by the ice cream parlor for a treat to celebrate our progress. If any would like to join me, I'd enjoy the company."

I turned to Gladys and Ollie. "I think I'd rather get started on the videos. Do you two want to team up with me?" I crossed my fingers. "I was thinking familiar faces would make the situation less awkward. After all, you've known most everyone in town for years. I'm more of a newbie and still adapting." I tried everything I could think of to persuade them.

Gladys gazed at Ollie who nodded. "Sure, we don't have any plans for the next hour or so," she said.

"Great. First, I need to stop by Glenn's to drop off the check for the furnace. Then, I thought we'd start with a visit to Meeka's Mementos." I shouldered my bag and walked with them to the exit door.

"Why not let me drop off the check?" Ollie grinned. "I have a funny story to share with Glenn. He's been asking for entertaining tidbits about my stuntman days."

"Sounds good. We can meet you at Meeka's, unless Glenn insists on a second or third story." A teasing lilt lifted my voice.

Gladys patted Ollie on the arm. "I'll text you where we go afterward because I know how you men like to gab."

Ollie snorted. "No more than you ladies."

I handed Ollie the check and thanked him. Gladys and I stepped across the street and up the block to Meeka's shop. Sweet smells of bagels and donuts baking wafted from Bagels and Buns next door. "We should stop in Lenny's for dessert treats first. I'm sure Meeka would like some."

Gladys chortled then winked. "I'm sure she's not the only one."

I scratched behind one ear. "You know me too well."

We popped in to find Lenny behind the counter. After a brief exchange of "how are you," we purchased a half-dozen custard and jelly donuts and then made our way next door.

The bell hanging above the door tinkled as we stepped into the giftshop. Soft and calming music piped through the intercom fit perfectly with Meeka's personality. She was like a Zen Buddha, gentle in her actions and wise in her advice.

"Ali and Gladys! How nice it is to see friends come to my shop." She wagged her finger. "You don't come around often enough."

"It's great to see you too." I held out my hand to shake, but all at once, Meeka wrapped her arms around me and squeezed.

"Friends give hugs, not handshakes. I'd rub noses too but stereotypical behavior is something my mom despises." Every inch of her shook as she threw back her head to laugh again.

Meeka was a member of the Alaskan Inuit tribe. Her parents moved to California before Meeka was born to open a general store. Meeka decided retail was in her blood. She came to Sierra Pines, and Meeka's Mementos was created. Proud of her heritage, whenever she got her hands on some Inuit art, she sold the items in her store. They varied with soapstone sculptures, paintings, hand-sewn wall hangings, and lots more. Walking through the aisles was like a visit to a museum.

A smile curled my lips. "Honestly, I'd take a little nose canoodling, and I'd never tell your mom."

"Hah. Good one. Now, I bet you're here to make me a star with your video, right? I got a call from Lucinda who heard from Clive that we're showcasing businesses to fight the bad publicity." Meeka rearranged a display of feather bookmarks on the counter rack while she talked.

"And with any luck, the plan will work," I said.

A scowl furrowed her brow and her eyes darkened. Gone was the cheery attitude. "It sure better. I'm tired of all the shop owners griping about poor sales. Nothing merry about this Christmas holiday, is there?"

"Even if the season makes up fifty percent of your yearly sales, griping doesn't do a thing to help, but it sure hurts the pocketbook." Gladys chimed in while she examined the angel figurine held in her hand.

Meeka plopped in the chair behind her checkout counter. Her shoulders sagged. "True. Hurts so much that my cash register feels lonely."

Slipping my phone out of my bag, I pressed the camera app and switched to the video option. "Let's see what we can do to make our troubles disappear."

After a quick interview where Meeka talked about her shop and the history behind it, she gave us a tour to point out the holiday gift items as well as those from the Inuit art collection.

"Sierra Pines is a wonderful community with caring people. Every year, we raise money for charity and gift baskets for needy families. Each shop owner donates something, whether merchandise or cash. We take care of each other. Thank you, and please come shop at Meeka's Mementos." Meeka finished her video clip with a wave.

I shut off the phone and smiled. "That was fantastic, Meeka. You are a natural in front of the camera."

She wiggled her shoulders. "I told you I'd be a star." She peered over my shoulder then leaned close to me. "Your special order should be here in a couple of days. I'll give you a call."

"We should probably hurry if we plan to film another merchant before it gets late. I have to bake cookies and start a list of items for tomorrow's breakfast," Gladys said as she strolled from the rear of one aisle.

"Oh, no." Meeka stiffened as she focused her gaze beyond us and toward the window. "I sure hope that woman doesn't stop in here."

I turned to follow her gaze. Tabitha Wells crossed the street and walked this way. I shifted my attention to Meeka. "Why? What did she do?"

"You'll probably think it's nothing." She threw up her arms. "She stopped here yesterday, going through my shop, picking up merchandise then tossing items back on the shelves. Even worse, you know what she said?"

I lifted my hands, palms up. "Was it bad?"

"You bet. She said my place was full of junk, and I had nothing worth buying."

"That's strange." Though knowing what I did about the woman, I wasn't surprised.

Meeka rolled her eyes. "Got even more strange. She backed into a display. Dozens of disposable cameras scattered everywhere. She mumbled an apology then stormed out of the store without offering to help clean the mess."

"Some people act crazy during the holidays. Maybe that's all it was," I said.

While Gladys made her purchase, I turned to stare out the window. Tabitha passed by the shop at a hurried pace, but not without a quick glance at me. Her face seemed tense as if she was angry. She spoke into her phone. Her mouth moved. It opened and shut, fast and sharp, like she was having an argument. In seconds, she disappeared from view.

Gladys tugged on my sleeve. "Are you ready?"

"Um-hum. Bye Meeka. Thank you." I followed Gladys out the door. The temperature had dropped and triggered a biting chill in the air. I pulled my collar up to my chin. I couldn't get over the angry look on Tabitha's face or the way she appeared to talk on her phone, as if she were disagreeing with someone. One of the Stiletto employees, perhaps?

We had one more stop to make before heading home, and we chose Opal Brier and her coffee shop. When Gladys suggested we shortcut the niceties and dive straight into the video to take a quick tour, I agreed. My head was pounding and stomach growling. It was not a pleasant combination.

"Let me text Ollie we're here. He can bring the car to meet us. We won't want to walk anywhere else. That weather has arrived early and boy is it nasty." Gladys nodded at the window and the swirling snowflakes and tree branches bending with the fierce wind.

Filming Opal and her shop didn't take long at all. She was just as much in a hurry as Gladys to get the job done. *Wheel of Fortune* was her favorite show, and she refused to miss it.

As promised, Ollie parked in front of the shop, waiting to drive us home. An icy coating covered the ground and frosted store front windows. I held on to Gladys's arm as we stepped carefully across the sidewalk. Hopping inside the Land Rover, I snuggled in the backseat. Heat from the vents quickly thawed the chill in my body.

Gladys twisted her head to face me. "Did you notice Tabitha when she passed by the store? She looked troubled."

I nodded. "You thought so too? She didn't seem to be having a good day."

Gladys tapped Ollie on the shoulder. "Watch the turn and don't go too fast. The road is slippery."

"Yes, sister dear. I'm being careful." Ollie slowed the vehicle and turned onto Englewood at a turtle's speed.

From the corner of my eye, I glimpsed an unfamiliar car idling across the street from the B&B. Within seconds, Nathan exited the vehicle and jogged across the lawn to the front door.

"That man is always in a hurry to get somewhere." Ollie shifted the Land Rover into park and turned off the engine.

"Yes, he is." I spoke in a low volume. Concern hit me in waves at different times. This wave was a whopper, and it drenched me. Another Uber lift, maybe? Who knew? His behavior was unpredictable and not at all easy to explain.

Sliding out of my seat, I took quick steps to the front door without slipping on icy pavement. No time like the present to confront him with all the questions I had—new questions. There had been so many in the past week. I tossed my coat on the rack and leaped up the stairs two at a time. Stopping at his doorstep, I took a deep breath. "Nathan?" I gave the door a gentle rap with my knuckle. After seconds of silence, I turned the knob. "I'm coming in."

He sat in the chair, scrolling through his phone. Angry lines deepened with the scowl on his face.

I gnawed on the tip of one finger and hesitated to move from my spot at the doorway. The image of a happy and carefree Nathan, the cousin I fondly remembered growing up, was hard to picture now. After all that happened, could I blame him for being sullen and angry? With a long sigh, I stepped across the floor. "Nathan?"

His head shot up, and his eyes widened. "Ali. I didn't hear you come in."

His eyes flickered, but then he stood, smiled, and gestured to the empty chair. "Take a seat." He moved to sit on the edge of the bed.

Once seated, I folded my hands and laid them in my lap. "You rushed out of that car and into the house before I could catch up. Is everything okay?" I struggled not to glance down at his phone.

"Sure. I'm holding it together as well as anybody who's just lost a spouse." His posture stiffened.

The sober expression returned, and I imagined his anger simmered just below the surface. I heard Julia speak to me. *Tread slowly and be kind.* "Is there anything more I can do?"

He studied me in silence, unblinking. "I know some don't believe me, even people back in New York, but I loved her. She was difficult. She had a mean streak and no patience for a sloppy performance in the business. She was jealous a good deal of the time. That emotion haunted her and dug at her confidence. But I loved the good in Izzie." He shifted to brace his arms behind him on the bed. "Did you know she donated a large portion of her earnings to needy children and the city orphanage?"

"No. I wasn't aware." My brow creased. Shamefully, I'd never once considered Isadora had good qualities. "Her death is such a tragedy. I can't imagine losing someone I love." How could I ask him about the note? Then again, how else was I to put my mind at ease? I wanted to believe him, believe *in* him. I pulled the note out of my pocket and laid it on his lap. "You must've dropped this. I found it outside your door last evening." My heartbeat raced, making it difficult to breath. I studied his face, searching for any reaction.

As he held the note, a scowl formed. He licked his bottom lip then lifting his head, he nodded. "I suppose you read what I wrote, and you want answers." His chest lifted and fell. "I called the insurance company to see what I needed to do to collect. Nothing wrong in that."

"Izzie's?"

"Yes."

I paused. "And Ace of Spades? Why did you call them?"

He raked fingers through his hair. A shaky laugh erupted. "This doesn't look good. I'm a living nightmare, you know? One horrible thing after another keeps happening, and the only good thing in my life is dead and gone."

I stifled my emotions. He didn't need me falling apart. "You've heard me talk about my aunt Julia. She once told me that life doesn't come in a neat and tidy package. Sometimes the wrapping is messy or stuff inside is broken. But if you can fix it, find the parts that work, and put them back together, then maybe life won't look or feel so bad." I shrugged and scooted closer. "I'm here to help you in any way I can, cousin. Even if what you tell me is difficult or painful, I'll listen and try to understand. Okay?" I squeezed his hand.

A low, breathy whistle blew from his mouth. "You remember in college how I loved to join those online gambling sites? Earning some extra cash to party and stuff was innocent fun." He raked fingers through his hair. "The fun is over. I have gambling debts. Lots of gambling debts. Ace of Spades is breathing down my neck to pay what I owe."

"How much?" I cringed.

"About five hundred thousand, give or take." He gripped his knees. "Each day that goes by adds another twenty. That's what they told me this morning. So . . ." He glanced at his watch. "In a few more hours, I'll owe them five hundred and twenty."

"Wow, that's . . ." I couldn't find the words.

"A whole heap of trouble, and that's what I'm in." He turned to face me. "I know what you're thinking, that I killed Isadora for the insurance money, but you're wrong. I have a plan. I put up my condo in New York for sale. It's worth at least a million. More than enough to pay off the debt and put a down payment on another place to live. Won't be as nice or big, but I won't need that much space any longer."

"And the insurance money? You can't use that to pay the debt?"

He shook his head. "According to Izzie's will, the insurance money goes to the St. Jude Foundation. Always thinking of children." I weak smile lifted his cheeks.

"That was really nice of her."

"Yeah, I went to Placerville. The bank there is handling the donation. I called the insurance company to let them know where to deposit the money."

I hugged him. "You are a good person, Nathan. I'm sure all this will be straightened out, and Quint will find justice for Isadora."

"Thanks, Ali. You're not so bad yourself, even if you were annoying when we hung out as kids." He winked.

"We are related, after all." I said goodbye and left him. Everything he told me was convincing. Why didn't I feel relieved? I remembered one incident when I stayed over to eat dinner at Aunt Betts's. Nathan bragged how he'd landed a deal for a reoccurring role in a series of commercials for a popular dogfood. He laughed and said he almost didn't get to audition, but then gave a performance worthy of an Oscar or Emmy when he told the casting director that his dog died that morning. He'd sobbed out the story. Saying goodbye to the best friend he had was too emotional and he'd almost called to cancel his audition. The director fell for it and let him try out for the part. Aunt Betts laughed at the story, telling Nathan how clever he'd been, while I sat in silence.

Nathan could tell a story and make it believable. He could lie. Was he lying now? The words I'd overheard Isadora say to him in two separate occasions echoed in my head. *I could ruin your career* and *say one more word about it, and I'll tell.* If she'd been referring to his gambling debt, was that enough reason for him to kill her? I closed the door to my room and dropped into a chair. Releasing all the pent-up emotion, I cried. I didn't know what to believe anymore. Hesitating, I then picked up my phone to call Quint. I couldn't decide this on my own—not when a murder was involved.

CHAPTER FIFTEEN

O DORS OF GREASE AND KEROSENE PERMEATED MY NOSTRILS. I covered my ears to muffle the scream of power tools coming from the work area of the mechanic's shop. Standing next to my vehicle, I shouted at Bobby Stillwater, owner of Retread Tire and Repair, trying to drown out the noisy background.

Bobby gestured for me to follow him inside the store where dozens of tires in all brands were on display. "No need to compete with all that racket." He wiped sweat from his brow with a handkerchief which he then stuffed in his back pocket. "Now, what can I do for you, Ali?"

"I need an oil change and maybe a new pair of wipers." After a quick breakfast, I'd rushed out of the house to come here. Yesterday's effort to relax with movies and wrap some gifts didn't help. Guilt was not an easy companion, and that's what consumed me. I'd called Quint and explained the note and Nathan's story.

Quint responded to the news with the professional attitude that he most always did. During our conversation, he never criticized or lectured me for talking to Nathan about it. Yet, I was left with a bitter taste in my mouth, as if I'd betrayed my cousin.

"We can take care of that, but you'll have a bit of a wait. One of my mechanics is out sick today." Bobby flipped the page on his clipboard. "Would you like a rental?"

"Sure. Business has been good, huh?" I pulled out my license and slid it across the counter.

Bobby raised his head and grinned. "Better than good. I've reordered tire chains twice in the past week. Tune-ups, repair work. I even have a snowmobile with a couple of dings and some scratches." He pointed to the vehicle sitting next to a Chevy Tahoe.

I raised my brows at a purple-painted snowmobile. Scratch marks raked the length of one side and a sizable dent marred the front. "Purple isn't a common color, is it?"

"Oh, I know a place over in Viola Springs that sells plenty." Bobby scribbled to fill another line of his clipboard.

I squinted and flashed on images of the pine tree, the grooves with purple flecks, and those narrow tracks. "Come to think of it, I noticed a purple one at Tahoe Pine Ski Resort on occasion."

"That's the one right there. Kyle Steele dropped it off about a week ago."

I took the keys he handed me. "Really? I heard he had an accident about a week ago and sprained his ankle." I hitched my breath, anxious to hear what I expected.

Bobby shrugged. "Sure. He was limping and griping to beat heck about it." He smacked the counter with his hand. "Now, let's get you to your rental. The Land Rover should be ready for pick up by ten. I'll call you."

I slid behind the wheel of a nondescript Ford sedan. "Thanks, Bobby." I turned out of the shop's parking lot and drove back toward Main Street. I'd spent so much time searching for evidence to prove Tabitha's guilt, I'd almost forgotten about Kyle. The argument with Isadora, his accident right after her death, and that stack of papers with Isadora's name and number were enough to make me suspicious. I wondered if Quint considered Kyle a suspect and if he'd given any thought to adding Tabitha to his list. Maybe my thinking was unfair, but as long as Nathan wasn't the only one on his police radar, I'd feel some sort of relief.

I parked in front of Lenny's Bagels and Buns and checked my watch to read a quarter before nine. I could easily fit in two or three video interviews. The view of Lenny loading trays of fresh-baked product into the showcase made me smile. No offense to Meeka, but Bagels and Buns was my favorite stop. Today, a sweet treat would be an added benefit in spending time with a friend.

I sat and drummed my fingers on the steering wheel, pressed by thoughts of the damaged snowmobile. When I'd gone after Nathan on Friday, Kyle mentioned the resort had one in for repairs, but he hadn't elaborated. And not being suspicious, I hadn't asked. That feeling changed. I picked up my phone and called the resort. Maybe if I asked nicely, Kyle would be more generous with his story. I needed details.

"Tahoe Pine Ski Resort and Lodge. How may I help you?" A perky voice sang into the receiver.

"Yes. Hello. I'd like to speak with Kyle Steele." I chewed on my lip while waiting. A rustling sound on the other end followed by muffled voices heightened my anxiety.

"I'm sorry, but Mr. Steele is out on the slopes with a client. May I take a message?"

My mind scrambled for an idea. "Yes, the truth is I'd heard someone at the resort had been hurt in a snowmobile accident and that the person could've been Kyle. I want to send flowers and my condolences." I winced. How lame was that?

"I'm afraid you're mistaken. As for Mr. Steele, his injury is not public information. No snowmobile accidents on the premises. I'd know because all accident reports come through me."

"But I just saw a damaged snowmobile at Bobby Stillwater's repair shop today. He claimed it belonged to your resort. Can you tell me, did a guest wreck it, or was an employee driving?"

"That information is confidential. Good day."

I exited the vehicle and stepped toward Lenny's. The snappy words and abrupt click to end the call brought my favorite resort employee to mind—Kristin Mulvane. I scrunched my nose. That conversation hit a brick wall. She gave me no confirmation whether Kyle or anyone else wrecked the snowmobile.

I opened the shop door, and the bell hanging above jingled. I waved. "Hi Lenny."

Lenny straightened and patted his hands. A cloud of powdered sugar settled around him. "Good morning, Ali. Bagels and donuts straight from the oven. Would you like one? Or a dozen?" He winked with a smile.

"A chocolate éclair would make me happy." I laughed and set my bag on the table next to me. "I bet you can guess my reason for coming here."

"The video." He nodded. "How about some treats first?" Plucking a sheet of wax paper from the box, he grabbed an éclair out of the glass case, handed it to me, then chose a cream stick for himself.

I slid my plate closer and bit into the éclair. Warm, sugary goodness exploded in my mouth. Our conversation was suspended for several minutes while we finished our treats. I dabbed my lips with a napkin and nodded. "Thank you."

"Always aim to please my customers. So, where do you want to start?" He swiveled side to side with arms up. "Not much space to cover, but we could include the kitchen area."

I snapped my fingers. "I have an idea. Why don't we film you talking about a typical day from the moment you arrive at the shop, preparing the day's baked goods, the chalkboard with your special deals, and then end with an upbeat message to thank your customers and praise for Sierra Pines and its welcoming, cozy feel. What do you think?"

"You're pure genius. Makes perfect sense, you coming from a family of actors."

I grinned. "Well, hold that thought until after you see the video."

Lenny's ease in front of the camera helped to finish filming in short time, which relieved me. I checked my watch and calculated that one more shop was all I could manage. "I should hurry. I've got one more stop to make before picking up my car from Bobby's."

Since I promised to buy Gladys a few colors of thread for her cross-stitch, Get Crafty was next on my list. Plus, that gave me the opportunity to cover two tasks. A border of craft items framed the store window. Every type of crafting imaginable was included. Cross-stitch, needlepoint, macramé, embroidery, decoupage, and so many more were displayed. Even the sign over the door—metal pounded into a block of driftwood with the name Get Crafty hammered into it—was a craft item. Sisters, Betsy and Lily Wheeler, owned and ran the business. They could talk about crafts all day and night, if you let them. I always came prepared with an emergency excuse in case I needed to escape.

I stepped inside and scanned the store. The sharp odor of burning wood teased my nostrils and teared my eyes. I took a path down one aisle then up another. By the time I reached the end of the third aisle, I stopped and listened. Faint notes of the Carly Simon song "You're So Vain" carried from the back. "Betsy? Lily?"

Betsy popped out of the shop's work and supply room. She wore a mask that covered most of her face. Tufts of bright red hair stuck out at all angles from the top and sides of her head. Skinny as a rail, yet she had the energy of a jack rabbit and the strength of someone twice her size. "Ali!" My name muffled out from behind her mask. She lifted it off her face and smiled. "How nice to see you."

I gave her a quick hug. "You too. I see you're working on a project but thought I'd take a chance to see if you and Lily want to film your video now? I have time to kill before I pick up my car at Bobby's."

"Sure! The project can wait a bit. A client over in Placerville is in no hurry."

I leaned around her to view the work room. "Where's Lily? I never see one of you without the other by your side."

"Oh, she's visiting our cousin in Cedar Grove. Nadine had her baby yesterday." Betsy shrugged. "I lost the coin toss, so I'm stuck running the store."

"That's too bad. Maybe you will get a turn after Lily comes home."

"Yep. Now, how are those two dear hearts, the Bellwethers? I haven't seen much of them in town lately."

"As feisty as ever." I chuckled. "Gladys is another reason I'm here, though. She needs several colors of thread." I handed her the list Gladys had written.

Betsy scanned the paper then glanced up. "Not a problem."

As she pulled bunches of threads out of several drawers, I had a hunch. "Gladys belongs to a group of crafters. Aren't you one of them?"

"Oh yes. I call Thursday evenings my hen time. Plenty of gossip and recipes to share." She turned to face me and laid the threads next to the register. "Seriously, I enjoy the break. They are a great bunch of ladies."

"I can imagine. Wasn't Dottie in your group? Such a shame what happened."

"She was, up until a month ago. Not sure why she quit." Betsy scratched behind one ear. "Maybe had to do with the SPACA group and her new position."

"Dottie was proud as a peacock to have the title. I wonder what went wrong?" I knew plenty, like the bitter attitude over losing the MC job for the Christmas event, but I hoped to learn more.

Betsy leaned forward, resting her forearms on the counter. "Well, I can't be sure, but there was something off about her the last time she came into the shop."

"How so?"

"I asked her about the craft group and how we missed seeing her. That must've hit a nerve. She got all huffy and claimed nobody in this town appreciated her. Said she was sick of the attitude and planned to leave town and go somewhere she had the chance to make something of herself."

My eyes widened. "Oh, wow. When did this happen?"

Betsy scrunched her forehead for a second then straightened and snapped her fingers. "The same day you found her at Schumacher's gold mining sight!"

I blinked. "What else happened after Dottie snapped at you?"

"She marched out of the store without buying a thing. Lily and I looked out the window and watched her approach a car sitting in front of the shop. Seems like she was arguing with the driver. Her hands were flailing in every direction and her voice raised loud enough to hear from inside the shop."

"Hmm. Did she get in the car?" Right away, I thought of the Uber ride she'd taken to the mining sight.

"No. The car drove off, and then Dottie walked across the street to Boxes and Bows."

"That's interesting." I tapped my fingers on the counter. "You don't happen to remember any details about the car, do you?"

Betsy clicked her tongue. "Now that you mention it, we did. Kind of plain, dark blue sedan. Maybe a Ford? Didn't think much of it to look at the license plate number."

My mind worked to process and sort the details. The car couldn't belong to the Uber service. Otherwise, why would Dottie argue? Betsy's description triggered another thought. Maybe because I was driving one like it, I wondered if the car could be a rental. Plain, dark color, the perfect vehicle if you wanted to blend in and go unnoticed. I did a mental eyeroll. Yeah, I was far out in left field with that line of thinking.

"I don't recall anyone I know who owns a car like that," Betsy said.

"Me neither." I struggled to take my mind off Dottie. Shaking my head, I pointed at my phone. "Look at me. I should be taping you instead of talking about other things. Let's get this done."

We finished a few minutes before my phone rang with a call from Bobby to say my car was ready. After paying for Gladys's order, I crossed the street to the rental. Alone, my mind turned to mull over Betsy's story about Dottie once again. All the complaints and her boast of leaving town were nothing new. We'd heard as much in Dottie's voicemail, and the fact she'd stolen SPACA money supported her plan to leave. The unfamiliar car and Dottie arguing with the driver, however, presented a new piece to the puzzle. I opened my phone and placed a call to Quint.

"Hey there, gorgeous lady."

"Hey back at you, handsome guy in a uniform. I have some news for you." I shared the details of my exchange with Betsy. "What do you think?"

"I think you should let me follow up on this, if there's anything to the story. Okay?"

"No problem. Just thought you should know." Of course, I didn't promise a thing about my plan to question Kyle.

I turned around at Pine Hollow Road and headed back toward Englewood. After a quick stop to pick up the Land Rover, I drove home. With plenty of daylight left and fresh powder on the slope, I could squeeze in a little skiing before talking to Kyle. Might as well take advantage and have some fun time.

Once inside the B&B, I let Gladys know where I was going then hurried upstairs to my room. I pulled on all my ski apparel and grabbed my bag and keys off the nightstand. Skipping down the stairs, I landed on the foyer floor with a thud, nearly colliding with Beth. "Oh! Wow, sorry." I winced.

She laughed. "No harm done." Shifting her gaze up and down, she added, "Say, are you headed to Tahoe Pine? Maybe I could ride along? The weather's beautiful for skiing, isn't it?"

"Exactly what I was thinking. Sure. If you can get ready in the next few minutes, that is. I hate to waste daylight." I waved an arm at the front door. "Meet me outside. I'll warm up the car."

"Thanks, Ali." Beth sprinted up the stairs. "I'll be quick."

I threw my bag in the back and cleared the passenger seat, tossing an empty sandwich bag, big gulp cup, and napkins left from yesterday's stop at a fast-food drive-thru in the trash. My shameful junk food indulgence for the month. I considered the dent Beth put in my agenda. Somehow, I'd make sure to sneak away before speaking with Kyle. There was no point in alarming her either. Part of my job as owner of the B&B was to keep our guests happy and safe, and provide the best experience for them to remember.

Beth skipped down the porch steps and cut across the lawn to the car. "Thanks again." She blew out air and relaxed her posture. "I'm so anxious to get back on the slopes. Skiing is like a drug for me, you know? I can't get enough."

I grinned. "I won't go that far, but I do enjoy the sport." I glimpsed her face as I backed out of the drive. She blushed and her eyes sparkled. "I bet you've been on some pretty impressive slopes."

"Oh yeah. Plenty. I think the ones in Aspen are my favorite, though." She bit down on the end of her glove and pulled it up to the wrist.

"Such a great release after being cooped up inside with cranky customers." I nodded.

"Hmm?" She frowned then widened her eyes. "Oh! You mean at the store. No, I, um, I work in the office. Hardly any contact with customers unless a call accidently transfers to me instead of the complaints department." She shrugged with a laugh.

"That call wouldn't be fun, I'm sure." I steered the SUV onto Lincoln. "Do you like your job?"

"Sometimes." Beth shrugged. "Like anyone, I had fantasies of a dream career. And like most people, I chose a profession that's more practical and dependable."

I thought of my family for a second. "I don't know. I think those rare individuals who landed their dream jobs might have been told to be more practical. Instead, they turned stubborn and got exactly what they wanted. My parents were and are like that."

Beth sniffed. "Well, a dose of luck might have helped. Some of us aren't quite so fortunate."

Her words trailed off into a mumbled whisper, but I caught enough of what she said. Poor Beth. I knew what disappointment felt like. I dreamed of becoming a screenwriter for major film productions and working for a director like Steven Spielberg or Martin Scorsese. I guessed fate had other plans. "I can't argue with that. Luck can play a part."

Within a half hour, I entered the drive leading to the resort. The dashboard clock read a little before eleven—plenty of time to ski, talk to Kyle, and get home before my nail appointment. I parked the car and switched off the ignition.

Beth slid out of her seat, stretched, and took a deep breath. "Don't you love this mountain air? So clean and fresh." She twirled around. "Maybe I'll move here someday. After I can retire, of course." She jogged in place then powerwalked across the parking lot.

After grabbing my bag from the backseat and locking the SUV, I quickly caught up to her. "The Lake Tahoe area is one of the most popular spots to vacation. Living here takes money. It's California, after all." I held up one hand. "Just my opinion, though."

"Yeah, I try not to think about that part."

Entering the lodge, I walked alongside Beth toward the rental kiosk, surprised not to find Owen behind the counter. In his place stood a tall brunette with stunning violet blue eyes. "Hi there. We'd like to rent skis for a couple of hours."

Within minutes, we had our equipment in hand. "How about we meet back here at one? I have some people I need to speak with after I finish skiing, but should be ready to leave by then."

I waited near the kiosk until she disappeared through the exit doorway. Turning, I smiled at the woman behind the rental counter and quickly read her nametag. "Hi Briana. Listen, I don't suppose you've seen Kyle Steele recently?"

"Sure. I was on a break and spotted him taking the trail on a snowmobile."

"How long ago would you say?" I glanced up at the clock on the wall behind her.

"Maybe a half hour."

I moved aside as another customer approached. Thanking Briana, I walked to the exit. With any luck, I'd run into him on the slopes, or at least when he returned to the lodge. I groaned at the long line of people waiting at the ski lift. The intermediate slopes must be the most used. Luckily, the wait was less than ten minutes. A gust of wind kicked up snow as I lifted into the next available car. Once in the air, I scanned the area below, searching for any snowmobiles. A half dozen sped along the trails. I had no idea which, but one of them had to be Kyle's.

The ski lift stopped at the top of the slope. I dropped down to the ground and pushed off, wind and snow biting my face as I picked up speed. The rush of adrenalin energized my mood. I wanted answers. I wanted all our problems to disappear—the murders to be solved and the town's business to return—so we could have a merry celebration at Christmas. The slope wound past a grove of trees. I leaned to the left and slalomed to follow the direction.

Just beyond the pines, Kyle stood off to the far side, next to his snowmobile. He leaned over the front of the vehicle, peering under the opened hood.

I careened toward him, and twisting my skis, I stuck my poles to stop. "Need some help?"

Kyle straightened to face me, and his gaze narrowed. "Unless you have a battery charger, I guess not." He shrugged and stuck his head back under the hood.

"Yeah, I'm no mechanic, but staring at the engine isn't going to help either." I slid my skis closer to him.

He faced me once more and ran his tongue across the top of his mouth. "You've got a smart attitude."

"Hah. Pot, kettle, black. Anyway, since I've interrupted you doing whatever it is your doing, I have a question." So much for sweet and persuasive. I could never squash my surliness when around him. "I've heard rumors about the infamous purple snowmobile that tangled with a pine tree. I figured you'd be the one to ask. Was it you driving? Hard to believe, given your dexterity with all snow related equipment." I smirked. Maybe taking jabs at his skills was a better way to get him to talk.

He puffed out his chest. "I don't wreck snowmobiles."

"But you took a tumble while on skis. I think you're a teensy bit off your game." I coughed into my glove to stifle the laugh.

"For your information, Tabitha was at the wheel. She took a turn too fast and lost control." He scoffed with a strong headshake. "Madder than I've ever seen her. Embarrassed too. She wouldn't talk much about it when I asked. Instead, she snapped at me to take it in for repairs."

"Hmm. I see." I ran my finger along my bottom lip. "That explains why I saw the snowmobile at Bobby's this morning. He said you brought it in about a week ago?"

"Yep. That was a crazy twenty-four hours. First, the Lane woman takes a dive off a cliff, then the next morning Wells wrecks the snowmobile." He slammed the hood shut then climbed into the seat. Giving the starter a couple of clicks, he grinned as the engine came to life. "How about that? Guess I have mental powers of persuasion after all. See you, Winston." He spun around to head back on the trail. Snow spitted from under the wheels, stinging my face and spotting my mask.

I rubbed the shield clear. "You did that on purpose." I shouted, but he'd already disappeared. "Guess it's time to have another talk with Tabitha." I finished my trip down the slope.

He could be lying, I thought. Afterall, if he wrecked it and was Isadora's killer, he wouldn't admit to anything that made him look guilty. Then again, telling the truth is what innocent people do. Why lie about Tabitha when Kyle knew I could check up on his story?

I pulled to a stop when I reached the lodge. "The real question is if Tabitha wrecked the snowmobile, why was she at the crime scene in the first place?" I muttered under my breath, shifting my gaze to make sure no one had heard me. She could've gone to search for any evidence she left behind. After all, she'd been upset. In a crazy state of mind, she could've killed Isadora, maybe by accident. Panicky people left clues behind sometimes. Tabitha wanted to make sure she hadn't.

I entered the lodge and returned my skis. Stepping away from the counter, I turned and found Beth waiting nearby. She pocketed her phone then wiped her eyes. No doubt, she was troubled. I wanted to ask, but thought it best not to unless she opened up to talk. After a few nights ago, when I found her crying in her room, I guessed this mood might be about boyfriend problems again.

The ride home was quiet, other than the radio playing. The half hour delay because of an accident on the road near the Cedar Grove exit put me in an anxious mood. Having to postpone my conversation with Tabitha was frustrating. At least I'd have time to shower and grab a bite to eat before my four o'clock appointment at Donetta's Nail Salon.

As I pulled in the drive, I snapped my head around. My plan to call Quint and give him an update about what I'd learned wasn't necessary. The cruiser steered to the curb in front of the B&B. Quint and another man whom I didn't recognize stepped out.

Beth went inside the house while I waited on the porch, wondering who and what the man accompanying Quint could be.

"Ali." Quint tipped his hat then gestured next to him. "This is Jerry Mackelroy, our IT expert who's been figuring out what's going on with all those online comments."

I stuck out a hand to shake his. "Nice to meet you, Jerry. Ollie certainly praises your skills." The thought crossed my mind that the department and especially Quint, must think the situation was serious enough to spend money on hiring Jerry. I knew how tight the budget was.

"How about we go inside?" Quint said.

"Oh! I'm sorry. Got lost in my thoughts. Please, come in." I opened the door and waved an arm as I stepped aside.

"Ladies first." Quint smiled and his eyes twinkled.

I felt the heat rise to my face, but hurried into the foyer. I hung my coat on the rack and extended my arm with fingers wiggling. "Let me take your coats then let's go to the parlor and get comfortable."

Once everyone was seated, I folded my hands and laid them in my lap. "I guess you found something, right?" My gaze settled on Jerry.

Quint cleared his throat, drawing my attention back to him. My brows knitted as I became worried. He rubbed a hand across his face and shifted in his seat.

"Let me tell her, Quint," Jerry said. "Ali, I checked and double checked to make sure. However, there's no doubt in my mind what I discovered." He leaned forward in his seat. "The IP address associated with your town's social media menace comes from here."

I frowned. "What are you saying?"

"He's saying all those comments might have been made by someone at the B&B." Quint added.

I loud rattle and crash made me jump in my seat. I turned toward the doorway.

Gladys held a hand to her mouth. A silver platter dropped and spun around at her feet. "Oh my."

My reaction exactly because adding to all our other problems, we had a cybercriminal living under our roof.

CHAPTER SIXTEEN

THE MINUTE OF SILENCE THAT FOLLOWED WAS DEAFENING. My throat tightened while I processed what Jerry and Quint told me. I opened and shut my mouth several times, not knowing where to start.

"Did you hear what I said, Ali?" Quint asked.

"Hmm." I nodded then, at once, shook my head. "That's impossible. Gladys, Ollie, and I would never do such a horrible thing. And I'm fairly certain, none of our guests would either. That's like shouting, 'look here, I'm the guilty one.'"

"I understand you're offended, but there's no way to finish investigating the issue without checking your home computer and laptop, as well as each guest's devices." Quint looked at Gladys. "That includes you and Ollie, I'm afraid."

I blinked. "Seriously?"

"Ali." Jerry stood. "It's quite possible you've been hacked. I can check the browser history on your home computer, see if there's unusual activity, run a couple of programs, and a few other things to find out. Would you be more comfortable if I did that first? Then maybe we won't have to bother your guests."

I nodded. "That would nice of you." With a side glance, I narrowed my eyes at Quint. He could've led with that suggestion instead of working me into a state of panic.

"The sooner we figure this out, the sooner our lives get back to normal," Quint said.

"As if." I grumbled under my breath and walked to the parlor desk. I booted up the computer and typed in the password. "Here you go, Jerry.

Might as well start with this one." I stepped aside. "There's a second computer in the library. I'll log into that one as well." I turned to walk toward the hallway.

"I'll come with you." Quint hurried to my side.

My brow lifted. "What? Afraid I'll delete something before Jerry can check?"

"Ali. Come on. Of course I trust you."

Quint's mouth curved down at the corners to form a pouty expression. I groaned. "Sorry. My mood has turned sour, and I'm taking it out on you." I paused in the library doorway and studied his face. "Do you really think someone in the house could be our cyber outlaw?"

He shrugged. "We won't know until Jerry finishes his thing."

I scratched my nose then entered the library. "What if he doesn't find anything? How does that explain his claim that someone remotely highjacked our IP address?"

"Not sure. I'm not the techy type, but then I have to consider a person in this house is our cyber guy or woman."

"Let's hope not." I flipped the power switch on the computer and waited for the sign-in screen to pop up. "What I'm counting on is Jerry finds a hacker." I clicked enter, and the home screen lit up. "There you go."

"Great. Let's see if he's made any progress." Quint led the way across the hall to where the noise of chattering voices grew louder by the second.

My stomach flip flopped as I entered the parlor to see three angry faces. Faith, Abby, and Margaret stood glaring at Jerry with their arms crossed. Ollie appeared unimpressed by the whole ordeal. Gladys, on the other hand, stood against the wall, twisting her apron into knots. We weren't exactly building those pleasant memories for our guests like I'd hoped to do.

"I'm sorry, Alexis. I was in the atrium talking to Ollie about this horrible situation and hadn't realized three of our guests were sitting on the back porch. They heard everything, and before I knew what was happening . . ." She threw up her hands. "Well, here we all are."

"And you suspect one of us?" Faith Ritter stood tall in a manner most likely meant to intimidate. If not for her short height and senior age, the effort might have worked.

Jerry wiped sweat off his brow.

Quint stepped forward. "I promise no one is accusing any of you."

"Not yet, you mean." Abby chimed in. "I thought this was a friendly

B&B."

"It most certainly is." Gladys shouted in a warbly tone. "We have one of the best rated bed and breakfast establishments in all of northern California. Or at least we did before all this." She waved an arm carelessly at the computer and Jerry.

"I don't understand. How could you know just by looking on our devices that one of us wrote the comments?" Margaret Smith asked.

Jerry tugged at his collar. Without removing his gaze from the screen, he shrugged. "I can't. Not for certain. Unless I stumble on some file or document or maybe a program that a person would be careless enough to leave on the device. Right now, I'm hoping for another answer."

He had my vote. On impulse, I offered a suggestion. "Gladys, why don't you unwrap that nut roll you were saving for tomorrow? I bet our guests could use a sugary pick-me-up about now. How about it, everyone?" I put cheer in my voice, hoping for agreement.

"I sure could use a snack." Ollie rubbed his belly as he chimed in.

"As always." Gladys rolled her eyes. "Come on, ladies. Follow me to the kitchen. You might as well come too, Ollie."

I sat in a chair at the far end of the parlor and waited quietly as Jerry tapped on keys and clicked the mouse, scrolling and scanning through files, while Quint hovered over him. Crossing my legs to get comfortable, I closed my eyes. At every turn, another obstacle popped up to put the B&B further in jeopardy. We needed a break.

"Woohoo!" Jerry bounced back and locked both hands behind his head. He grinned from ear to ear. "We got him. Or her. Can't know for sure. Anyway, there's a hacker who remotely got into your IP address through an open path." He twisted around to face me. "You see it's like your IP address is your house. And the pathways are the rooms in it. If any are open—"

I held up a hand. "You don't need to explain. Just tell us you can stop him or her."

"Not completely." He frowned.

I sank into my chair and moaned. What was the point? "You know there's a criminal but you can't prevent him or her from doing more damage?"

"I can do plenty. There are malware programs and firewalls to set up, for instance." He nodded at Quint. "I'm getting paid enough, thanks to the sheriff's department. I'll upload the programs on the computers belonging to every business owner, and, with a little monitoring, you all can keep track of the hacker's activity."

"Huh. Seems like we could've done most of that by ourselves, but I am grateful it's a hacker and not someone in this house." I searched for what to add. "Any chance you can find out where this is coming from?"

Quint raised a hand. "I can answer that one. Word from Sacramento authorities gives us a lead. Activity similar to ours has been happening for the past several months in their city as well as in Folsom and as far south as Stockton. My guess is this could be related."

"But no one has been caught. That's discouraging." I couldn't picture an end to this. On the plus side, no one at the B&B was guilty of hacking and trashing our town businesses.

Quint and I left Jerry to finish and took seats at the kitchen table to nibble on nut roll and drink cups of decaf. The others had gone out or to their rooms, tired of waiting for more news about the cyber bandit, Gladys explained.

"If you'll excuse me, I've got some knitting to catch up on," she said.

"I'm relieved and worried at the same time." I pinched crumbs off my plate and stuck them in my mouth.

"I know what you mean. Picturing Gladys or Ollie as hackers gave me heartburn." Quint laughed.

"Heartburn? More like a bad horror movie haunting you." I laughed with him.

He reached across the table and took hold of my hand. "I'm sorry for making you worry and for ruining your afternoon."

"Don't be."

"I am. The mayor is breathing down my neck and demanding answers."

"Playing politics. Such a hardship, right?" I gave his arm a playful nudge.

"Stop. To change the subject, how was your morning?"

"Better than this afternoon." I winked.

"You never quit, do you?" He spoke in a warm tone and leaned back in his chair. A lazy smile curved his lips.

I shivered. He was sexy and handsome as ever. Still, the sobering thought of my trip to the resort kept me focused. "To be honest, my morning wasn't much better." I continued the conversation by relating everything I'd learned about the snowmobile accident and Kyle's version of the story. "One of them drove and wrecked that vehicle. Kyle or

Tabitha. I'm not sure what to believe."

"Or anyone at the lodge could be guilty as charged."

"Yeah, always the one to complicate matters." I wagged my finger. "You know what else I'm thinking?"

"I can't imagine." He pushed his plate and cup aside. With elbows on the table, he cradled his chin with both palms.

I tossed my napkin at him. "If you're not going to take me seriously—"

"Okay. I'm listening. See?" He pointed to his lips that drew in a straight line.

"I'm thinking about Tabitha. What if she is the killer, and in a moment of panic, she forgot to cover her tracks or left some clue behind? Then the next morning she went to the murder scene to search for whatever it is. She panicked even more and lost control of the snowmobile and bam! She hit the tree." I smacked the table for dramatic effect.

"Bam, huh?" Quint stood and stretched. "I like that. Maybe I'll use the word bam in my final report when the time comes."

"Fine. I'm done. I have a nail appointment in an hour and no time for you and your snide remarks." I lifted my chin then grabbed dishes off the table and carried them to the sink.

"Awe, I was teasing and you know it. I'll question Tabitha and Kyle, see if I can get more details." He wrapped an arm around my waist. "I promise, if you turn out to be right about Tabitha, I'll apologize."

"Whatever." I gave him a peck on the cheek before leading him down the hall.

Jerry came out of the library as we reached the foyer. "All done. Let's move on to the business owners while there's plenty of day left."

Quint tipped his hat and walked to the door. "Thank you for your cooperation, Miss Winston. I'll call you tomorrow." He paused and turned. "Pink?"

I frowned. "Hmm?"

"I really like pink nail polish." He winked then disappeared through the doorway with Jerry close behind.

"PASSION PRETTY PINK IS THE PERFECT CHOICE FOR SUMMER." Donetta fingered the dozens of bottles of polish lined up on the shelf and hummed a tune. "Ah, hah!" She plucked one bottle from the middle of the bunch and set it in front of me. "Nothing says Christmas like cranberry crush, don't you agree?"

I stared at the deep red color of polish. "I've never worn such a bright color. You don't think it's too showy? I mean for everyday wear. I could see the color would be right for a party or evening out."

"Ali." Donetta pressed my hand. "You're overthinking this. Please trust me." She opened the bottle and stirred. "If you were going to a party, I'd add a coat of gold or silver glitter."

"You've never steered me wrong before." I set my hand, fingers splayed, on the tray.

She swiped her long brown tresses into a messy bun then began to work her nail magic. "Polished and Pretty has been my business for twenty years. I've cared for thousands of customers, and never once did I receive a complaint." She tipped her head. "Well, there was one time, but how could I know the woman was allergic to acrylic?"

My gaze wandered while she continued to chat about her family and gossip about town business. The shop was small but quaint. An antique loveseat with cherry wood accents and flowery cushions sat in the waiting area. Smells of cinnamon candles and the mint chocolate steaming from my mug of cocoa were like an aphrodisiac. Donetta certainly knew how to pamper her clients.

"All finished." She announced with a wave of her arm. A smile brightened her eyes. "I am the Picasso of nails, don't you think?"

I lifted my hands in front of me to examine the results. "Okay, I'll admit you were right." I waved a polished red finger. "Come summer, though, I want that passion pretty pink."

"You got it." Donetta stood and walked behind her desk. She pulled out an iPad and entered some numbers.

I slid my credit card toward her. On the far side of the counter, coupons and fliers covered the area. I glimpsed the top of the tallest stack. The name and logo of Tahoe Pine Ski Resort and Lodge were stamped across the top, with the description of discounts and perks underneath. "Doesn't look like these are going very fast." I scribbled my signature on the iPad and pocketed my card.

Donetta scoffed. "Sad, isn't it? That woman is so desperate for business. I told her to take out ads in the paper and the tourist website. Won't get much action in here. My clients are locals and most of them don't ski."

I tapped one perfectly polished nail on the counter. "You mean Tabitha Wells? I thought the resort business was booming." Nothing like a fishing expedition because I knew very well Tabitha was in over her head.

"The way she acts when I see her, all anxious and fidgety." Donetta's eyes widened. "Have you seen her nails? Bitten down to the nub. The sight of them makes my heart ache."

"Has she ever mentioned anything about the resort? Or maybe talked about other things that bother her?"

"No, not that I can recall." In a second, she snapped her fingers. "Wait. I do remember a conversation when I ran into her at Lucinda's the other day. The subject of the holidays and what people had planned came up, and she got all teary eyed, saying she wanted to go visit family in Missouri, but her job wouldn't allow it." She placed a hand over her chest. "Gets you right here, doesn't it?"

I exchanged goodbyes with Donetta and wished her a happy holiday before leaving the shop.

Five o'clock arrived and daylight disappeared with dark clouds that covered the skies and promised more snow. The air was crisp and cold and invigorating. As I stepped onto the sidewalk, I lifted my chest to take a deep breath. When the traffic light flashed green, I hurried across the street to Meeka's. She'd sent a text message letting me know the engraved items arrived this afternoon.

Lining the sidewalk, Western Redbud trees twinkled with gold lights threaded through their branches. Store front windows came alive as shop owners turned on their own holiday light show. I stepped inside Meeka's to find her placing glass tree ornaments on a shelf. "Hey there."

"Ali." She turned to greet me then set the box of ornaments on the floor. "I can't wait for you to see how they turned out."

"Me too." I'd been worried and excited all at once for several days. These gifts had to be perfect. I tensed as Meeka opened the boxes and slid both across the counter.

"What do you think? Nice, right?"

"Oh my. Wow. Better than I ever expected." I held up the bookmark in one hand and the telescope in the other. Each had the engraved inscription I'd requested. My eyes moistened and I quickly placed the items back in their boxes. I sniffed. "Thanks, Meeka. They will love these."

We moved on to a more serious conversation when Meeka asked about the cyber mess. "Has Jerry the computer guru got an answer to our problems?" she asked.

"Not yet."

"He came by a little bit ago and put some software program on my computer then talked a bunch of jibber jabber techy stuff I didn't understand." She placed both boxes in a gift bag and handed it to me.

I laughed. "Computer gurus have that problem of talking over our heads. Just keep an eye on the thread of comments on your website. If you see any suspicious activity, tell Quint."

She snorted. "Like that will help. Proactive works better than reactive."

"Huh. That's very wise of you." I patted my handbag. "I should get going. I promised to drop off fliers at the theater. Florence said she'd be there this afternoon and evening."

Once out the door, I jaywalked across the street to reach the theater. After passing through the lobby, I faced the stage and searched the area for Florence. "Hello? Anybody here?" My voice echoed to answer me. "Huh. That's weird." Taking a walk down the aisle, I reached the stage and set the fliers on the podium nearby. I was tired to the bone and had no intention of waiting around. Since it was close to dinnertime, I guessed she could have gone out for a bite to eat. Still, why hadn't she called or texted to let me know?

I turned to retrace my steps when the lights flickered. All at once, darkness blanketed the room. My body stiffened as I clenched my bag and hugged it to my chest. "Probably just an electrical short. Nothing to worry about." I tightened my muscles and pulled my shoulders back. "Florence? If you're anywhere in this building, you better answer me." A slight breeze and the light shuffle of footsteps passed by me. I gasped. "Florence? Is that you?"

CHAPTER SEVENTEEN

MY BODY SHOOK. I MANAGED A TINY STEP FORWARD, which I hoped would take me away from the stage. If I kept moving, maybe I'd eventually end up at the exit door. "This is crazy. The lights went out. So what?" I waved my arm to the side, feeling for a chair. When my hand touched a metal frame, I weakened with relief.

I'd gotten no further than a few steps when the lights flickered then popped on. I shielded my eyes against the glaring fluorescents. A lump formed in my throat, making it difficult to breathe. Whatever happened seemed to be over. I released the grip on my bag and sat in the closest seat. No doubt, my nerves were frazzled. The past week and a half had been filled with one disturbing or puzzling event after another. I bent my head and rested it in the palm of my hand for a moment. Regaining my composure, I stood and walked over to the podium to check the stack of fliers. One had fallen on the floor. I bent over to pick it up and frowned at the scribbling across the top.

"Stop nosing into matters that don't concern you." I read and reread the message. The warning was clearly meant for me. The truly frightening thing was that someone had written it while I stood close by and in the dark. Someone who might be the killer. "Right here in this room." I felt a chill, and my arms grew all goosepimply.

"Ali. Whatever is going on? I returned and found the lights off. You shouldn't be traipsing around in the dark. You could get hurt."

I jumped at the sight of Florence. "Oh, hey, there you are." A tittering sound escaped my lips.

"Are you all right?" She knitted her brows. "You seem upset."

I stuffed the flier in my bag and cleared my throat. "I wasn't stumbling around in the dark. The lights went out after I got here." I stepped around her. "The fliers are there on the podium. Sorry, but I'm in a hurry to get home."

"But—"

I waved and kept walking. "Really, I need to go. Talk to you later."

"I thought maybe we could talk about the visit with Mr. Mackelroy."

"Later." I smacked the theater door open with both hands and charged out of the building. Right now, I needed the warmth and safety of my B&B to calm me.

Consumed by my thoughts, I stepped off the curb and into the street. A car horn blared and tires screeched. A hand grabbed my arm and yanked me back onto the sidewalk. I steadied my feet to keep from wobbling.

"That was too close." Beth stood next to me. Her chest moved rapidly and her smile quivered.

I squeezed her arm. "Oh my, if you hadn't been here . . . thank you. I think you saved me."

"I don't know if I'd put it that way, but you're welcome." She turned her head to glance up the road then returned her gaze to me. "Did you drive? Maybe I should walk you to your car. Or better yet, drive us back to the B&B?"

"Yeah, maybe you're right. I can't stop shaking." I clenched my hands.

"Almost getting hit by a fast-moving car can do that to you." She managed a half smile.

"I parked the Land Rover across the street in front of Bagels and Buns." I assured her I was fine to drive since the B&B was only two blocks away.

Once inside the house, Beth excused herself. I went in search of Gladys in the kitchen where I figured she'd be. Since Julia passed, Gladys became my go-to person for comfort as well as sage advice. I was desperate to tell her about the note and being thrown into darkness for what felt like an eternity.

Gladys stood at the window overlooking the backyard with hands braced on the sink ledge. Her shoulders lifted, then dropped as her body shook.

"Gladys? Are you okay?" Concern for my dear friend replaced my worries. As she teetered to one side, I rushed forward to steady her. "My goodness, what's wrong? Are you hurt?"

Tears trickled down her cheeks. She swiped them away with the back of her hand. "No, dear. I'm only hurting on the inside, thinking about your aunt."

I clutched my throat. "That's a relief. I mean I'm sorry thoughts about Julia make you sad but glad you aren't physically hurt."

She tilted her head then pointed. "From your face, I'd guess I'm not the only one feeling hurt. Now, don't deny it. I can always tell."

I lifted my chin. "Oh? How's that?"

She shrugged. "Instinct. Come. Sit at the table. I'll put the kettle on to make us chamomile tea." Her brow hiked. "Unless you want something stronger like hot toddies? I could certainly use one."

I gave her a thumbs up sign then pulled out a chair to sit. "A hot toddy sounds perfect."

After lining up bottles of honey, lemon, and whiskey on the counter, she took a seat across from me. "Now, talk to me."

I dove into the details of my story, maybe embellishing at times for dramatic effect. After all, the actor's persona was in my blood. "That's about it."

"My stars. Thank goodness Beth was close by." She gave her head a harsh shake.

"I should've been more careful, but that note panicked me." The kettle screamed and I jumped in my seat. "Guess I'm still shaken."

Gladys poured hot water into two mugs and added the other ingredients. Placing a wedge of lemon and a cinnamon stick in each, she brought them to the table. "Well, you're home now. Safe and secure. Ollie and I would never let anything happen to you." She patted my hand.

A smile wavered then faded. I sipped my toddy while attempting to rid my mind of the troubling images. The note, however, shouldn't be dismissed so lightly. The words were a warning. People didn't ignore them if they were smart. "What about the warning note?"

"I'm thinking of your aunt and how she always defended the truth no matter the danger the situation might put her in." She wrapped fingers of both hands around her mug.

"So, you think I should keep going to find the truth, despite the warning?"

"I think you'll do so no matter what I say. Just be careful, dear."

I agreed on one thing—I didn't plan to risk my life.

The pounding of footsteps reverberated from the hallway and into the kitchen. Nathan paused as he stared at us. Dark shadows underneath his eyes gave him a haunted appearance. At once his gaze shifted to the counter. He licked his bottom lip then took a path to the other side of the kitchen. He reached for the bottle of whiskey. "Mind if I have a glass?"

Gladys set down her mug. "No, of course not. Help yourself. Liquor glasses are in the top cupboard to your right."

I studied the back of him. His hand shook as he poured a generous amount of whiskey into the tumbler. Without another word, he walked out of the kitchen and up the stairs. Did men who murdered their wives, wallow in pity and tortured thoughts? I wasn't sure, but Nathan certainly was tortured. I made my decision. I'd keep quiet about the note because if Quint found out, he'd do everything in his power to keep me from snooping, and that's the last thing I wanted to happen.

Morning came with a jarring headache. I hadn't slept well. Those thoughts about my visit to the theater I'd tried so hard to dismiss invaded my dreams. My solution was to keep busy and go investigate before I wimped out. First, I'd take another trip to the resort and visit Tabitha, even though I'd promised a certain sheriff to let him do the job. People are intimidated by men and women wearing badges. That was my reasoning. Besides, Tabitha and I had formed some sort of friendship, or at least I hoped so. We had much to discuss, and I was determined to get answers, which apparently was a common occurrence with me nowadays. I cornered people, demanded answers, and moved on. Quint needed to put a badge on my chest and deputize me because I sure was acting like an authority figure.

I ventured into my bathroom and opened the medicine cabinet. Popping two pain reliever tablets in my mouth, I downed them with a glass of water. Nearing the bottom stairs, I counted the chimes of the Moose cuckoo clock. *Nine o'clock.* Some B&B proprietor I was. Two late mornings in the past week. If I didn't watch, this could become a bad habit.

Stopping in the kitchen, I grabbed an apple out the bowl. "Morning, all." I greeted the Bellwethers, Abby, and Faith who sat around the table eating their breakfast.

"You should have a proper breakfast, Alexis. Come sit with us," Gladys said.

I waved as I passed through the doorway. "No time. I have errands to run before noon. Save me a couple of muffins. They smell yummy."

Powerwalking to the foyer, I grabbed my coat off the rack and kept moving. The earlier I got to the resort, the better the chance I had of catching Tabitha in her office, at least before she ran off taking care of her duties.

I'd considered calling to ask questions over the phone. Two reasons stopped me. First, I wouldn't see any emotional reaction on her face, one that hinted she was lying or uncomfortable. Second, all calls went through her assistant who would tell me to make an appointment. Even if Tabitha was willing to talk to me, I'd need to wait until who knew when.

The traffic on Lincoln Highway backed up. A flatbed truck loaded with mulch from Digmoore's nursery had pulled out of the parking lot, causing a trail of six or more cars to follow at a snail's pace ahead of me: so much for catching Tabitha at an early hour. At least the sun shone brightly, and the forecast called for warmer temps. Feeling optimistic, I decided that after my talk with Tabitha, I'd treat myself to a mug of mint cocoa from Tahoe Eats and Beverages and sit by the fireplace. Little pleasures might help to erase those unpleasant thoughts about the warning note. That was my plan.

As I passed at a crawl by Bobby's repair shop—I honestly could've walked faster—a glance to my right made me press on the breaks and swerve into the shop's parking lot. "Guess I don't need to drive to the lodge after all." I tapped the horn and quickly powered down the window to holler hello.

Tabitha looked up from the papers she held in her hand. With a flicker of a smile, she lifted her arm and waved.

I rushed out of the SUV and caught up as she reached her car. "What a coincidence. I was on my way to the lodge to see you." I spoke in a breathy tone. "Got a minute?"

"I stopped by to pay a repair bill, but I'm in a hurry. I'm due back at the lodge in an hour for a staff meeting." She licked her bottom lip. "If you need more time, maybe you could schedule an appointment through my assistant."

I grew solemn. "I think you need to hear me out, first." I was impatient to get answers and desperate to clear Nathan's name, if that was even possible.

Her shoulders sank. "Very well. This better be good. I expect punctuality from my people. It's important I show them the same practice."

I motioned to the wooden table that sat on the strip of land between Bobby's and Digmoore's. "Let's take a seat over there to give us some privacy."

Once situated, I dove into the conversation, starting first with what Kyle had told me. "Is it true you wrecked the snowmobile?" I waited while she fidgeted with the papers in her hand. "I also talked to Donetta. She claims you are worn down from your efforts to boost the resort business. Tabitha, whatever is wrong, you can tell me. I'm a great listener."

"Oh, my." A long breath released from her quivering lips. "I am, I'm so very tired and anxious. Stiletto corporate is such a monster. Working for them has been a nightmare. So much pressure to do better, sell more, promote more. I've been leaving coupons all over town, at airports and hotels, buying ad space in travel magazines, anything to help. It's driving me mad. When Isadora made her threat to badmouth the resort, I snapped. I knew if too much negative publicity got out, I'd be fired. Or worse yet, people might start to dig into the resort's activity and find some things I'd done that aren't exactly what you'd call professional. Stiletto knew and warned me if any of that information got out, I'd be done. Anyway, I tried to reason with Isadora, but you saw the way she responded, didn't you?" She shuddered. "I had to muster all my willpower to keep from slapping her face."

"Don't be ashamed of your reaction. She pushed most everyone's buttons, mine included."

"Really?" Tabitha sniffed and dabbed at her eyes.

"Many times." I patted her hand and softened my voice. "I bet you were crazy with anger, and that's why you wrecked the snowmobile. Right?"

Tabitha gripped my fingers and squeezed. "You don't understand. When I heard she'd fallen off the cliff, and the sheriff was investigating to decide if it was murder, I panicked."

"How did you panic?" I strained to get the words out while removing my hand from her uncomfortably tight hold.

"That's the unlucky part. You see, I was snowmobiling on the trail running by that cliff two days before. I always keep an extra pair of gloves and a stocking cap in my backpack. When I returned to the lodge and checked my bag, I found the flap open. One of my gloves was missing. I figured it had fallen out while I was on the trail." She paused and ran the back of her hand across her cheek. "Hearing about Isadora made me worry that if the investigation led to finding my glove and the sheriff learned about my shouting match with Isadora . . . Don't you see? He'd have every reason to suspect me." She gave her head a hard shake. "I couldn't let that happen. I didn't kill her."

"Why would the sheriff think the glove is yours? Seems like a long shot to me."

"I have my initials embroidered on all my ski gear. Hard to miss." She shrugged.

"I see. So, you went to the crime scene to search for your glove?"

She nodded. "When I didn't find it right away, I went crazy. That's when I wrecked the snowmobile."

The explanation was totally believable. I wasn't sure how to take the news. I felt happy for Tabitha and disappointed for Nathan. My list of suspects was dwindling. I squirmed in my seat. If I were to believe Tabitha told the truth, that is.

"I know you think I might be the killer and want to clear your cousin's name." Tabitha's lips thinned to a narrow line.

"I'm sorry. In trying to help Nathan, I'm alienating friends." My mood sank and embarrassment filled me. I traced a knot hole marring the table surface. "If you aren't the one, then who is?" Without meaning to, I voiced the thought aloud.

"Kyle Steele would be my number one suspect."

My head shot up. "Why? I mean, I know he's not the most pleasant person to be around. At least not for me. Why would you think he killed her?" I was fishing for information, again. After witnessing the tense scene between him and Isadora before she got on the ski lift and then the suspicious timing of his injury, I had plenty of reasons to cast a curious eye on him. Though I wasn't sure if that was enough incentive or reason to commit murder. Not even Tabitha's behavior warranted enough reason. I leaned away from the table. Only Nathan fit the profile of a killer with the perfect motive, but was Isadora's threat to blab about his gambling debt and ruin his career enough? My heart sank. Without acting, he had nothing left. Plenty of advertisers would cancel their contracts, arguing he was no longer a respectable role model. I imagined that was a powerful motive. Even though I couldn't picture him as a killer, my view or opinion wasn't the one that mattered.

Tabitha cleared her throat to grab my attention once more. "As a manager of such a large staff, I need to do background checks when each employee is hired. Sometimes, even after." She lifted her chin. "I'm not being nosey, mind you. Managing the resort and keeping all parts of it running smoothly is my primary concern."

"Go on. You were saying something about Kyle?"

"Hmm, oh yes. The day Isadora and I argued and she, well, you know, I noticed something. I'm a keen observer of human behavior. I caught the reaction on their faces when they met. Kyle looked surprised or maybe shocked, not the way you'd look if you saw a complete stranger. On the other hand, Isadora seemed not to react at all. Then again, she was an actress. After a few seconds, the situation changed. They addressed each other with miss and mister, like nothing was wrong. Anyway, I decided to do a little digging. I had plenty of personal info on Kyle already." She lifted her chin in a proud gesture. "I'd make a great detective. I'm thorough and don't stop searching until—"

"Tabitha, maybe you should hurry? You have a staff meeting, right?" I urged her, anxious to learn what she'd found.

"Yes, of course. What I discovered went back several years and far away from Sierra Pines. Kyle and Isadora were business partners who launched something relating to the movie industry. Whatever happened between them must've gone wrong because another article I read explained Kyle was arrested for extorting money. He was released a couple of days later." She narrowed her eyes. "I confronted Kyle, threatened to fire him for lying on his job application since he didn't tell me he'd been arrested. That's when he spilled the whole story."

I gripped the edge of the table. Why had I never heard of Isadora's time in Paris? I figured I was about to learn. "What happened?"

"Kyle claimed Isadora stole money from one of their investors then planted it in his room as a way of getting back at him. He says she can be extremely vindictive when pushed. And clever. She trashed his room, breaking furniture and making the scene look like someone had broken in."

"I can see her doing that."

"Right away, he called the Paris authorities to report a break-in. However, Isadora also made a call to the gendarmes. She explained her former partner had committed a crime and stole money from one of their investors. Things happened pretty quickly after that. Kyle let the authorities search his room, totally unaware they were looking for the stolen money Isadora reported. Twenty-thousand in US dollars was hidden under the mattress. He was arrested, but fortunately his lawyer managed to get charges dismissed. Something about a technicality and no search warrant. Plus, the investor in question did not want the publicity of a trial. He was satisfied to have his money returned. Kyle was released after an agreement to pay several thousand for damages to his hotel room. By then, Isadora had returned to New York. He hadn't seen her again until that day at our lodge."

"Wow." I puckered my lips and whistled.

"A big wow. I mean, what are the odds of meeting each other here? I asked him if he talked to her any time after that meeting inside the lodge. He swore he hadn't."

"That's not true." I explained the argument I'd witnessed near the ski lift. "Isadora was upset and crying. Kyle tried to comfort her, but she lashed out at him, warning to leave her alone because she knew how to ski. I thought it strange when Kyle responded by saying it wasn't that easy. Why all the squabbling about something so trivial? Guess that wasn't the case." I suddenly wondered if this explained why Kyle had Isadora's name and number scribbled on that stack of papers.

"No. The argument could've been about what she'd done to him in Paris. I wish I'd known they'd argued. I would've told Sheriff Sterling when he questioned me about any suspicious behavior at the lodge." Tabitha traced her finger across her lip. "I should call him."

"Good idea. He already knows about the argument, but background details are important." My phone buzzed with a text from Gladys asking me when I was coming home. I quickly typed to answer. "I need to go. You too, if you're gonna make that staff meeting on time."

"Thanks for hearing me out, Ali." She extended her hand to shake.

"You bet." We parted ways and I turned my vehicle around heading back to the B&B. As far as motives go, Kyle Steele's ranking on the suspect list moved to first place, or at least he tied with Nathan. Wasn't revenge also one of the most popular motives? His anger and resentment over Isadora's efforts to send him to jail might have built over the years. Possibly seeing Isadora rekindled those feelings. Could he have acted on the idea? Isadora would never apologize. Humility wasn't part of her character. I pictured the scene in all its cinematic drama. Kyle followed her down the slope, confronted her at the cliff, and demanded an apology. She laughed in his face. His outrage grew out of control and he shoved her, sending Isadora to her death. I shivered.

However, one detail about their argument bugged me. Why comment that she didn't need his help? Or was the line something to cover up what they really talked about?

When I entered the house, I nearly collided with Gladys who stood in front of the foyer mirror. "Oh! Sorry, Gladys. Going somewhere?" I flipped my gaze from head to toe, studying the details of her appearance. Tailored dress, hat and gloves to match, and her hair styled in an upsweep with a silver clip—she looked sharp.

"Get changed, Alexis. We're meeting Ralph and Owen in an hour at Dominic's for lunch."

I blinked. "We are? When did this happen?"

Gladys caught me up to speed. "Florence called for an emergency meeting, five minutes after you left. I explained you'd gone to the lodge, but she insisted to meet without you." She rolled her eyes. "After all that drama, the only topic of discussion was to tell us the video had been uploaded to the town website. Like an email wouldn't possibly do. I swear she makes up excuses to meet so she has the opportunity to pound that gavel. Ridiculous."

"About Dominic's?"

"Oh! Of course. How silly of me. Ralph and Owen were at the meeting with their sweet little girl, Sophie. They wanted to go out and celebrate. Sophie received all A's on her report card. Isn't that wonderful? Anyway, at Sophie's request, we are invited." She waved an arm. "So, go change. Wear the red dress you bought last month. Very festive, don't you agree?"

I tugged at my ear and processed the lengthy monologue of information she'd given me. "All right then. I'll be down within twenty minutes." I hurried upstairs to my room. Dominic's was in the town of Camino, a twenty-minute drive from the B&B, if traffic was light. We'd arrive with minutes to spare.

As I stepped inside my room, I grinned. The red dress, along with a red beaded necklace and my reindeer earrings lay on the bed. "Oh, Gladys Bellwether. What would I do without you?"

WE SAT AT A CORNER TABLE away from the kitchen doorway and next to a window that provided a view of the mountains. Dominic always gave us special treatment. In return, we advertised his restaurant to all our guests.

The amber glow of stained-glass lights gave the room the perfect ambiance. Add scented candles, romantic music, and the peaceful sound of an indoor waterfall, and you had the perfect venue for couples in love. Or in our case, people who crave fine dining and authentic Italian cuisine.

I sniffed the air as the smell of pasta dishes baking wafted from the kitchen. "I'm starving. Thanks for inviting us." I tapped Sophie on the nose. "And you, superstar. How about those A's? Congratulations." I held out my hand for a high-five, which she returned with an ear-to-ear grin on her freckled face.

"Thanks, Aunt Ali."

"Aw, did you hear that? I've just become an aunt." I winked at her while everyone around the table laughed.

The conversation hummed while servings of pasta, garlic bread, and salad were served. This was another moment to enjoy and steer my mind away from problems that weighed heavily on me. Lifting my glass of tea to my mouth, I froze. Near the front of the room, Kyle sat across from a familiar face. Beth was chattering on about something while he smiled, his chin cradled in both palms. I'd never seen Kyle so pleasant or engaged.

I forced myself to look away and set my glass down without taking a sip. I laughed with everyone at whatever Owen had said.

"Is everything all right, Alexis?" Gladys touched my hand. Her brow furrowed with deep creases.

"Absolutely." I dapped my lips with the napkin. "Maybe a touch of indigestion is all."

"It's no wonder with everything that's happened," Ralph said.

"No, I definitely think it's the generous amount of garlic getting to me." I nodded. "Did Ollie ever tell you the story about eating an entire loaf of garlic bread for a midnight snack? He was miserable for days."

At once, talk steered away from me. Thank goodness. I made every attempt to relax and stay involved in the conversation, but questions about why the ski instructor and our guest were together, chatting like old friends, bothered me.

"Thank you for coming to Dominic's. I hope you've had a wonderful time." Our server distributed checks and left.

Once on the road, I settled back in my seat, relieved that Ollie offered to drive. I had too much to think about and little ability to concentrate on the road. Kyle and Beth had one thing in common—their passion for skiing. Maybe they struck up a conversation about skiing while at the lodge. I remembered Gladys mention Beth and Abby left the house after breakfast. Beth could've had plans for a morning run down the slopes, bumped into Kyle, and their conversation continued over lunch. Most likely, the situation was innocent. unless Kyle was the killer. The nagging and worrisome thought refused to get out of my head. Beth's life could be in danger.

As we turned onto Englewood Boulevard and approached the B&B, I spotted Quint's cruiser parked out front. "Now what?"

"We have company. How nice," Gladys said.

"I wouldn't call it nice just yet." I popped open the door and climbed out of the SUV. Lately, too many visits from Quint spoiled the B&B's holiday spirit.

As we approached the front door, the sharp sound of two men shouting could be heard through the walls.

"What in the world?" Gladys turned the handle and led the way inside.

I looked over her shoulder and could see Quint and Nathan standing in the parlor. Their faces flushed red. "This can't be good."

"Not at all," Gladys said.

"Maybe I should break them up." Ollie came alongside me and rolled up his sleeves.

I patted his arm. "I don't think that will be necessary, but thank you for the offer, Ollie."

All at once, Nathan marched out into the foyer. As he looked our way, he halted his steps. After a pause of maybe two or three heartbeats, he moved forward once more, his head bent to look at the floor.

"Nathan." I reached out, but he jerked away.

"Leave it alone, Ali. I'm done here." He yanked open the door and rushed outside.

"Done how?" I called after him.

"He's upset, dear. Let him cool off." Gladys stroked my back.

As Quint approached, I threw up my arms. "What was that all about?"

He folded his hat and held it in front of him. "I came to ask him some questions about the lab report. A blood sample taken from Isadora's clothing matches his. I asked him how that could've happened. He claims he cut himself shaving and the blood must have gotten on her when he tried consoling her with a hug. That was the morning of the day she was murdered. Pretty convenient story, huh?"

"Or totally reasonable and truthful. Gladys and Ollie, could you give Quint and me a moment alone?" I gestured for Quint to return to the parlor while Gladys and Ollie walked to the kitchen.

Once seated, I asked, "That's the whole story? He was angrier than I've ever seen him."

"Isadora received some bad news that morning."

"What sort of news?"

"She received a call letting her know the movie she was promised a part in was canceled due to financial problems. Nathan says she was inconsolable and at the point of losing control. He swears no one knew what to expect from her when she was like that." He raked fingers through his hair. "This case seems to get more confusing with each new piece of evidence."

I grew quiet. What else could Nathan be hiding? "All those secrets he keeps are damaging. He must see that."

"I told him as much. I said by not telling me everything, he was holding up the investigation of his wife's murder case. That's when he blew up, saying he shouldn't have to tell anyone about such personal stuff between him and his wife when it didn't relate to her murder. Of course, I disagreed. That's about the time you guys came inside."

I shouldn't keep secrets either. Maybe I was holding up the investigation too. "Quint, I need to tell you something about what happened to me yesterday at the theater."

CHAPTER EIGHTEEN

M Y PHONE ALARM INVADED MY PEACEFUL SLUMBER with the tune "Grandma Got Run Over by a Reindeer." I smacked the screen then shoved a pillow over my head. "What was I thinking in choosing that song?" I lifted the corner of the pillow to peek. The clock read six am. After giving myself another minute to acclimate, I tossed the pillow to the side and peeled off the covers.

I promised Gladys I'd help with the holiday baking this morning. Her goal was twenty-dozen cookies. Half would go to the church Christmas dinner this Saturday, which happened to be Christmas. I couldn't believe we had three days left to prepare. I still hadn't finished buying presents or wrapping them. My to-do list kept growing.

Slipping into an old t-shirt and sweats, I pulled my hair into a messy bun. Baking a few dozen cookies should keep my mind off of my conversation with Quint last night. Calling his response a lecture would be an understatement. He went into protective mode and told me not to go anywhere alone until he'd arrested the killer. That idea was impractical. I didn't need a body guard. He said he'd hire one, if need be. I ended the conversation with the promise to be careful and not hold back anything else that should happen to me. In the meantime, I gave him the note to be analyzed by the lab, even though my fingerprints were all over it. He scolded me for that too.

I entered the kitchen and prepared to bake. "Morning. So, what do we start with? Cutouts? Thumbprints with jam? Chocolate chip?"

"Good morning, Ali. I hope you slept well." She waved a floured hand. "As you can see, there are eight pans of cutouts to frost. Why don't you start with those while I prepare breakfast?"

"My goodness. Did you work through the night like Santa's elves?" I stirred bowls of red, green, and white frosting and lined up bottles of sprinkles.

"Of course not." She grinned. "I've been up since four."

"I can't believe your energy. I swear, Gladys, you need to tell me your secret." I spread red frosting on a Christmas bell then added silver sprinkles.

She shrugged. "Clean living maybe? Most likely good genes. My mother and grandmother lived to be one hundred. I plan on reaching at least a hundred and ten."

I chuckled. "Sounds like a wonderful plan."

Within less than two hours, I finished decorating. Washing my hands, I heard footsteps approaching the kitchen and the chatter of voices. "The breakfast crew is here."

"Just in time." Gladys filled the last warming tray with scrambled eggs. Everyone but the Smiths entered and grabbed plates off the stack.

"Did Margaret and Paul leave already?" I asked.

"Yes. Right around the time I got up this morning. They had a change in flights and had to be at the airport by six. They told me to tell you they had a wonderful time and would be in touch about the book," Gladys said.

We all sat at the table. I listened mostly to the conversation while my gaze focused on Nathan. He was smiling and laughing. What happened to cheer him up, I wondered.

"I don't care for the beach. Give me a ski slope and I'm in heaven," Beth said.

"You and Kyle Steele have lots in common, then. He eats, sleeps, and breaths the sport." I laughed.

"Being a ski instructor, he better enjoy it," Abby said.

"Speaking of Kyle, I spotted you at Dominic's together." I sipped my coffee—hard to miss how her jaw tightened and eyes darted away for a moment.

"We met at the lodge and got started talking about the resorts we'd been to. Before long, we decided to continue the conversation over lunch." She lifted her chin and smiled.

Just what I expected her to say, but I worried Kyle might have another motive. Until I knew for sure he wasn't the killer, I remained suspicious. "Well, I have some last-minute shopping to do. Gladys, I'll be back soon to help some more with the baking." I set my dish in the sink and walked out of the kitchen.

"Ali, hold up a minute." Nathan rushed to meet me in the hall. "I wanted to tell you I sold the condo and paid off all my gambling debts."

"That's fantastic, cousin." I squeezed his arm. The grin on his face was such a pleasant change. "Sorry you had to sell your condo, though."

"I'm good. Paying that debt is like a hundred pounds off my shoulders."

"Or five hundred thousand pounds." I laughed.

"Yeah, Good one. Anyway, I just thought you should know." He stepped back toward the kitchen. "Have a good time shopping."

After a quick change of clothes, I drove into town and parked in front of the jewelry shop, Gems and Baubles. I had the perfect gift idea for little Sophie. The girl loved seahorses, and I'd noticed necklaces and bracelets with seahorse charms in Bonita's shop.

As I stepped inside, Bonita stood at the counter waiting on a customer. I waved and kept moving to browse the store. The place was somewhat cluttered with its narrow aisles. Only one customer could pass through at a time. Items were crowded together on the shelves like a line of dominos. One shoulder bump could cause them all to tumble. Most of the time I visited, I only admired the selection while keeping my hands at my sides. Today was different, though. I came to buy.

Fingering the children's jewelry items, I picked up a box with a matching set of seahorse bracelet and necklace. They were uniquely adorned with tiny turquoise stones placed in the horse's eyes.

"Ali! So nice to see you." Bonita approached. She jingled with each step as the copper bracelets and necklace she wore moved to match her rhythm. Soulful brown eyes, wide and innocent like a deer's, warmed in color as she smiled. "Your Gladys was here only two days ago doing some shopping." She winked. "I won't tell you what she bought, not even if you twist my arm."

I laughed. "Then I won't ask." I held up the box. "I came to purchase a gift for Ralph and Owen's little girl, Sophie. What do you think?"

"Um, yes. That girl always goes straight to my selection of seahorse items. She'll love this choice. Anything else I can show you? Christmas is only three days away, you know. Not much time left to shop."

"Oh boy, don't I know it. I woke up this morning thinking the same thing." I followed her to the front of the shop. "Good thing I only have Ralph and Owen left to buy for."

"The bookstore."

"Hmm?"

"Ralph was in here last week and talked about him and Owen catching up on reading. Every year, they make a Christmas wish list of book titles." She rang up the jewelry and handed me the package. "Not sure what they haven't purchased, but Toby at the bookstore should know."

"Gee, thanks. That saves me time and worry over what to get. Too much has been happening lately. I can't seem to catch up with all I have on my plate."

"Ah, you mean the murders of Isadora Lane and Dottie Sample."

I gasped. "How did you know about Dottie?" I figured everyone knew the details of Isadora's demise.

"Well, Charlene told Margie who told me. You know how it goes."

"Yeah, I really do." I shoved my wallet back in my bag.

"Such a shame." Bonita wagged her head. "I liked Dottie. When she last came to my shop, we didn't get a chance to talk. Something made her rush out without saying a word."

"Oh? How's that?" I hadn't heard this story. Most of them had been trivial and not worth much as far as Dottie's case went.

"Well, let me think." She tapped her lip then pointed at me. "Two of your guests came into the shop. One mentioned her name. Abby? The other was tall, long dark hair, sort of athletic build? Anyway, they came in to ask about jewelry. Bracelets, I think. About that time, Dottie came in and stood nearby, waiting her turn. Then, Abby made a comment and the other lady laughed. For some reason, Dottie's face turned almost white. She looked shocked or surprised or something not right. Without a word, she ran out of the store. I noticed, but the other two didn't pay any attention. Weird, huh?"

"I can imagine it was. Well, I should be on my way. I have a bookstore to visit. Thanks, Bonita." I waved goodbye and hurried out of the shop. My mind was racing. What could've upset Dottie that day? From Bonita's description, I knew the woman with Abby was Beth. I needed to talk to both of them, find out if they said something that could've upset Dottie. Maybe there was a clue in there somewhere that could lead to discovering Dottie's and Isadora's killer. I crossed the street and closer to the bookstore, Books and Such. I had a very strong hunch that Dottie figured out who murdered Isadora and that's what got her killed. I shuddered. No wonder Quint was so worried. Whoever the murderer was wouldn't hesitate to make sure no one found out his identity—no one including me.

After twenty minutes, I had made my book purchases and was on my way home. With any luck, I'd find Abby and Beth, or at least one of them, at the house. If not, my talk would have to wait. I hated waiting. However, if I learned something important, I'd call Quint. It was about time I heeded his warning and quit my snooping. After all, he was the one with the badge.

Opening the front door, I pulled up short. Quint stood in the foyer talking to Ollie. Both were too engaged to notice me. "Hello, gentlemen." I set my bag and packages on the floor and hung my coat on the rack.

"Ali, I was telling Ollie the news about the cyber hackers." Quint waited as Ollie excused himself, then he walked across the foyer to meet me.

"Oh? Good news, I hope. Why don't we go to the parlor and sit?" I stepped away but he caught my arm.

"I haven't much time. A call came in a few minutes ago. An altercation at a gardening supply store in Cedar Grove escalated. Shovels were their weapons of choice, I guess."

"Wow. Who knew gardening could be so violent? I hope everyone's okay."

"The situation's a mess, and I'm heading there now to make an arrest."

"Won't the men involved be gone? I sure wouldn't stick around."

"The owner acted quickly. He coaxed them into the stockroom by offering free supplies if they promised not to press charges. Then he locked the two inside and called the sheriff's office."

"Smart. Now, what did you find out about the cyber mess?" I moved to the foyer bench and sat. My legs were tired from standing for the past hour or so.

"A bunch of young activists wanted to make a political statement about greedy capitalists who only want to make a buck."

"Seriously? I wasn't aware shop owners in our town were greedy capitalists. Shouldn't they aim for bigger targets like Wall Street?"

He shrugged. "Like I said, they're a young bunch and obviously misguided. After leaving a trail of comments and hacking into several websites, they were bound to get caught. Thanks to Jerry, getting caught happened today. Arrests have been made. We'll probably read about it in the papers tomorrow."

"Thank goodness. That's one problem solved." I glanced up. "Anything new about the murders to report?"

"Unfortunately, no. I followed up by talking with Kyle and Tabitha. They confirmed what you told me. I get the feeling one or both might be holding back."

"You mean leaving out parts of their stories?" I scowled. "Makes sense if someone's guilty."

He glanced at his watch. "I need to go." He backstepped toward the door. Narrowing his eyes, he pointed. "Stay out of trouble. I don't want to be getting a call about you too."

I saluted. "Yes, sir, officer. Will do." After the door shut, I leaned against the wall. Nathan hadn't brought a curse to Sierra Pines. Now maybe the townsfolk would stop spreading that rumor.

With the cargo of handbag and packages loaded in my arms, I went up to my room. Shoving the gifts in the closet, I returned downstairs. I needed a midmorning snack and quiet time in the atrium to relax before resuming my role as assistant baker. The kitchen, though, was empty. A note left on the counter from Gladys explained she had to run to the market for more supplies. I blinked at the sight of a dozen supersized cookie tins stacked on the table. "How does she ever do it?"

I grabbed a plate from the cupboard and added three thumbprint cookies from the pan left to cool, then poured a glass of milk. As a last-minute thought, I added a couple of grapes to my plate. Stepping into the atrium, I set my snack items on the table. "I have a special treat for you, pretty bird." I grinned and passed one grape through the cage bars.

Blackbeard whistled and squawked. "Love snacks. Birdie love snacks."

"My, you're in a talkative mood today." I handed him the other grape. "So, what's new in your life? Hopefully full of good things." I sat in my chair and nibbled on a cookie. "I, on the other hand, seem to have nothing but trouble. Maybe you could give me advice about that? You certainly are cool and laid back."

Perhaps the idea gave me comfort, or telling my account of this morning's events helped me process. For whatever reason, I chatted to Blackbeard about Dottie and her strange behavior when visiting Bonita's shop. "I should talk to Abby and Beth, right? Get their sides of the story. Maybe they have something important to add. What do you think?" I paused and steadied my attention on the bird.

He hopped around the cage and squawked, talking mostly about nothing. Snacks being the most used word. I was ready to give up. "No one seems able to solve this mystery. We might have a killer who's never caught and will roam the streets of our town forever. How scary is that?"

"Get out of town. The heat's too close. Get out of town." Blackbeard rambled, his head tilting side to side.

I straightened in my seat. "What did you say, pretty bird?"

"Snacks. Birdie love snacks." He squawked.

I most definitely heard him. He'd said the words get out of town and the heat's too close. Parrots gained their vocabulary by mocking others. Who made those comments in front of him, I wondered? And what exactly did they imply? I gobbled the remaining cookies and gulped down the milk. Too bad the bird couldn't tell me who said the words. They seemed ominous. Of course, they could be from a movie. Ollie often carried his portable tv out to the atrium or screened porch and watched television. "That's probably all it was." Or at least I hoped so.

I carried my plate and glass back to the kitchen. Gladys had returned so we immediately got started on round two of the baking marathon. Two hours later, I sprawled out in a chair, tossed my towel on the table, and closed my eyes. "I'm done. Can't frost another cookie."

"For once, I agree. I am tired to the bone," Gladys said. "Why don't we pour glasses of lemon punch and make our way to the parlor? I think I hear voices and laughter coming from that room. Might as well join in."

Entering the room, I was pleased to see Abby. She and Faith were engaged in a game of scrabble. I was anxious to interrupt with my questions, but thought it might be rude. I nodded at Gladys. "Why don't we sit over there with Ollie? He seems lonely."

Gladys scoffed. "Poppycock. As long as that man has a plateful of food to keep him occupied, he'll never be lonely."

I grinned as she continued walking toward him anyway. Theirs was a love-hate relationship. The downfall of siblings growing up together, I guessed.

"Ali, why don't you take my place at the board? I've exhausted my vocabulary, and Abby has beaten me three games out of three." Faith laughed and shook her head.

"Sure. Why not? I need to exercise my brain before it turns to gray mush." I sat across from Abby and picked up tiles. "I was talking to Bonita this morning."

"Who?" She lined up letters on the board then raised fists into the air. "Ten points! I'm on fire."

"Bonita owns the shop, Gems and Baubles." I managed to add four points to the board.

"Oh, right. Beth and I stopped by to look at jewelry. She wanted to buy something for her sister, I think."

"Do you recall an older lady with short curly red hair, about five feet tall? According to Bonita, she rushed out of the store like it was on fire." I frowned as Abby racked up another twenty points. No wonder Faith couldn't win. The woman across from me played like she could win millions on a game show. "Anyway, I thought maybe you'd remember if something was said to make her run like that."

Abby shrugged and concentrated on the board. "Hmm, I can't think of anything peculiar. Beth and I asked to see some bracelets. We were admiring and talking about the beautiful diamond ones, tennis bracelets you call them. That's about it." She whistled. "Thirty points! How about that?"

I added letters to hers and leaned back in my chair. "Ten for me. That's a grand total of fourteen compared to your sixty. Not exactly giving you competition, am I?"

"Don't feel bad. I won the state scrabble championship back in college. Guess I should've mentioned that before, huh?" She winked.

I wiggled my finger at her. "A true hustler. Good thing we weren't playing for money." I stood. "Wish I could stay to finish, but I need to get a room ready for our new guests."

"Maybe another time," she said.

"Or maybe not." I called over my shoulder and waved as I walked toward the staircase. Nothing had been gained from our conversation, and I trusted Beth wouldn't be able to add any details that mattered. So much for that lead. I pulled towels and bed sheets out of the linen closet. Gladys had added our signature scented soap and shampoo to the bathroom, as well as other toiletries. After making the bed and hanging the towels, I opened the cabinet to retrieve copies of the brochure on local attractions and our B&B printout of breakfast options, available activities, like the video room and game night, and placed them on the nightstand. After checking the mini fridge for bottled water, I stood back to give the room a onceover while running through my mental checklist.

During the phone call yesterday, the Tunakas, Katsu and his wife Emiko, commented they'd seen our video showcasing all the wonderful people and sights in Sierra Pines, and they were excited to visit. I couldn't have been more pleased. I moved a pine scented candle closer to the middle of the dresser table then left the room, whistling "Jingle Bells" as I walked toward the attic stairs.

My eye caught sight of Beth in her room, standing in front of the mirror. Rethinking my idea, I knocked on the door. "May I come in?"

"Oh! Ali, yeah. Of course." She waved her arm while examining herself.

"Only if you have a minute. Looks like you're ready to go out." Her parka, gloves, and hat were laid out on the bed.

"Just doing some shopping in town." She pivoted on her heel to face me. "What's up?"

I sat on the window bench seat. "I wanted to ask you about your visit with Abby to Gems and Baubles last week."

"Yes?" She returned to viewing herself in the mirror and ran a brush through her hair.

"I talked to Bonita, the owner. She mentioned how Dottie was in the store at the same time as you and acted very strange. Can you remember if something was said or done right before she ran out?"

She paused for a second then rummaged through her makeup bag and pulled out a lipstick container and eyeliner. "Nothing comes to mind. Why don't you ask Abby?"

"Already did." I braced my arms on the bench.

She applied lipstick and then traced her eyes with liner. Turning, she smiled. "Like I said. Nothing comes to mind." She pulled on her parka and zipped it up. Grabbing her bag, gloves, and hat, she took long strides to the door. "I'm kind of in a hurry. Talk to you later." She vanished out the door.

"Huh. A lot of fussing and primping just to go shopping." I stood and walked out of the room. Maybe she had another date with Kyle. That thought made me worry. Beth was an adult, though. I couldn't play nursemaid or den mother to every guest under my roof.

Hitting the top stair, I could hear the house phone ringing in my room. Sprinting across the hall and into the bedroom, I grabbed the receiver. "Hello? I mean Sierra Pines B&B." I spoke in a breathless tone.

"Yes, may I speak with Kimberly Cedar? This is a representative of Sacramento airport security."

I scowled. "I'm sorry. There's no one here by that name." I waited and heard the shuffling of papers.

"That's the name I have. Miss Cedar reported a missing suitcase when she arrived on a flight last week and asked that we mail the luggage to your B&B, if it was found. Unfortunately, the item ended up in Kansas. I wanted to let her know, but she isn't answering her phone."

"I see, but I still can't help you. There is no guest staying here with the name Kimberly Cedar. Maybe she confused the name of our B&B with the one she's actually staying at."

"Possibly. Thank you for your time. I'll keep trying her number. She'll answer eventually, I'm sure. Have a good day."

"Huh. How strange." I set the receiver down. Rather than taking a quick nap as I planned, I headed back downstairs to find Gladys. Maybe she'd heard of the name. Could be Kimberly Cedar called to make a reservation, but we were booked at the time. Gladys might have taken a call.

I found her sitting in the atrium talking to Ollie. "Hi Bellwether siblings. Catching some afternoon sun?" I sat next to the back wall.

"Sharing some memories too." Gladys patted Ollie's arm. Her eyes filled with warmth. "We sure have some good ones, don't we Ollie?"

"Absolutely the best." He answered with a wink.

"I just had the strangest phone call and wanted to ask you guys about it."

"Really? Do tell." Gladys took a sip of her drink.

I explained the conversation with the man from airport security. "Do either of you recall getting a phone call from a Kimberly Cedar? Maybe last month? We were booked full then."

"No. Can't say that I do. How about you, Ollie?" Gladys turned to him and waited.

"Nope. None by that name."

"It sure is odd. I suggested to the security gentleman that maybe Miss Cedar was confused about the name of where she was staying."

"That makes sense. Remember, there's Sierra Crest B&B twenty miles east of town." Gladys nodded.

"Get out of town. The heat's too close." Blackbeard squawked from atrium.

I blinked. It was as if Blackbeard intended to voice his opinion on the matter, and I had to agree. The heat was getting too close.

CHAPTER NINETEEN

I SAT IN THE BACK ROW OF the theater next to Gladys and watched the rehearsal with interest. This would be the final practice before tomorrow evening's Christmas Eve event.

"Places, everyone!" Florence's command, accompanied by a sharp clap of her hands, made all the children scurry to take their positions on stage. Feet shuffled and tiny voices whispered with a few giggles thrown in, until Florence pounded the gavel that she kept with her at all times.

Florence gestured to the accompanist who sat at the baby grand, Sierra Pine's pride and joy, Eveline Brightworthy. The fact was widely noted that Eveline had once played with the Cleveland Orchestra when she lived there in the nineties. Nowadays, she starred in her own local television show on the public broadcast system where she'd play various classical and contemporary songs for thirty minutes once a week. Some folks in town really loved the program.

Gabbie Ebbings, a daytime soap star on *The Raging Storm* and a pop vocalist who'd won a Grammy for her album last year stood off to the far side of the stage, flipping through pages of her script. She was our celebrity M.C.. Florence had decided home-grown wasn't good enough for our event and was able to persuade the actress to say yes to our invitation just as she'd done with Isadora, promising a full write-up in the *Hollywood Star Gossip* magazine. Florence was thrilled. Gabbie added a splash of glitter and glamor to the program. Florence's words, not mine.

"Miss Ebbings, would you care to join the children's choir? The song you're included in is up next." Florence spoke in a sugary sweet voice.

"Buttering up the star of the show," Gladys said. "As if Miss Grammy and Tony Winner cared a hoot."

"You know Florence. She always caters to the rich and famous." Poor Florence. It was sad how much she tried, but most of those on the receiving end seemed oblivious to her efforts.

"Well, someone should tell her to stop. It's embarrassing to watch." Gladys stood. "I need some refreshment. Would you like me to bring you anything?"

The theater had a concession stand in the lobby filled with snacks and drinks. Unless there was a movie or play, the stand was closed. However, the owner agreed to open for business during our rehearsals. "I'll take a small container of caramel corn, please."

Our portion of the program, which included Gladys, Ollie, Minnie, and me, was rehearsed earlier. A short skit about Christmases past where each of us told a town story, along with dramatic touches, didn't please Ollie. He was assigned a scene with Minnie where he had to kiss her. He griped about being a confirmed bachelor who shouldn't be subjected to such behavior. Minnie, on the other hand, was blushing and giggling the whole time. She never hid how she felt about him.

After the choir's last song, Ollie, dressed as Santa, would hand out toys to the children. For the last portion of the program, announcements of those charities to receive donations would be made. Each SPACA member had been assigned a turn to present. After the program ended, all of us would visit homes where needy families received our gift baskets filled with food and other staple items.

Eveline played, her fingers racing across the keys with graceful flourish as the children and Gabbie sang "Let it Snow" which ended with squeals and clapping from the choir.

Before Florence could bang her gavel to dismiss them, the stage emptied, and children scampered out the door. "Next we have Ollie distributing gifts. Yada, yada, yada." She flipped through pages while nodding and babbling. "Okay then, afterward we announce charity donations. Who starts?" She glanced up and her eyes flittered to view the theater.

"That would be me." Ollie raised his hand.

Florence scowled. "Nonsense. How can you possibly change out of your Santa outfit quickly enough to start the charity portion of our program?" She snapped her fingers and pointed. "Ali, you will take the lead. All the announcements are on cards and you each will collect yours before the start of the program. Please don't lose them. That's about it. Rehearsal is over. Get plenty of rest, people. Tomorrow evening is the big moment."

When the gavel pounded with extra force, I winced and nearly choked on a kernel of caramel corn. Stuffing the half-eaten snack in my bag, I then moved sideways, following Gladys, to reach the end of the row and into the open aisle.

Eveline stood waiting with her hands crossed in front of her waist. "Gladys, I'm so glad to see you. It's been ages." She leaned forward to give Gladys a kiss on each cheek.

"I'd say nearly a year." Gladys squeezed my arm. "This is Julia's niece, Alexis Winston."

"I do believe we met once. You were visiting your aunt right before starting college."

"You have a great memory." I laughed. "I wish I did. I've heard you're from Cleveland and played with the orchestra."

"Yes. So many years ago. Have you ever visited?"

"No, but my Mom and Dad have. They had parts in a small production performed at Playhouse Square."

"Beautiful theater. I miss some of the sights, but I've grown to love Sierra Pines and the Lake Tahoe region. When I get lonely for the hustle and bustle of the big city life, I visit Sacramento." She smiled.

"Well, I should get going. It was nice to meet you, Eveline," I said.

"Alexis, if you don't mind, I'd like to stay a bit and visit with my dear friend." Gladys hugged Eveline. "We have lots of catching up to do."

"Sure. See you back at the B&B. I plan to have a relaxing afternoon and read a book."

Wet and heavy snowflakes fell from the sky, coating every inch of me with a thick layer. Ollie and Gladys had taken the truck and left the house early for the rehearsal. I offered to clean up the breakfast mess and drove the Land Rover to the theater. Last-minute shoppers filled the stores and traffic was bustling. No surprise, I had to park my vehicle a block away. Checking out the clock tower in front of the town hall, I hustled a little faster. Ten after twelve. Florence had insisted going through most every part of the event's program, and that took two hours. She was thorough if not annoying.

I told Gladys the truth when I said I planned to relax, read a book I'd been trying to tackle for the past month, and enjoy my afternoon. No sneaking around to snoop on possible suspects because for now I promised myself to let Quint do his job. We'd see how long that promise lasted. Besides, I made plans for later this afternoon—a carriage ride to the town park with Quint. I recalled our first date and the picnic surprise he'd arranged. He pulled up in front of the B&B with a horse-drawn carriage, and we rode to the park. Twinkle lights adorned the gazebo while dinner and a bottle of wine waited for us at the table. Without a doubt, I enjoyed the most romantic date ever. Yep, nothing and no one would ruin my afternoon, not when I had Quint and that ride waiting for me.

"Ali Winston! Do you have a minute? I'd like a word with you."

I'd whisked by the Taffy House and pulled to a screeching halt at the sound of my name. Turning, I faced Margie, the owner. Annoyance must've covered my face.

"Well, don't look so disappointed. I only wanted to warn you that one of your guests nearly ran me down this morning. I don't care if she or he is an out-of-towner, a little respect for our laws would be nice." Both hands anchored to her hips while a sour expression deepened the lines in her forehead.

"I'm so sorry. Did you recognize the driver?" I wondered how she knew it was one of our guests if the car drove by so fast.

"Well, not exactly. But I'm sure it was no one from town. And the vehicle was not familiar." She lifted her chin. "I recognize most every resident's vehicle. After all, Bobby runs the only car repair service in town, and everyone would rather go to him than take their business to Placerville."

Bobby was Margie's brother. She always bragged about how much money the business made and how smart and talented Bobby was. Plus, on slow days at the Taffy House, she closed early and played receptionist at Retread Tire and Repair. I guessed she saw most every car that came into the shop. "But you can't be sure the driver was one of my guests? As I see it, the person could've been anyone driving through town, maybe on their way to one of the ski resorts." I spit out the snowflakes landing with a fury on my face.

She huffed. "Well, it's a reasonable conclusion for me to make. Just thought you should have a talk with your guests."

I blinked as Margie marched back inside her shop. "Okay then." I continued my walk to the Land Rover. Margie was a pleasant person but critical of any outsiders and not ashamed to hide the fact. Most likely, I remained on her waiting list to be accepted as a citizen of Sierra Pines.

Taking her observation and conclusion lightly, I moved on to other thoughts, like that carriage ride scheduled for this afternoon.

I parked in the drive. As if Mother Nature waved her wand, the snow stopped and sunlight broke from behind the clouds. Once inside, I shrugged out of my coat and kicked off my boots. Leaving the items in the foyer entrance to dry, I then sprinted up the stairs, stopping for a moment to check on Nathan. We hadn't seen or talked to one another since yesterday morning. He was happier than I'd seen him since before Isadora's passing. That thought consoled me, but like anyone, I worried the mood might not last.

The door was ajar. Pushing it open, I peeked in the room. "Nathan? Are you here?" No sound or sight of him. I decided he might have gone into town. No reason to worry.

Pushing on, I neared the stairs to the attic. Glancing to the left, I did a double-take and skidded to a stop. My breath hitched, and I tiptoed into Beth's room which was in total chaos. Clothes scattered across the bed while dresser drawers stood open. I listened for the sound of the shower running or something to let me know Beth might be here. Silence made me tense even more. I didn't have any idea if she was the messy, leave-it-until-later kind of person. She'd been in such a hurry lately, like yesterday when I'd asked her about Dottie. I tapped my stockinged foot on the hardwood floor for a few seconds then sprinted downstairs.

Grateful to find Ollie and Gladys had returned, I let go of the breath I'd been holding. "Thank goodness you're back. Have either one of you seen Beth this morning?"

Both shook their heads.

"Not since yesterday afternoon, come to think of it," Gladys said.

"Thanks." Without explanation, I went to the parlor. Abby, Faith, and the Tunakas sat chatting. "Hi everyone." I jumped right into the topic on my mind. "I don't suppose any of you have seen Beth this morning?"

"No. I haven't spoken to her since we went to dinner yesterday," Abby said.

Everyone else shrugged and shook their heads.

On a hunch, I asked, "How about Nathan? Have you seen him this morning?" Getting a consensus of no, I backtracked to ask the Bellwethers that question and got the same answer.

"Why do I feel like such a mother hen?" I muttered under my breath. There went my peaceful afternoon, I thought.

As I approached the foyer, my pocket buzzed and the sounds of Christmas hummed from my phone. I lifted the device and stared at the screen. The number was unfamiliar, but panicky thoughts running through my head made me answer anyway. "Hello?"

"Ali, thank goodness you answered. You need to help me."

I cringed at the high-pitched tone. "Who is this?"

"Me, Beth! Please, you need to come and help me."

My heartbeat raced as I gripped the phone tighter. "Beth? Where are you?"

In between sobs, she managed to get words out. "Nathan kidnapped me. I tell you he's insane. He brought me to the cliff where Izzie died, and he swears he'll do the same to me. All because I heard him talking on the phone telling someone that he needs to leave town quickly before he's arrested for murdering his wife. Ali, I'm so scared."

Suddenly, Blackbeard's rant about getting out of town made sense. I hitched my breath at the silence from the other end. "Beth? Beth, are you still there?" I shoved my feet into my boots and grabbed the coat off the rack, still damp from my walk. *Nathan.* How could I have been so wrong? Nathan was family, my cousin. Hit with the idea, I fought to accept it. Nathan was the killer. Nathan, the one who'd fooled me into believing him, trusting him.

"I don't want him to hear me, and I don't have much time." Her voice softened to a whisper. "Ali, you're the only one who can talk sense into him. Please, come. Before he—No, please. Stop!"

A rustling sound covered her words and then the line went dead. I raked fingers through my hair. I should tell Gladys and Ollie, but that wasted seconds. Beth might not have seconds. Instead, I pulled open the front door and rushed to the Land Rover still parked in the drive.

BY TRAVELING FAST ENOUGH TO SET A RECORD, the trip to Tahoe Pine took me thirty minutes. Fortunately, I spotted no one manning the highway with a radar gun to catch speeders. I parked then sprinted across the lot and into the lodge. Risking no time in renting skis from Owen, I grabbed a pair leaning against the wall outside.

"Hey! What do you think you're doing? Those are mine." I woman cried out from behind me, but I ignored her and hurried to the lift.

The blood rushing to my head caused a dizzying sensation. I struggled to keep steady on my feet. This was all my fault, or at least mostly my fault. If I hadn't been so hellbent on proving Nathan's innocence, maybe I would've seen the signs for what they really were. Now, it might be too late, unless I arrived at the cliff in time to save Beth. If words wouldn't work, maybe a dose of pepper spray would distract him long enough for her to get away. Even if I took her place, Nathan would never do anything to hurt me. I had to believe at least that much.

I jumped into the next available car that already had one occupant. No time to wait for riding solo. I settled into my seat, attempting to slow the adrenaline pumping through my veins. I feared I would pass out if I didn't get myself under control.

With a deep breath, I opened my eyes. Peeking at the person next to me, I scowled. The profile looked familiar. My eyes widened as she slowly turned to face me.

"Hello, Ali. So nice of you to come." Beth's smile stretched tightly.

"Beth? I don't understand." My brain raced to catch up to what was happening.

"Oh, poor Ali. You had no idea, did you?" She shifted in her seat and patted my arm.

I flinched and jerked away from her touch. "You tricked me."

She laughed in a way that reminded me of the sinister villain in one of the Bellwethers' old black and white films. "Wait. Where is Nathan?"

"Oh, don't you worry. I'm sure you'll both be together soon."

"If you hurt him, I'll—"

"You'll what? Run to save him?" She laughed. "If you'd only kept your nose out of it. I tried to warn you. But no, you just couldn't stop. I knew with that sense of determination you'd eventually figure it out. Besides, I can't leave town with those loose ends hanging, can I?"

I had to keep her talking. My hand touched the phone in my pocket. If only I could slip it out and dial 9-1-1. I shifted to my side, hiding the pocket with the device tucked inside. "Why? Why would you kill Isadora?" On the phone, she called her Izzie. I should've caught that slip. No one who'd met her once called her anything but Isadora, and even then, anyone, including Nathan, who called her the nickname rubbed her the wrong way. Using Izzie, I figured, was an intended jab.

Beth's gaze wandered to look out over the slope. "We knew each other back in New York. Izzie had already gained success while I was still strug-gling to make it in the industry. Every part helped." Her eyes darkened.

"I thought you lived in Cleveland."

"Like I said, clueless, aren't you?" She snapped at me then calmed once more. "I took the name Beth Rawlings from a bit part I played in an off-Broadway play. Of course, I knew she wouldn't recognize me. Me the one who got a role in a major production, a role Izzie wanted. I was a nobody to her, a nuisance she needed to get out of her way." She heaved a sigh. "After she spread all sorts of lies, I couldn't get hired anywhere for anything. I was blackballed in the industry.

"That's when I decided to fight back. Nothing gives you purpose more than wanting revenge. I lost weight, died my hair, saved up money by taking part time jobs here and there, and hired myself a publicist. I finally snagged my first role in over a year. It's a tiny part in a play that most likely will close in a week due to poor attendance." She jabbed a finger at my face. "But you know, I could be so much further in my career if it wasn't for that selfish, cold diva your cousin married."

I swallowed hard. "You followed her and Nathan to Sierra Pines to kill her?"

"No!" She flashed angry eyes at me. "I came to get an apology and ask if she could see her way to recommend me for a part in her movie. Yes, I heard all about the plan to take a major role in a Hollywood production. I deserved to get a piece of that pie, trust me." Her words turned surly. "I followed her down the slope and saw my opportunity when she stopped by that clearing. Of course, she laughed in my face, then told me there was no movie. She came to Sierra Pines hoping to get money from that pompous fool, Kyle Steele, to help finance it. Can you believe that? The great Isadora Lane, begging for help. She claimed he had money stashed away from some stupid scheme they pulled off in Paris. Only he refused to give her a penny. Even after confessing that pathetic story, she was so full of herself. She told me I was a nothing actress who should go home and take a job waitressing." Beth sniffed and wiped tears from her eyes. "Bragging about her success, her marriage, and dangling that diamond bracelet in my face. I couldn't handle it. I snapped and ripped the bracelet off her wrist and shoved her." She hiccupped. "I didn't mean for her to fall off that cliff. I didn't mean for her to die. But I'm glad. I got my revenge and I'm going back to New York. As soon as I take care of—"

She reached out to grab me. I leaned out of reach. "Wait. You didn't tell me what happened to Nathan."

"I'm not stupid. I know what you're doing." She nodded. "A few more minutes won't matter. By now, your sweet sheriff is searching Nathan's room. I planted the bracelet, broken in two and with just a trace of blood. You'll never guess whose blood, and neither will your sheriff. Not right away. I left an anonymous tip on the sheriff's voicemail. By the time they get a second call, letting them know Nathan is here at the resort, you'll be dead and Nathan will be arrested for yet another murder."

My eyes widened. "Dottie saw you wearing that bracelet while you shopped at Gems and Baubles, didn't she? That's what made her run. What happened? You realized she recognized it, so you lured her to the mining sight to kill her too?" I fumbled with the phone in my pocket, punching buttons out of desperation. Forget calm, cool, and collected. I was in a full overblown state of panic.

"Of course not. I didn't start out to be some kind of serial killer." She spat out the words. "She tried to blackmail me. Your friend wasn't a sweet, little old lady like you all thought."

I didn't take the time or dare to correct her. No one would've described Dottie as sweet. "Then what happened?" My gaze darted all around the lift car, searching for something I could use as a weapon and paused to focus on the pair of skis resting next to Beth's.

"I met her at the mining sight. You know, I was ready to give her the money, believing she would keep her mouth shut after that. She said she planned to leave town and how no one appreciated her. She'd be long gone and never say a word, if I gave her the money.

"But then she had the nerve to demand more. Can you believe that? She wanted twenty thousand, or she'd go to the authorities. One thing led to another. I don't know." She stood and the car rocked. Gripping her head with both hands, she twisted back and forth. Her voice rose. "I picked up the rock, and when her back was turned, I hit her. I was so angry. Why can't people do what they promise? What the heck. It doesn't matter anymore what I do." She lifted one of the skis and swung at me.

I dodged and weaved, shaking the lift even more. With each swipe, I reached to grab hold of the ski, but it slipped from my grasp. The car careened, almost ready to dump one or both of us out. The ground was far below, hundreds of feet. Death was a certainty, but all I could think about was that romantic carriage ride with Quint.

CHAPTER TWENTY

IN A DESPERATE, DETERMINED EFFORT, I gritted my teeth and latched onto the ski and jerked it from her hands. The car suddenly shifted, moving back and forth rather than side to side. Beth fell back and landed on her rear in the seat.

"Don't you move. Or else." I brandished the ski like a warrior on the battlefield. "I won't hesitate to hurt you." I scrambled to think how this would play out. We were only a third of the way across to reach the other side and the lift drop-off.

As if my prayers were answered, the car started moving in the opposite direction, beginning its descent back to the lodge. I felt my nerves melt into uncontrollable sobs, but I gripped the ski harder and glared at Beth. She cowered in her seat, eyes darting like a scared rabbit. From outside the lift car, I spotted Quint, Gladys, and Ollie. Gladys waved but I didn't dare return the gesture or take my eyes off of Beth for more than an instant. I had a strong hold of the ski, ready to act at her slightest move.

The car ground to a halt. Deputies grabbed hold of Beth's arms and lifted her from the car. As I dropped the ski and on wobbly legs attempted to get out of the car, Quint wrapped his arms around me and helped.

"Ali Winston, I don't know what I'm going to do with you."

He nuzzled my neck. The warmth of his breath comforted me. "I know. I promise that won't happen again. I was worried about Nathan. I'm supposed to watch out for him, you know. It's my job, and then I thought he'd—Nathan! I can't believe I forgot." I yanked myself out of his arms. "She kidnapped Nathan and left him at the cliff where, you know, and she planned to make it look like he killed me, but she was going to kill me first." I sobbed. "I don't know what I'm saying. Please, you have to send someone down there. He may be hurt."

"Okay, okay. Calm down. Everything will be fine." Quint spoke in a soft tone. His words came slow and easy.

My sobbing quieted. "I'm okay. Honest."

Quint snapped his fingers and ordered two men to take a snowmobile back to the crime scene to find Nathan. "I'll just be a minute."

I watched as Quint helped Beth into the back of a cruiser and spoke a few words with the deputies who then rode off.

All at once, Gladys ran at me, crushing my body in her vicelike grip. "Gladys. I'm all right. You can stop holding me."

"Yes, well you know we can't lose you. Why didn't you tell us where you were going? If it wasn't for the phone call, I don't think we would've figured it out in time."

"What phone call?" I studied her face.

"The airport security from Sacramento? A different person, a woman, called and again asked for Kimberly Cedar. I explained we had no one by that name staying at the B&B. She insisted we did, then she described Kimberly as tall, athletic build, long dark hair and a mole on her cheek. Pretty accurate description, don't you think? Anyway, mentioning the mole got my attention. Right away, I told Ollie we needed to search her room. You'll never guess what we found." She paused, waiting for me to answer. When I only nodded, she continued. "Tucked in the back of her suitcase was a pair of brown wool gloves with blood stains on them. Can you imagine how frightened I was? I couldn't find you or Beth or Nathan anywhere in the house. Of course, I called the sheriff right away to be sure my hunch was right. Sure enough, a picture from the New York DMV has a photo of a Kimberly Cedar on file who is a perfect match for Beth Rawlings. Now, unless she has an identical twin, Beth is Kimberly."

"How did you know to come here? That's what I don't understand, though I'm eternally grateful you did." I shivered and rubbed my arms.

"Oh, good question. Would you believe we got a phone call at the house from Mr. Farley? He complained that the Land Rover was blocking his way to plow the parking lot. Perfect timing, as if the gods of fate did us a good turn."

"Thank goodness you found me before it was too late." I shuddered. Just as Quint and Ollie approached, I explained to all three how Beth, aka Kimberly, knew Isadora so well. "She wanted an apology, not revenge. Turns out she got more than she bargained for. Even Dottie's death wasn't planned. Our dear friend got too greedy and demanded more money than she'd asked for in the beginning."

"We can take your statement later. Right now, I want to get you back to the B&B." Quint took my hand.

"Not yet. I have to know Nathan is all right." I stood my ground, and Quint didn't argue. Even the Bellwethers kept quiet.

In another twenty or so minutes, the snowmobile trailed down the slope and back to the lodge, stopping feet away from where we stood. Anxious, I ran over to meet Nathan as he got out of the vehicle. A bandage covered his forehead and blood crusted on his check. His smile was weak, but he grabbed my hand and squeezed.

"I'm so glad you're okay." I squeaked out the words. "Seems I'm always rescuing you, cousin."

"I worried about you too. If anything had happened, the family would've disowned me." He heaved his breath and tried to smile. "Sorry. I shouldn't joke."

"I'm sorry for doubting you and thinking for one second you could've killed Isadora." I sniffed.

"Stop. I'll always be grateful for you being there when I needed you, little cousin. Especially today." He laughed then winced and gingerly touched his forehead. "Ouch. That hurt."

I circled my gaze to search for Quint. He stood exactly where I'd left him. His face was almost void of emotion, except for that tiny flicker in his eyes and the firm set of his lips.

"We should get you to the hospital." One of the deputy's spoke.

Nathan grabbed my hand. "I'll probably head back to New York right away. I want to spend Christmas with Mom and Kinsey. But I plan to stay in touch and call you now and then. Is that okay?"

"Of course, more than okay. We're family." I gave him a quick hug then waited until he got into the back of the EMT van. I retraced my steps and nudged Quint in the side. "You know I'm still looking forward to that carriage ride, Sheriff."

"Good because I don't have a backup plan if you cancel." He stroked my cheek with one knuckle.

I stood on tiptoe and planted a kiss on his lips. "Perfect."

A grin broke free from that stern face. "Now, are we ready to get out of here? I'm starving. How about lunch? We can catch the midday special at Sunrise Eatery, if we hurry."

I linked my arm through his. "You bet. Gladys? Ollie? Care to join us?"

"I'm always up for a good meal," Ollie said.

"Is there a time when you aren't?" Gladys smacked his belly.

"Hey, now. No need for that, sister dear."

I chuckled as we all steered toward the parking lot. Now that the sticky matter of murder was solved and those pesky cyber bandits were behind bars, maybe holiday spirit would return full force and brighten the moods of everyone in Sierra Pines.

THE OVERHEAD LIGHTS IN THE THEATER DIMMED and spotlights played on the stage. Two dozen young people stood together, wearing festive dresses and suits. A colorful array of red bows and glittery tree ornaments were strung from end to end just below the curtain top.

As Eveline sat straight as an arrow, hands perched on the keyboard, Florence gave her the cue to begin. The opening of "We Wish You a Merry Christmas" carried from the piano and children sang with cheerful faces. After they finished, Gabbie climbed the steps and took her place at center stage. She opened with her solo on the first verse of "Let it Snow" and the choir joined in after. All and all, the music portion of our program turned out nice. Everyone in the audience clapped and whistled, especially the parents.

"It's so wonderful to hear the children sing," Gladys said.

"Our Sophie sounded like an angel. Don't you agree?" Ralph beamed with pride.

We all nodded as Florence motioned for Ollie to come back stage.

"Showtime, folks," Ollie said and hurried to put on his Santa costume.

The curtains were drawn closed once more while, as arranged, a few of the younger men who'd volunteered carried the Santa chair and gift boxes filled with toys on stage.

"Ho, ho, ho, Merry Christmas." Ollie shouted in his best Santa voice while the pounding sound of footsteps echoed across the stage.

Soon, the curtains opened, and we all laughed to see Ollie leaning back in his chair, patting his round belly.

"Didn't need to stuff his waist with much padding, did we?" Gladys snickered.

The next hour flew by as children hurried on stage to retrieve their gifts. When the packages dwindled down to very few, Gladys, Ralph and the rest of our members hurried down the aisle. We took our positions in line to announce charities and hand out checks.

I shuffled off to my seat to wait for the others to take their turns. When Ollie, who fell in line last, finished, I closed my eyes. We'd made it, despite all our hiccups and snafus that fate threw at us. As the gavel pounded, my eyes popped open.

"I have one other announcement to make before we end the evening. A very special one."

Gladys nudged me in the arm. "Something's up. She's supposed to end the program and tell everyone good evening. I hope she's not going to give some long speech about town spirit and all that."

"We've always supported one another in our town."

"And here we go." Gladys crossed her legs and arms.

"That's what makes us so special. Our caring and understanding is what makes us strong." She sniffed and dabbed the corner of her eye. "I'm sorry. I get all choked up at times like this. Anyway, my announcement calls for Alexis Winston to come up on stage. Ali." Florence beckoned me with her arm.

"What in the world?" I looked at Gladys who only shrugged. Sliding my way passed the row of chairs, I hurried down the aisle to the stage. My cheeks were burning with embarrassment. Everyone who knew me was well aware I hated being the center of attention.

"Now, Ali, the town would like to present this check. Everyone who could, donated when they heard how you might lose the B&B. We love your cozy establishment and want you to continue your aunt Julia's legacy. So, please, accept our gift and keep the Sierra Pines B&B running."

Clapping and cheering echoed throughout the theater and pounded in my ears. I blinked away tears to clear my blurry eyes. "I don't know what to say other than thank you. Thank you so very much. You all are wonderful and kind."

I spotted Quint standing near the back of the stage. His arms folded across his chest and looking sharp in his uniform. I waved the check and grinned.

He nodded and gave me a thumbs up sign.

Yes, Christmas spirit had returned to Sierra Pines, and I was truly thankful.

EPILOGUE

The Hollywood Star Gossip

Well folks, guess who's in the news again? Gabbie Ebbings, star of the daytime soap, The Raging Storm *and Grammy winner for her pop LP* Love You Always. *Before you all get excited for some juicy gossip, this is not your typical tabloid drama. My dear friend, Florence Greeley, invited Gabbie to act as M.C. last month in her town's Christmas charity event. In a humble gesture, Miss Ebbings accepted. Not bad, huh? One of our own, joining in the holiday spirit. Kudos to Gabbie for shedding the bad girl behavior in this second act of her life.*

But wait. There's more. I can't disappoint you, can I? Afterall, gossip is in our magazine's name. You might remember the town Sierra Pines featured in my column a couple months ago where murder was at the center. Well, here we are again. Another murder, you ask? How about two? Yes, two. Poor Sierra Pines. The town can't seem to escape the curse of a murderous plot.

Adding a bit of history to the story, I can say this tidbit excited me. Sierra Pines is located in the heart of gold mining territory. It even boasts one of the first discoveries of gold back in the mid-eighteen hundreds. How's that for a claim? Pun intended. Here's where it gets macabre. One of the murders happened at this gold mining sight. Not exactly what a tourist would expect to find. And on that note, I'll leave details of the ski slope murder for another day.

Tune in to my web mag tomorrow and learn more about what Gabbie is up to next. Think dueling soap stars, money and prizes, and plenty of entertainment. Until then . . . see you in the stars.

—Tiffany Bertram, the voice of Hollywood